PROUD   PATRICK

Michael Aloysius O'Reilly

MORNMOR Publishing

Chapel Hill, NC 27516

ISBN: 9781792011887

For nothing can be sole or whole
That has not been rent.
—W.B. Yeats

I

The Golden Anniversary

At the whine of the piper every Sullivan turned to the double doors. In kilt with thickly veined legs extending to scuffed Oxfords a thin, a sixtyish geezer squeezed his bag like a one-winged chicken and began wending through the family tables. He was followed by Barnaby and Bridget who both paraded slowly as age demanded but with a benevolent regality, a pomposity perhaps borrowed from black and white movies of kings and queens. The Shelburne's oaken paneled walls—now shivering with the piper's whine—were hung with portraits of Irish heroes past: Parnell, Daniel O'Connell, Michael Collins, Wolfe Tone, Jack Kennedy--dour visages in thick textured oils, their black eyes followed any and all passersby flinging mute challenges: *Here am I, dead but upon the wall. What are you willing to withstand to gain a place on these walls?*

The family rose from their seats. First the grandchildren, then the children and their mates. Even Patrick stood. The patriarch, with the stem of his Martini held between wrinkled thumb and index, his head tilted back, with pursed lips and an arch gaze upon all, paraded mincingly past the tables without precisely recognizing or acknowledging anyone. The celebration long planned, including tonight's opening grand march, their coming together in Dublin, the culmination of fifty years of marriage: who would not, despite the day's earlier loss, be suffused with more than a little bonhomie--with or without the aid of gin? Over and behind the chairs reserved for the honorees there was, push-pinned onto an oaken panel, a ten-foot banner with large green and black felt-pen strokes. This was the work of granddaughter Shannon, Jenny and Matt's oldest. She the one most doted upon. She therefore bestowed with the greatest promise. All agreed that Shannon was to be the Sullivan family's artist. Every family has one. She was theirs. The clan already possessed her--tenderly, proudly—as having the artist's somehow different soul—but with nary a blemish in sight. As a young artist having not yet found her own soul, she was excused to have painted--extracted from the universal Irish soul—a gaudy border of four-leaf green clovers. The banner read:

All Hail the King and Queen
Of the Sullivan Clan
GRANDPA AND GRANDMOMSABOMB
Fifty Glorious Years

Rosemary leaned to Patrick, whispered: "We are the only ones, the ones who know that nothing has changed."

"Dougie knows."

"Okay. Dougie too."

"Kevin knows.' Corrected himself. "Kevin *knew*." With locked eyes they traveled separately down so many lost decades that Time now forced upon them. Patrick took Rosemary's hand: "I walked out on this big nothing. And I'm glad I did."

Rosemary, with narrowed eyes, raised her white wine over Patrick's brow, and drizzled a thin but continuous streamlet of Pouilly-Fuissé: "Wrong, you jerk. You walked out on me."

Patrick stood slowly and, not removing his frown heaped down upon his big sister, queried Matt while expunging the white wine that had flooded an eye: "Where's the loo?"

"The loo I don't know. The crapper's down the hall. On the right."

II

Chicago

Patrick Sullivan remembers a summer day on Whipple Street. The reminiscence visits in nanoseconds: a tableau of six naked siblings in the small dining room of his boyhood home. That June afternoon when the Sullivan children were bare of clothes, bare as the grey sycamore on the lawn was free of bark.

The oldest of the six, Rosemary, does a kind of a hop-about as she is whacked with the aluminum egg flipper. Patrick, avoids Rosemary's yelps, squints his eyes, hears the metallic squeak of a sprinkler next door and a fly buzzing to escape at the screen door. A mosquito floats among the nudes. Patrick has just turned eight. He looks out the door to their sycamore and floats to where he can place his back against that tree and sit like an indolent monk. Where he can take in the quiet afternoon and watch a robin feed its young in a high nest while barn swallows flit under the Hartigan's sprinkler. He smiles in the warmth and peace of the beautiful June afternoon. He daydreams even as Rosemary dances to the thwap-thwap of the egg flipper on her pink skin.

Rosemary and Jenny scream like opera ladies when they get their whacks. Jenny, even then the empathic sibling, screams when another is whacked. Dougie and Patrick don't scream. Patrick smiles while Dougie plays dead with eyes wide open.

Kevin and Larry sit; diapered witnesses with thumbs in their aghast mouths like lollipops not sucked. Too young to be adjudicated felons, but not too young to learn about felonious conduct, Kevin is almost three and Larry eighteen months. They stroke their cheeks with rayon bunting and watch today's inquisition occasioned by the discovery that MomsaBomb's rainy day stash--in the pink chalk piggy bank--has been found empty. The pink chalk piggy bank that Barnaby won ten years ago for his fiancée throwing baseballs at milk bottles made of lead. Those were the best days of her life. Now not so much as a nickel for the pay phone in the foyer remains in the pink chalk bank.

MomsaBomb knows who did it. Or at least the gang involved. This is an inside job. By her brood. Confessions, as the children dance, are encouraged with the egg flipper. Patrick is glad, though not visibly so, that today Barnaby's rawhide belt is nowhere in sight. Struck upon a buttock,

7

the sterling silver buckle imparts a pink intaglio-welt of not-so-transient beauty: a hooded and fanged cobra.

Rosemary, whose ninth birthday party was just a week past, is first in line—"Oldest first!"--for a truth-inducing whacking. Patrick will be second. Then Dougie, Patrick's Irish twin. Then Jenny. Larry and Kevin are spared the lashing—but not the spectacle.

"Filthy goddamned good-for-nothing Irish pigshit brats, look at me!" Patrick turns to MomsaBomb. She bares her teeth; he thinks of a snarling dog. "Tell me who did it." MomsaBomb knows that the more removed a child is from the innocent baby that God blessed her and Barnaby with, the more corrupt that child has become.

Rosemary's scream precedes the belt: "Mommy, I didn't take anything!"

"Balzac! Shakeshit! Bullshit!" Thwap-thwap. Scream, scream. Rosemary's screams might shatter crystal were there some. She jumps as if on hot coals. Patrick, in preparation, freezes his smile. Begins the work of believing that he cannot be hurt. That he must smile at all costs. Patrick knows that he will win. But it will still be a bad day. Not the worst day ever. But very bad.

With the flipper held high, MomsaBomb's glance darts down the line to Jenny. Jenny who, though yet untouched, is bawling. Her crimson face leaks like an August tomato split in the hot sun. "Quit your caterwauling!"

MomsaBomb is always easiest on Jenny. And Rosemary too is spared a lot of that which Dougie and Patrick are not. "Boys are worse than girls." What MomsaBomb always says: "The prisons are full of bad boys but how many girls are on murderer's row? Answer me that one."

Today, MomsaBomb seeks a confession. If the guilty one can be convinced to blubber the truth, justice will have been served. The only thing worse than the transgression itself is the refusal to own up to it. A sense of personal guilt must be infused into lying children. Or forever the mother must live in the knowledge that she has failed in her holy calling.

Rosemary, held by a wrist, tries to dance away: "I swear I didn't do it, Ma." The hits of the metal flipper on her butt, back, and thighs have a tinny percussive quality, a primitive music. Patrick thinks of the wild-eyed drummer on Ed Sullivan while watching Rosemary get her whacks from the corner of his eye. MomsaBomb says the drummer is a dope addict. Patrick hears the flipper clack upon a tooth.

Dougie gets Patrick's eye, does his Wild Man of Borneo face: eyes wide, one finger up a nostril, the other digits crammed into his mouth. Patrick turns away. To laugh is terribly dangerous. A calamitous invitation to be struck before his time. He casts an eye back. Dougie becomes a happy Porky Pig: silently, with lips puckered and smashed nose, he roots in the air. Patrick can't help but look at Dougie. MomsaBomb sees Dougie

8

and swats down the line, slashes him across the face. A perfect red square colors his cheek and a bloody freshet appears then dribbles haltingly from the wick of his lips.

Dougie does his dead thing.

MomsaBomb does not care about a little blood, she knows he will heal: "Serves you right, funny boy."

But when she turns back to Rosemary, Dougie flashes Patrick his Goofy grin and Patrick, smiling wide, dreams of raspberry jam-filled pastries on First Fridays: breaking fast in the classroom, after Communion, having stockpiled plenary indulgences against the   possibility of eternal flames. Perhaps the best moment of any month because Barnaby always finds he has many quarters to dole to his kids for chocolate milk and sweet rolls on First Fridays.   That day when all temporal punishment can be erased forever. Heaven guaranteed; foretold.

With Rosemary on the floor, reaching for her limbs and unable to stand, squawking guttural cheeps, MomsaBomb turns to Patrick. Patrick does not know who did it. Perhaps, he thinks, he may have fortuitously acquired some pennies. Maybe he took a couple nickels and dimes. *Forty cents maybe. Not a dollar! I would remember taking a whole dollar.* He resolves not to cry. Nor to cop to a minor offense. *Smile!* Because Dougie probably did it. Or Rosemary.

Bridget swats Patrick like Bob the butcher at the Jewel Tea flattening meat. Patrick, standing beside himself, commands his eyes: *Stay wide, look at nothing. Stare at the crucifix: Thou shalt not blink. Smile.* The whacks are aimed and not aimed, catholic; he feels much and little and nothing. The hurts hurt but someone else is getting hurt. He flies to a land where warm white surf spills itself over beaches of endless black lava sand, where there are red-faced monkeys high in the palm trees. Or to Grandma Power's house where she has made him cinnamon toast and tea (from a bag used only once) with clover honey. He folds his hands as they chat, her sweetest boy.

"Grandma, I love you."

"And I love you, my little Paddy-cake."

But Patrick's beatific smile makes it worse for him; MomsaBomb spits as she swats which only happens at her maddest moments. Patrick stares at the whitish crescents in the armpit of her sun dress and remembers that we all have salt in our blood. Sister Mary Prudence said that. Barnaby says that ladies' sweat ruins dresses; he can't get out sweat marks at the Cleaners. Has to tell the ladies to throw out that dress: "We are helpless, Mrs. Moran. No dry cleaner in the world can save wool with sweat marks."

"You dare to smile? Paddy, okay, I'll fix you good!" She swats her mightiest. He falls under the table. His forehead hits the lion's claw. She drops the utensil. Pounds on his back and butt with her fists. Hearing her heavy grunts, Patrick knows she is losing. He is removed to where the hits are on someone else: *She is so stupid, she thinks she is beating me. Ha ha. Our little game.* His teeth clenched as hard as possible, front teeth bared: *Ha ha! I will win. Again. I always do.* "Paddy, you did it, now admit it!" She shakes his shoulders as if trying to discharge something stuck in his throat. "And stop your *goddamned* smiling!"

"Ma, I can't help it."

"Yes, you can."

Seizing a dense shock of red hair, she elevates him, retrieves the aluminum flipper. Eyes flared, she whacks him, a rolling moving target, on the butt, the face, the back, and then the butt again. She looks him in the eye. Panting hard, he is too heavy to dangle. He lets himself slump to become more of a load. She is catching her breath. Her face clouds. *It's almost over.* With a pant of disgust, she pushes him to the floor. A dizzying pain comes and goes. Patrick is not so numb that he cannot nudge Dougie with a toe. *Look at me: Didn't hurt, didn't hurt.*

Dougie's turn.

Calling on reserve power, she screams while beating her third born. But Dougie does not cry. Dougie never cries. Nor will he talk. He's dead. It's been a long, long time since Douglas Sullivan shed a tear. Dougie has killed the whole idea of crying. He doesn't smile like Patrick. He looks dead with eyes wide open. MomsaBomb kicks him after he has fallen but with Dougie it's like trying to hurt a football. Patrick, holding his smile and watching askance, is struck with the stony quiet of Dougie's deadpan: Patrick can smile through anything but Dougie plays dead like you should call the doctor and the priest.

***

At age six, Patrick held his smile through a fractured clavicle; his shoulder clicked where the hurled griddle struck him. MomsaBomb told him to tell the doctor he fell from the roof. That he was bad to go up there. And sorry. Bridget Sullivan told Dr. Slattery that, in her opinion, the break might even be a punishment from God the Father Himself for Patrick's going up on that roof. Dr. Slattery said it was a small miracle that her Paddy had knitted so perfectly. He told Patrick he was blessed with special healing powers. Patrick was proud. He had powers. He was a miracle. Uncle Aloysius, who is a priest and gives his blessing each time he visits Whipple Street, told Patrick that his greatest greatest grandfather was an olden time King of Ireland. Were he still in Ireland, he, Patrick, the clan's first born male, would be king. Rightful King of the proud and mighty Sullivan clan. Late that night, the night after the afternoon when Dr. Slattery pinched his cheek and said his bones were miracle bones, Patrick floated over his sleeping brothers and sisters, to the plaster ceiling of the ten-by-ten bedroom the six Sullivan children shared, a pin-striped dormitory of mattresses, where the ungrateful six dare not stir, nor get up to pee and certainly not to ask for water until dawn. There, delighted to have left his body behind, Patrick, feeling angel wings lift him, escaped through the hoar of the window, noiselessly levitated over the blue mercury street lights, looked back on sleeping, icy Chicago, then soared through the black universe with a warm wet wind in his face and—discovering himself to be the proudest, highest-flying boy in the world--said 'How do you do?' to an astonished Man in the Moon.

***

MomsaBomb, of course, knows that Dougie is faking death. But she is learning that Dougie only comes back to life when Dougie chooses to come back to life. Disgusted, or perhaps because her arm is tired, she moves to Jenny. From the floor, Dougie looks up to Patrick, his glistening eyes proclaiming yet another victory, and mouths: "Didn't hurt, didn't hurt."

Patrick mouths back: "Did so. Did so."

Jenny screams how much she loves MomsaBomb and to please stop but such emotional appeals have the opposite effect. ("I know what's in the black hearts of bad children," she has said many times. "And I know what's good for them.") Jenny cries like one abandoned in an infinite desert. Rosemary cries because it hurts. But Jenny's desperate pleas derive from an innocence that cannot be shattered, a clarion innocence that proclaims a monstrous mistake. Her screams embrace the injustice, deny the moment; her innocence negates the possibility of such. All this is a terrible confusion, a nightmare that must end in sweet, healing forgiveness, her enfolded in the supple mercy of Jesus' universe. All the children are hushed hearing Jenny. MomsaBomb slackens hearing Jenny.

The telephone rings. Once. Then again.

MomsaBomb steps back from the six. Her nostrils are flared white and her brow is beaded with fat drops of sweat. She hisses, whispers as if the ringing phone could already overhear, that Jenny and Rosemary had better "Stop your blubbering! None of you are hurt. You're all filthy liars. Just wait till I hang up 'cause then you're going to really get it."

She picks up the phone. Rosemary and Jenny, sniffling, quiet themselves, comfort themselves, and reach out to hold Kevin and Larry. Kevin, though never beaten, cannot stop a hiccoughing kind of sobbing. Larry is wide-eyed witness to a world he never anticipated. Patrick hopes it's Grandma Powers who is calling to say she is on her way to visit. But it is one of Chicago's Finest who wants to know if there's a problem because a neighbor has reported screams coming from the Sullivan house. "Why no!" MomsaBomb says in affable offense as if she's been asked if she's a relative of President Truman. "No, Officer, no trouble here. Certainly not." She hangs up, then hangs her head. Her upturned palms limp on her knees. She begins to sob, her breasts, heavy with Larry's milk, heave. Her tears make the children feel horrible. They are the miserable brats who have

11

brought their MomsaBomb such piteous sorrow. The time of the great anger, they sense, has passed. The six supplicants advance to the angry goddess at the phone table. Larry, having recently learned how, crawls to her. They crowd as close as they dare for she could yet strike out. Rosemary holds MomsaBomb's vengeance arm while her other hand holds her own ankle. Where it still bleeds.

MomsaBomb cries through splayed fingers: "See how you pig shit brats made the police call?" Patrick strokes her beautiful hair which had a smelly Toni perm done by her lady friend Evangeline just last week. He, as the oldest boy, knowing he should be brave, takes the lead and begs her not to cry. She blows her nose and sends the four oldest off with the command to get dressed again: "Do you think you can do that? One simple thing?" Upstairs they can hear her wailing sorrow, heaping damnation on them, and onto her life with Barnaby. Barnaby who has left her alone with six brats. Patrick's heart breaks to hear the sorrow she bears.

Rosemary gives Patrick an evil look: "Paddy, you caused all this."

"Horse manure," Patrick whispers back. "I bet Dougie did it."

Dougie says: "Ish ka bibble. You're all babies."

"Up your hole with a rubber hose."

From the bottom of the stairs, her wailing gives way to nasal warnings: "Wait till your father gets home because then you're really going to get it, all of you. He will find the liar. So watch out if it's you. Mister Smiling Face Sullivan. Little Miss Brown in the Pants."

But, at eight o'clock, when Barnaby arrives home (to pork chops slathered with mustard then simmered in Campbell's chicken with rice soup), she is watching Perry Como croon like a shy virgin on the flippety floppety Motorola and never once does she mention the felonious invasion of her pink chalk pig.

***

"Patrick, don't be a dried turd; only remember the good times." What Larry likes to say: "Those were good times back then. Great old times."

Patrick long ago interred this scene. A family trait. No Sullivan ever looked back.

III

Thanksgiving Day

On Whipple Street, it was Barnaby and Bridget's turn to host the extended family on Thanksgiving Day. Always a great day: Barnaby did not have to work at the dry cleaners and the Sullivans were not obligated to go to Mass. The Saturday baths were pushed to Thursday and began at eight in the morning. Rosemary was first, locked the door and filled the tub within two inches of the rim. She then lay motionless while others pounded on the door. MomsaBomb asked through the door if she was now a fish. "Maybe Esther Williams?" Barnaby, last out of bed, hollered that there was no hot water.

MomsaBomb laid down the law: the Sullivan children were to eat at a side table and when MomsaBomb lifted her right index finger to her chin, it was the signal that the food was running low: *family hold back.* Start a fight and the relatives will bite our backs all the way home. "Douglas, Paddy...you had better be listening. We are not pig-shit Irish, you hear? All your cousins are spoiled rotten brats so--all of you--must make MomsaBomb proud."

Patrick and Rosemary watched MomsaBomb start dinner. Though barely ten in the morning, the oven had warmed the kitchen. By hanging near, they hoped to be awarded with odd jobs. Treats happen for those doing odd jobs as MomsaBomb created the greatest feast of the year. There was a twenty-pound Tom turkey, turnips, parsnips, and cranberries squeezed from a can open at both ends. Mashed potatoes and sweet potatoes both, the latter dotted with hot tiny marshmallows; creamed corn, and the oyster and sausage dressing that Grandpa Powers loved. Dessert was pumpkin pie with whipped cream from a can. Alone in the kitchen for mere seconds, Patrick squeezed the nozzle, filled his mouth with sweet billowing foam and a surge of carbon dioxide that tickled his nose.

As the guests began to arrive, Dougie and Patrick jostled to establish ownership of the coat concession. MomsaBomb, glowering, pinched firmly the thin meat of their shoulders: they were to share evenly the riches of the day.

Father Aloysius, Barnaby's big brother, gave both of them silver dollars then squared himself: "Hit me, I only want your best." He lifted his black silk bib revealing not skin but undershirt. The boys gasped then looked at each other.

"Hit!"

Dougie hit first. Then Patrick. Father Aloysius encouraged him. Laughed. Again and again till he insisted Patrick try: "Big boy, come on." Until they wouldn't hurt their knuckles further.

14

"Four hundreds sit-ups," he whispered. "Then the Mass for the Dead, then Confessions for an hour, then a three hour walk. Try it. *Wimps.* They're softies, Barney! Your boys are wimps!"

Grandpa Powers gave both boys quarters. Uncle Alex and Aunt Evie arrived but all Patrick and Dougie got for their troubles were kisses. Bishop Quinlan, Father Aloysius' best friend, was last to arrive. Patrick and Dougie dropped to their knees and kissed his ring. Patrick hoped that all of Whipple Street realized that the black Cadillac at the Sullivan's curb belonged to a Bishop. The Bishop tipped both boys with uncirculated dollar bills.

***

MomsaBomb's unforgettable ritual on Thanksgiving was the creation of éclairs beginning with the kneading then mounding of sticky dough, her floured fingers disappearing then reemerging. The children could watch so long as they did not push or shove. Flour soon covered the kitchen table and the linoleum acquired a dusty patina. MomsaBomb read from a yellowed handwritten recipe, that of a Great Aunt now dead. Patrick and Rosemary, this and every Thanksgiving, tried to read the ingredients but could not decipher the 19th Century script. "Irish people aren't like we are today," advised MomsaBomb. "Their handwriting is funny and they went to the bathroom out of doors." Rosemary and Patrick nodded their agreement, felt privileged to share facts historically arcane. There was no dessert more famous in the entire Sullivan family. Even the aunts and uncles said so. MomsaBomb said that they were right. She also said, before they began to arrive, that they were all big mouths. All her brothers and sisters wanted to do on the phone was yak. Didn't they know that the Mother of Bell Telephone was clicking off the minutes costing nickels and dimes all the while that they yakked about absolutely nothing?

The morning's ritual consisted of tiers of unfolding events: after the éclair shells have been baked MomsaBomb cooled them on cookie sheets in the boot room which was not heated. Once the milkman delivered milk when it was ten below zero and milk flared out the bottle top like vanilla ice cream without a cone. MomsaBomb wouldn't pay. Said the milkman was a dummy and it wasn't the Sullivan's fault that the milk was ruined. After that, Barnaby had to stop at the dairy store and carry milk home, a chore he forever rued, carrying six and seven gallons, after working and slaving for "you kids" all day.

Carrying bags to the garbage cans in the alley, Patrick passed two trays of golden pastry puffs with jagged peaks cooling in the boot room. Next they would be filled with vanilla pudding. Then MomsaBomb would replace the crowns, lather their jagged peaks with chocolate frosting, and tease each to a beckoning peak with a bent finger. Patrick's hunger was enormous. He wondered whether tonight, when dessert was served, he would get more than one éclair. He dreamed of two. Perhaps even three.

His nine-year-old belly after all could easily accommodate six. Or more. He counted, touching each peak: thirty-six unfilled shells. Perhaps after company left there would be as many as ten for him to devour? Patrick knew that he must be on guard to get his fair share. Douglas was a hog pig. Always had been. And Rosemary a terrible obslay. (But she could be nice too as she was teaching Patrick Pig Latin and Barnaby giggled when they spoke: "You characters, you really crack up your old Dad.")

MomsaBomb was the greatest cooker in the world. The Sullivan kids knew that in their blood. Didn't she send her éclair recipe to Royal Pudding company with a letter telling them that if they showed an advertisement in the *Saturday Evening Post* or *Life* or *Look* of a mother making these éclairs with her six children watching hungrily then they could use that idea to sell about "a million, maybe even a *billion* boxes" of their puddings? Or so she limned in the letter. For her grand idea, the president of Royal Pudding would surely send MomsaBomb a thousand or ten thousand million dollars. With the money, she would buy a sofa and rugs and new clothes "for each and every one of you brats". Royal Pudding did send a letter in return. She read it and then tears flowed. Told the children crowded around that Royal Pudding said "no, but thank you" for the interesting idea and here are some nickel-off coupons so you can enjoy more Royal Pudding.

"They're stupid," said MomsaBomb. "Stupid, stupid." She sat and they stroked her hands. All agreed that Royal Pudding was a stupid bunch of ignoramuses and so the Sullivans switched to My-T-Fine (after using the coupons) and Royal Pudding lost the Sullivans as good customers forever. MomsaBomb always was on the lookout, when perusing magazines for several years after, to see if her recipe had been stolen by "those jerks" who owned Royal Pudding.

Dougie and Patrick watched her as she scooped out the gooey insides of the eclairs. Dougie's hand was slapped for trying to eat a handful of the goo which would only turn to a rock in his little stomach: "There's company and I don't want any of you puking your guts, okay?"

She ladled vanilla pudding into each cavity, restored the crowns and topped them with frosting. Dougie and Patrick were awarded the licking of the chocolate frosting pan. They fought, but only with words, over who was hog-pigging the most but MomsaBomb did not hit anyone. Even her voice, this day, was unusually calm as she sipped an ice drink from Manhattan: "You two, cut it out or Bishop Quinlan will hear."

At noon Patrick, taking a bag of trash to the alley, passed the finished éclairs where they rested on cookie sheets in the boot room. With a deft swipe at the tray, he liberated one from the outside rim, and crammed it into his mouth. All at once, the entire éclair. He chewed madly, with his back to the house, so that no nosey brother or sister could see. He swallowed quickly—lest he be detected--with little time to savor

16

the taste remembered from prior holidays--the almost unbelievable goodness, this mixture of chocolate, vanilla pudding and pastry, baked by the greatest éclair maker in the world.

In the boot room, before re-entering the steam of the crowded kitchen, he licked his lips furiously to hide any trace of chocolate or pudding and rearranged the tray: one éclair would never be missed. Or had she counted? He floated into the kitchen—smiling beatifically, a saint-in-training approaching the altar for Holy Communion.

Later, but only a half-hour later, he offered to take to the alley a quarter-filled bag of eggshells, gizzards and carrot peels. On this job, he ingested a second éclair. Again he chewed furiously. If MomsaBomb opened the door with a rinsed-out milk bottle, he knew he risked being slammed to the wall. But Grandma Powers and MomsaBomb had made another iced drink from Manhattan, with cherries inside that have been totally ruined by whiskey, and no one seemed to be thinking about éclairs except Patrick. Grandpa Powers, Barnaby, Bishop Quinlan and Uncle Aloysius were watching the Bears and the Lions hitting each other in the mud on the flippety floppety Motorola. He could hear them booing and cheering in the living room.

He saw Dougie go to the boot room and come back in looking down at the floor like he had just lost a penny.

Was Dougie sneaking éclairs too?

Then Patrick saw Rosemary return from the boot room. This was extremely suspicious because Rosemary never volunteered to go near the cold alley or touch a garbage bag.

Sitting on Grandma Power's lap, her arms working around him while she peeled sweet potatoes, Patrick saw Dougie enter then return from the boot room: his face was flushed as if just slapped by the hand of God. Patrick blanched as he realized that Dougie was still swallowing. *He will eat them all.* Patrick became a maelstrom of inside screams. Then quickly proceeded to create volunteer trip after volunteer trip. On the most gluttonous excursion, he devoured three éclairs in mad, choking succession. Lest Dougie, that sneak, rob them all.

The platters, rearranged to disguise lacunae, were shrinking by the hour. By three o'clock when the table was set with the China plates with the beautiful red roosters and water glasses from Ireland where the Sullivans were kings in the olden days, twenty éclairs have disappeared. But in the kitchen the laughter was raucous. The Tom's roasting pan had fallen from the open oven door and the golden gobbler had slid across the linoleum coming to rest under the Formica table. Grandma Power grabbed it with her bare hands, put it on a chair, and commanded it to "stay right there, damn you! This turkey must be a Mason, Bridget!"

Aunt Evie shook so hard that she had to hold her boobs in her dress. The priests, Barnaby, the uncles and Grandpa Powers rushed from the football game to see the cause of all the shouting. Barnaby asked four times if MomsaBomb was sure the turkey was dead. MomsaBomb laughed so hard she got the hiccoughs. Today, it was clear that she really loved her children because she kissed and squeezed each about six times.

At six o'clock, when the éclairs were finally served, there was still one for everyone in the family. MomsaBomb looked to the children's table, with a wry smile, and announced that "someone's been sneaking". Dougie, Rosemary and Patrick shook their red-faced heads in innocent protestation, were indeed grievously offended by the very suggestion. Patrick pointed at Dougie. Dougie kicked Patrick under the table. Rosemary smirked. But MomsaBomb only laughed because the ravaged batch of éclairs proved once again that she was, in the eyes of her loving children, the best cooker and the best Mom, not just in Chicago, but in the whole round world.

***

Late that night, after the company was long gone, after the children had had turkey sandwiches on toast with mayonnaise and lots of salt and finished off the last of the pumpkin pie with whipped cream from the sputtering can, Patrick awoke. Heard Barnaby's swears and MomsaBomb's screeches. Heard fists hitting flesh. Patrick squeezed shut his eyes, said mile-a-minute prayers to the Trinity and the Virgin Mary.

IV
Riverside Drive

Patrick Sullivan at age 45 ran East Coast sales for a Napa winery at a time when the wines of Napa Valley were taking their place next to the great wines of France. The French greeted Napa's success with denial and arrogance. But the consumer and the critics for the most part cared little about French pique. Prior to August Discipio, Patrick's hero and boss, California had only produced brandy-fortified wines that eased the afternoons of alcoholics. August Discipio's wines deliberately reached for the stars. His wines caused amazement first in California then in the rest of the country and of late in Europe and Asia. The neighboring wineries of the valley followed him like so many grateful lemmings. Followed him over a cliff of glory. August Discipio, a man with steely grey eyes, a man who forever marched forward without a false step, was a black and white contrast to Barnaby the Boozer.

Beginning ten years earlier, August's odyssey became Patrick's odyssey. Patrick nominated August as his mentor and hero. No hotel or steak house, no airline or cruise line was free from the assault that Patrick mounted to win them over to Discipio wines. In recent years, a stroke had ended August's travels. No longer could he regale foreign dignitaries, millionaires and politicos with stories of his conquests not always entirely true for as he aged he spun gloss upon his commercial victories. Though he probably had not read a book since college, he intuitively knew that storytelling was an art and that art is nothing if not exaggeration. A kind of jeweler in his senior years he polished the diamonds of his career while drinking the twenty and thirty year old wines of his glory years, and did not hesitate to embellish history. Embellishments his interlocutors would repeat following a lunch or dinner with the great man. How legends start. The mixing of truths, the making of myths. But then came the stroke. Italian families are all about the glorious future of their sons and August's son, Carmine, from the night of August's embolism had seized his birthright, and already dreaming of the time he'd take over the business, occupied with big eyes and envy the oversized boots his father's life had created.

On this June night, toward the midnight hour, Patrick sleepily rode the elevator returning to his co-op on Riverside Drive. This following dinner during which thirty bottles of cabernet and Bordeaux had been consumed with the Manhattan Oenophiliac Barristers. ("We're the MOB", he was told five times--Patrick's count--by red-faced members.) Though the night had been a commercial success, heretofore heathen lawyers gravitating from pagan Bordeaux to the recently baptized Cabernets of Napa Valley, Patrick felt broken.

Rebecca heard his key in the door.

"You're not in bed?"

"Pat, we need to talk."

"I can't. I'm destroyed. The dinner went on and on." Patrick was still able to run a mile or three each day despite the aches and clicks of popcorn knees. Having nothing to do with running his muscled arms and chest were—had always been—firm. Sculpted. All day and all night in a state of flex. With no effort. Stasis. Just the ways things were. In the locker room, surrounded by mirrors, he'd muse while thinking of Barnaby's whitish flab.

"It's Melissa."

"Melissa. Why am I not surprised?" He dropped his briefcase and jacket on the white sofa. Flopped with legs stretched before him.

"Pat, she's in her room. In front of Mannie's shrine. Praying. Or something."

Patrick asked: "Proving again that I live in a mausoleum?" Rebecca indeed also kept photos of her dead husband, Mannie, everywhere, even in the master bedroom.

"She's locked herself in."

"She wants to be alone."

"I'm worried sick."

"She won't break."

"My astrologer said this morning that Melissa's day would not be good."

Patrick, slowed by an eighteen hour day, pushed himself down the railroad flat's hall. At Melissa's door, he stood in a low haze of jasmine, sandalwood, and vanilla bean that floated through the jamb. He knocked. Rapped repeatedly. Pushed. The door, locked from inside, would not budge.

"Melissa, let's talk."

Nothing.

"I haven't heard a sound for an hour."

"You had your ear at the door?"

"I did."

"She's stoned."

"Force it."

"Let's wait her out."

"No. Pat, please."

"I have to sleep."

He shouldered, then kicked the door; fumbled unsuccessfully at the hinges with a screwdriver. "Stand back." He kicked the door's center

21

panel till he had opened a square foot of a hole. With elbow bent he reached in and turned the knob. Upon opening they saw perhaps twenty candles and, within the haze, naked Melissa. Unconscious on her eighteenth birthday. Under dead Mannie's smiling visage. And other dead men, in poster form, Melissa's Trinity: John Lennon, John Belushi and Jimi Hendrix. On the night stand, Patrick's bottle of sleeping pills, lying on its side, empty; his nighty-night pills kept in reserve for monthly red eyes back from California.

On the West Side Highway, Patrick's Mercedes reached a hundred and twenty. Rebecca, in the backseat, cradled her wrapped-in-a-blanket daughter, implored her, demanded that she not "give up, don't you dare... If you see a white light beckoning, you must not go!" Melissa moaned a little, nothing more.

At Presbyterian-St. Luke's, Melissa's tiny belly was pumped till six in the morning. Then wide-smiling Dr. Rangsnathan appeared: "So sorry, you must be mother and father. Little girl, she need psych eval. Cannot do here. Very troubled these kids. No ambition." His is an idiot laugh. "You sign here. Bellevue has bed. She be fine. You are wine man? Sikhs don't do alcohol. I am very bad Sikh to so love wine. Yuk or yum, I drink them all. Which is very very best vintage? I buy only that. You know! Tell me now! She be fine. I don't like cocktail. Wine! I think all wine to be yuk or yum. Either one. Just like life, Mr. Sullivan?"

***

Silently they watched Melissa's gurney glide into the ambulance even as the first sun sneaked over Washington Heights. Back at their co-op, Rebecca found what she had missed when scooping up her unconscious daughter. Found a lengthy epistle in which Melissa revealed that Rebecca had won worst mother and Patrick, in the place position, a "bastard" of a step-father award. It was they, Patrick and Rebecca, who had poured the sleeping pills down Melissa's gullet, the two of them, it seemed, like a couple of French peasants fattening their goose's *foie*. The letter ended with an unfinished line: *"You are both total..."*

That long day, as neither thought of sleep, Rebecca in a straight back chair repeatedly mused for and demanded answers of herself and Patrick. She stabbed herself with what she could have and certainly should have done, while dully overlooking the Hudson where petroleum barges, their hulls almost submerged, arduously plied the river. On the bosky Jersey side, a green world beckoned. Patrick sat on the sofa, sunk into the down cushions his chest buffeted with throw pillows. Melissa was not the only subject. The couple reviewed their five years of marriage. Reviewed too the night before.

"I tried to be a father."

"Sure."

"I did. You know I tried."

"We failed her, Pat."

"*'We'* did?"

"Last night speaks for itself."

"Mannie ran the first shift."

Rebecca's eyes looked slowly up from the deep red veins of palmate philodendron, shivered somehow without moving a muscle, then and returned to the plant. "Ok. It's all on me."

"Mannie too."

"I married him. It's all on me."

Into the late morning, in a dispirited way, hardly for the first time, they revisited the tedious arguments that had comprised their marriage like so many shriveled apple parings. Patrick declared: "She needs to work things out. All alone."

"I should abandon her?"

"You are too close. You have always been too close."

"Pat, how can anyone be too close?"

"At her age, every Sullivan kid was on his own."

"You're going to hold up the glorious Sullivans to me?"

"I am. Melissa needs to be spun off into the universe."

"While she's still in Bellevue? Or should I wait for her release?"

"She'll be out in a week. Spin her off, Rebec."

"That's really not possible. Not for a Jewish mother."

"So stop being a Jew."

"That's sick."

"I stopped the Catholic thing."

"You're dead. Do you know that?"

"No." Patrick looked longingly into the bolsters of the down-filled sofa, wondered how many geese had lived and died to provide him comfort that day. "It's Dougie who's dead."

"What?"

"I'm the one who smiles." Patrick smiled weakly.

"You're out of your body."

"Probably."

"Stone cold bastard."

"I have to leave."

"What's more important than this?"

"Carmine. I'm picking him up at Laguardia."

"Really, fuck Carmine."

"The source of many bucks."

"Pat, we could live in a cottage on the shore. Maybe in the desert."

"Maybe. Maybe."

"If you wanted to…"

"*If* I wanted to."

"But you don't."

"Honestly. No."

"Which means?"

The apartment was a freeze frame. Their life had often devolved to this, the tedium of no will. Patrick knew the feeling well. *I never wish to touch, nor be touched, by you again.* "Rebek, if not for testosterone, I don't think I ever would have married. Either time. Not Annette, not you." She whitened. "I'm sorry. But there's the truth."

"You're sorry. And you're right. You're the original son of a bitch."

"I'm out of here."

"You're not really going to leave?"

"Look what I've done to your life. To Melissa. I peddle wine. Beyond that, there's not a helluva lot going on."

***

He packed for two weeks, then from the front door watched Rebecca's tears drip-irrigate the begonias in the window box. She crossed to him, measured him, spoke slowly: "You are such a liar." She slapped him. Open hand but roundhouse. Patrick erected a faint grin. Then smiled broadly. She held her palm, caressed it, shivered, cradled her breasts within crossed elbows. He stepped into the foyer. His cheek still stinging. The sting a kind of thrill. He felt like returning. To bed her.

He did not.

Awaiting the elevator Rebecca said softly: "Your whole family is standing next to you. Right there."

"I've risen above them."

There was no more to be said. Not by Patrick. He had already gone to a conversation with a yakky aging rental agent pointing out the conveniences of a one-room executive suite with phone, fax and a Murphy bed. "All you need, Mr. Sullivan for a solid, profitable commercial life. A perfect life in the Apple. Should I call you Patrick? Pat?"

V

LGA

Crossing Central Park, the car phone rang.

"Paddy Sullivan, my most favoritest oldest brother." Larry's voice, his cheer.

"Are you in Dublin?"

"Almost. We're at O'Hare."

"So...*bon voyage* and what's up?"

"I want to hear the magic word."

"It's still no."

"Wrong answer."

"This kid's got many bottles yet to sell."

"I've got four hundred cars to move by August and I'm still going to our beloved parents' anniversary."

"You're a great executive. I'm not."

"Paddy, I want you in Dublin."

"*So* Barnaby can punch me in front of the grandchildren? Surely you jest."

"Paddy. How old are you? His slug-the-kids days ended years ago."

"I doubt it."

"He's mellow, he cries a lot."

"After how much juice?"

"The old guy loves your ass."

"He doesn't know what my ass looks like."

"I showed him pictures from your wedding."

"Lar, I've got to go."

"Paddy, it's their Golden."

"I am so indifferent that words fail me."

Larry shouted: "Paddy, do I have to stop in New York and drag your butt to Dublin?"

Patrick shouted in return: "Why this? You know I don't care if they live or die."

"*Paddy*. Come for the rest of us. Jesus, Mary and Joseph, we're all going. Except you and Kevin. You are about to earn my Asshole of the Year Award." He whispered: "Come for me."

"Bro, I'll meet you and Paulie somewhere. Ever been to St. Barths?"

"All your nephews and nieces think their Uncle Pat is the case of wine that comes at Christmas. *They don't know you.* How long can you hold out?"

Twenty-five years? "It's not about holding out."

Patrick pushed the End button. *Lar, you'd punch me to hear me say this but I've forgotten just about everything about back there.*

Having rung off from Larry and his insistence that Patrick come to Dublin, Patrick crossed the Triborough Bridge to collect Carmine Discipio at LaGuardia. On his cell phone, Patrick left a message for the East Coast team: "Hey, out there! This end-of-year battle, it's a big one. Guys...you too Abbie in Boston, I didn't forget you, babes--it's stand-up-time once more at Discipio Winery!" *Once more, dear friends, unto the....* Patrick felt himself inserting a knife in his own belly, and twisting. That his only future was years and years of such bluster. "I will take us to Maui where we will drink Dom Perignon in the pool and I promise you that your loved ones will forget every night that I got you to stay on the road making numbers." He tromped on the gas pedal, the needle edged toward a hundred entering Astoria. *Twenty-four years out of Georgetown, and I suffer a bulimia of clichés. I have murdered my bibliophiliac self. My portfolio, however, is good--even after I give half to Rebecca. (No pre-nup! Was I mad?) With what I have now, I can buy a small hotel on a tropical island. Victoria. Does she desire--as do I—a return to shameless nights?*

***

In the private plane terminal, Carmine Discipio approached leaking enthusiasm: "*Hola*, Senor Sullivan, how would you like us to own half Chile's vineyards?"

"Half the vineyards or half the country?"

"It's the same thing. Vineyards are all they have down there. I met this guy: Bolivar. Yesterday, Bolivar called His Holiness the president of fucking Chile on my car phone. Can you believe it? To clear the way for my buying half the fucking country. Patrick, I will be a goddamned Don. Zorro."

"Zorro sliced up the Dons. Zip, zip, zip?"

Carmine, in black shirt and black linen suit, looked with both misapprehension and confusion then continued. "We don't have to lay out a peso. Do they have pesos or dollars down there? Anyway it's an all-stock deal. Now I need you, Patrick, to get our stock price up. *Way, way* up."

Carmine's black silk shirt with the top three buttons not done displayed a jungle of chest hair. From his neck hung a golden bejeweled wine goblet. In his mid-forties, he wore his black and silver mane slicked back with pomade like a silent screen star; this sheen along with a rat tail,

27

and dense, wild black eyebrows, was the result of a makeover by an Iranian in Beverly Hills. The PR department thought Carmine needed to become an icon if Discipio was going to spend many millions each year on television. Slim ("Pecker" as he was known) Peckinpah, the Discipio PR head, described the desired look: "We need a guy who looks like he rides the vineyards all day on a black horse. A guy who, when he spots a beautiful woman is capable of getting off that horse and taking her. Right there in the dirt. Her ecstasy between rows of purple clusters." Carmine was more than just pleased with the icon assignment and was rarely out of costume.

"Pat, two weeks from now, when the Board of Directors asks you about this plan, you know, 'Is this a crazy idea?' Charlie Dodd will ask you that sure as shit. At that moment I need you to say: 'Charley, this is money in the fucking bank'. I'm not stopping with Chile."

"Such as?"

"Discipio Oregon and Washington. Discipio Australia. Discipio Tuscany".

"Your father agreed to this?"

"My father has a big name and a farmer's brain."

"But…your father agreed to this?"

"My father is veg. I am now Discipio."

"Your father has a great heart."

"I will be bigger than three of him." He leaned in: "When we get really big France is there for the plucking."

Patrick stopped in the mall outside Duty Free. Turned to Carmine. "This is the not the ride I signed onto."

"Which was?"

"In an ugly world we made something beautiful."

"You can always jump ship. Rats do that."

"I've thought of it."

"Well?"

Patrick closed his eyes and saw Rebecca as he waited for the elevator. In her eyes and sagging lips, the despair unto death felt by one facing abandonment. "Carmine, I think it's time."

"Time for?"

"For you to work out a parachute. For this rat."

VI
JFK

"Dublin. One way."

The freckled Aer Lingus agent had strawberry blond hair with locks below her shoulders. She had darting blue eyes and fair skin that revealed the bloodlines of the 9th Century Norse who had raped the coast of Ireland. "You are emigrating, Mr. Sullivan?"

"To the land of beauties just like you."

"I'm just a normal girl."

"I like normal. Let's meet in Dublin? Think of lust-filled nights together. You could save me, me a lonely émigré."

Not looking up from the keyboard, she replied lightly: "Go fook yourself. Mr. Sullivan."

Rebuffed he thought a second. "Give me a round tripper too. Make it out to Kevin Sullivan."

***

In Business Class, the plane still on the tarmac, Patrick dialed Kevin.

"Kootenay Bait shop. All our worms are fat and juicy."

"It's your big brother."

"You haven't called in a year."

"And you? You got broken fingers?"

"Touché."

"I've decided we need to reconnect to the clan. In Dublin."

"Larry's been calling. No way. Really, Patty I don't want to go and can't afford it anyways."

"If I go you have to go."

"You are going?"

"I have a certain feeling. Nothing I can put in words. This might not work but anyway there's a round-trip ticket to Dublin with your name on it. You fly tonight. Out of Spokane."

""You did *what*?"

"Erin go bragh."

***

The jet lumbered over Long Island Sound. By Nantucket he was awash in dreams more real, more vivid, than their premieres in decades long past. A sleep deprived Patrick took two blue pills and quickly drained two splits of Champagne. His head starting to spin, he fantasized falling though the window, in a gyre hurtling toward the white-caps below.

The stewardess's voice stirred him: "Brandy, Mr. Sullivan."

"Two, darlin'. Sit and have one with me."

"Nasty boy."

***

Somewhere over the North Atlantic Patrick emerged from the Aer Lingus blanket. His left parietal lobe throbbed as if being drilled by a jackhammer. He thought back to the Champagne and the sleeping pills. Brandy. Wondered what had happened to the common wisdom that alcohol is not to be enjoyed at 35,000 feet. He looked upon an endless blanketed floor of clouds. Then sleep took him to a time just after he had begun with August Discipio. His trip to see Kevin. To Durango and the white collar lock-up where Kevin had been sentenced for interstate trafficking, sixteen to twenty-four months.

***

Durango is a minimum security institution with an electrified perimeter but no guard towers. Patrick and Kevin were free to walk the grounds. His clothes were not the institutional green Patrick had expected; Kevin wore a "Free Me" white T-shirt, white pajama pants that billowed like a genie's and Jesus sandals; a snake pendant climbed toward his Adam's apple. He wore granny specs and shoulder length blond hair that framed his viewlike blinders.

"I hate to see you in here."

"At least you came."

"No Rosemary?"

"Nope."

"No Jenny? Larry?"

"You're the only one."

"Did you ask them?"

"Brothers and sisters need to be asked?"

"I did." The yellow aspen leaves of autumn rustled as they walked a lane. Patrick asked: "What about your parents?"

"I think you mean '*our*' parents? Barnaby did write but only once. Told me what a dumb ass I am. Guess what: *I know* I'm a dumb ass."

Kevin had grown a foot since last Patrick had seen him last on Whipple Street when he was ten or eleven. His middle and neck had thickened. "Starch," said Kevin. "The main thing they give you here is starch. The only good thing is my job in the library. Lady Chatterley's Lover is the *numero uno* meat book."

Kevin at that visit was more stranger than brother; Patrick knew little of his doings the past fifteen years. He remembered him best as when he left him; an eleven-year-old that New Year's Eve when Patrick jettisoned the family and Chicago. Patrick was taken back to a letter received at Georgetown, a letter Patrick had kept in his billfold for years until it finally shredded. He had first read it sitting in his dorm room at the Evans House.

Dear Paddy,

It's getting bad here since you left. Mostly because I'm lonely. I miss you!!! I have Sister Faith Mary and you know how mean she is but when I'm at school then I hate going home. In my writing class I wrote a poem. Here it is.

Patrick rat trick
Hides in the attic

Larry ate the berries
When Mother baked the pie

Kevin speaks to angels
Lying on his side

I hope you like it. I received a VG for Very Good from Sister Faith Mary but she should have given me E for Excellent.

Also if I didn't tell you there is a boy in my class now whose name is Jesus (I just bowed my head) but for Mexicans naming a kid after God's son is not a sin. Did you know that fact?

Since Rosemary got her job taking care of defektiv children Jenny just calls Pranzo's Pizza each night and we get to have pizza for dinner. Which is one good thing anyway. Do you like Pepper O'Nee? I love it. Larry and I still play War and now we are learning Monopoly.

I want to ask you something--can I come to live with you at college?

Missing you a lot,

Your brother,

Kevin

P.S. Say hello to presdent Kenndy if you see him.

You lucky dog.

"So..." Kevin asked, 'What happened to you and Annette?"

"I was mad at her all the time. All the time. She's still the perfect sweetie, a great mom. You'd know that. *If* you had ever come to New York.'

Kevin ignored Patrick's dig.

***

Kevin never did come to New York. At age 19 he had fled Whipple Street. Like Patrick had done at 18. But Kevin had fled westward and lived—at different times--in the Haight, Maui, Big Sur. Once he had offered that he was living "Up in Oregon" as if that was a postal address. He was maybe with a woman, maybe not, no one in the family ever knew much. Like Patrick, he never spoke to his parents. Kevin's need to talk to family descended only upon Patrick. Usually between two and four in the morning.

"Where the hell are you?"

"Some people have a house." Kevin's voice full of slurred sentiments. "Bro, do I miss you! I love you so much!"

"Give me your number so I can call once in a while. During human time."

"Can't do it."

"Why not?"

"Cause I'm leaving."

"When?"

"I don't know. These people they don't know I'm using their phone. I don't think they care. If they do, I'll pay them."

"Who are they?"

"Super together people."

"So where can I call you?"

"You need to be closer than you are. Under a hundred yards." He laughed the pothead laugh. Kevin's favorite gag, age five: "How do you call someone who doesn't own a phone?" Patrick remembered this better

33

than any recent event. Kevin rolling on the kitchen floor, clutching at his belly, spitting out the punch line: "Very loudly."

"Kev, I love ya guy, but I'm going back to sleep."

"But I wanna talk!"

"Not now!" Fumbling in the dark Patrick slammed the phone down. Annette, awake also, and living a life getting smaller by the day, spoke quietly: "That was Kevin?"

"Someone answering to his name."

***

They watched a basketball game. Kevin pointed out the players by criminal offense: an embezzler playing center, a stockbroker-market rigger at a guard position, and several petty drug offenders at the others.

Kevin gave the details of his bust: "I had retired—from the business, if you know what I mean--when these two guys I met in a bar started to talk up a buy. They were very persuasive. I decided: okay, one last deal before I retire."

"It was entrapment?"

"Indeed it was. So my lawyer came up with this brilliant defense---that I was *really* just stringing them along. To entrap them? So my lawyer puts me on the stand and I said, 'In fact, your honor, Ms. Judge, I was--civic citizen that I am--simply collecting evidence for some future court. Perhaps this very court of yours, Ms. Honorable Judge. I was just about to make a citizen's arrest when....' The judge—what a total bitch--started laughing. Right there in the courtroom. Best joke she'd heard in a long, long time. Great lawyer I had. He charged me five grand. Up front."

"Where'd you get five grand?"

"I had to do one more deal."

They walked a stone path. The time was late September and, though the afternoon was warm, snow already had settled upon the higher elevations. Kevin said that he walked the path a lot. To get out of the cigarette smoke and the incessant click-click of ping pong in the game room. They moved to an isolated patch of lawn and sat. Kevin talked of life in the Durango pen: "All these guys in here, they're all a bunch of compulsive liars. Paddy, I hate it so much."

"When do they let you out?"

"Maybe March. April. Want to know Jimmy Carter's visitors today? Every Cub's batting average? The UN General Assembly opens today, I bet you didn't know that." Kevin, recumbent, stared into the trees. "I've started to write stories again."

"Animals? More animals?"

"Forever and always."

***

Kevin wrote animal stories even before high school. Rosemary would enclose them with her letters. She also told stories of Kevin's doings. How Kevin had immolated Barnaby's wedding watch in the coal furnace. How he had boiled goldfish on the stove. How two baby pigeons were found dead in the garage with straight pins piercing their brains. Rosemary wrote that Kevin denied everything but all the evidence pointed at him. Barnaby dismissed it as, "Boy stuff, stuff all kids do."

Bishop Quinlan took MomsaBomb's side and arranged to have Kevin examined. The psychiatrist prescribed electric shock. Rosemary thought this involved two or three treatments. But quickly Barnaby had had enough of psychiatrists and their foot-long bills: "Those witch doctors don't know their anuses from holes in the ground. Kevin's looking for attention, that's all."

Kevin's IQ was the buzz of The Play Pen. "How's that boy who's a genius? Wazzisname again? An IQ of one-hundred-and-forty?"

"One-forty-eight," Bridget corrected.

"Knowing you two, Barnaby, Bridget: I mush tell you that I am not at all surprised. No, goddammit. Not at all!"

And Barnaby, with a flick of his pinkie finger, signaled: "Fat! One more for my friend and me." And Fat Callaghan poured another round.

***

Patrick ended the Durango visit and drove to Denver to catch a plane. Kevin was paroled in the spring then disappeared for two years. Their relationship devolved to waiting for the next call. Whenever Patrick thought of Kevin he thought of the animal stories. And then shook his head in wonder. After Rosemary moved out, Kevin sent Patrick his high school stories. Patrick sent back notes, for the most part limited to corrections of grammar. The stories, in their envelopes going back and forth from Chicago and Georgetown, comprised what they were to each other--a postal relationship.

Any humans found in Kevin's stories had been scrupulously included as filler like a French novelist is careful to include the furniture in each and every room. Somewhat necessary to the narrative but hardly central. Kevin's one and true universe was, again and again, a perky menagerie of animals forever saying sweet things.

Then once in Jackson Hole, Patrick led a tasting for forensic scientists, coroners all. The finishing act in a week-long conference, he led them through Chardonnay and Sauvignon Blanc, Pinot Noir and Cabernet Sauvignon. They asked technical questions, the chemistry of wine, and when the seminar ended in the early afternoon, Patrick decided to make a weekend of it and drove north into Idaho. Drove his rented convertible with the top down and let sun and wind clean business from his brain. The road north to Kevin's town was sinuous and lightly traveled as it followed the coursing Kootenay. The sun shimmered on rushing water and diving birds fed on insects flitting over the roiling surface. Patrick could disappear till Monday back in New York.

He almost missed the turnoff, a shotgun-peppered road sign on the gravel shoulder.

Snakeskin

Population 27

Driving across a suspension bridge he quickly came upon his destination. More shack than house, the sign read:

Kevin's Bait Emporium
Worms & Other Nutrients, Beer

Kevin nearly lost his mind when Patrick pulled to the door. The screen door slammed and 6'2" Kevin bounded into the convertible to give Patrick a big wet kiss.

They caught up while sitting at a picnic table on the banks of the river. A guy named Joe, a Nez Percé from up the road, stopped to talk. His skin was olive, dry leather. His cheeks were hollow and his chin bore occasional white whiskers.

"Kevin told me about you. You are the wine guy."

"That's me."

"You sell wines for a hundred dollars a bottle?"

"Some."

Joe was dazzled. Struck by the unfathomable mystery of such a product. He spoke of his son, only four, who had some sort of a blood disease. "The BIA didn't do nothin'. Gave me a prescription. His mother moved back to the res. Bitch."

Joe left. They watched him walk down the road to his sick son.

Kevin erected a tent for Patrick close to the river. "You will sleep the best sleep of your life." Then he brought a cooler of beer from the shop and harvested some trout from lines he had strung along the bank. "Illegal. But delicious." From his shirt pocket he pulled out Red Skelton, a pet chipmunk.

"Why do you call him Red Skelton?"

"Watch." Kevin tickled Red Skelton's belly. The pet stood on its hind legs and shook. The tickling caused the chipmunk to giggle and shake.

While Red Skelton searched the table for crumbs, Kevin gutted four trout and roasted them over an open fire. They ate not speaking of Chicago, a subject neither cared to return to. They devoured all four trout, two bags of potato chips and eight beers.

Patrick asked: "You still writing about animals?"

36

"You bet. Winters are long on the Kootenay. I've had time. Time is my best friend. Paddy, it's weird, sometimes I don't know anything. Other times I know everything." His look was of one sharing a mysterious formula: "Maybe just after seeing a tree squirrel fly. Everything is so unbelievably clear to me. There have been days, and nights, the past couple of years, when the stories just kind of wrote themselves. The customers...I just take their money and don't even gab any more. Who needs other people. I haven't been with a woman for a long time. Stories keep flowing from me like I'm a river or something."

"Kev, you're kind of babbling."

"Sorry." Kevin's eyes narrowed then flared: "Don't say that. You of all people."

"Gotten anything...published?"

"No. No high falutin' magazine in the whole country understands what I feel in me. It's somehow...maybe you'll understand—it's sacred? What's been going on in me. And private?"

In the gloaming the only sounds were river water over rocks and the whir of bats hunting mosquitoes in the pines. "That's what I do out here. If I have something I like after writing half the night, it's more than what I had when I started the night." A dreamy Patrick listened through the fog of the beer, let the dark adumbration of hills take him over. Kevin went on: "You will hear the coyotes tonight, we've got lots around here. I listen to them. The things they say, I'm amazed at their talk. I write what they say to me. Sometimes I only have curlicues and doodles to look at by three in the morning. Other times good stuff pours out of me--like God lives in my fingertips? Paddy, can you imagine how good that feels?"

Patrick, his stomach filled and his mind quieted, could only reply: "I guess."

They sat in silence on the picnic bench facing the black ripples in the murmuring current. The night air cooled after the sun had fallen. When Kevin started to speak again, his voice was different; Patrick heard a hushed timbre emerge: "I hope you don't think it's crazy. But the writing, it is more than making up stories. It's like...like when we were kids, Paddy, and I'm happy when I'm doing it." He laughed a soft laugh. "I am going to tell you a story I wrote last winter. First let me tell you that I wrote it after ten days in a snow cave. Not talking once. Joe took care of the emporium." He looked into the river waters, then continued: "I call it 'The Tale of the I Shall Be Pleased Boy'. Paddy: are you listening?"

"Sure."

"You really want to hear it?"

"Really."

"Paddy, when I wrote this...I had this feeling...like I was on the other side?" His face wore a huge grin.

Patrick looked off at the river and asked: "'The other side' of?"

"Doesn't matter. The other side."

He spun his story. Without any paper. Recited the fable as the night deepened.

"There once was a boy who had been brought to a small village next to the ocean by an old sailor. The old sailor said he had won the boy in a game of dice. The sailor was dying and wanted to leave the boy with the villagers. Because the boy's fingers were joined by skin like webs, the old sailor told them the boy was lucky. But the villagers called him Frog Boy and only laughed when the old sailor and the boy passed by.

"Then the sailor got drunk and fell from a cliff into the sea. So the Frog Boy was forced to walk the streets begging for scraps, always smiling and saying 'Please'. In his rags, he walked the lanes and byways of the coastal hamlet, his cry from the lane plaintive but friendly: 'Please, I shall perform for thee. Just a little scrap for me?' And the Frog Boy performed any trick requested.

"One day the miller's boy said: 'Frog Boy, I want you to jump from the roof of my father's shed.'

"And the Frog Boy said: 'I shall be pleased.'

"And he jumped from high on the shed and the miller's boy bellowed a harsh laugh to see the Frog Boy lying in the dirt of the hard ground. He asked him to jump again. And the Frog Boy jumped again. And again. Jumped so many times that his legs shortened up in him causing him to waddle as he walked. Still the Frog Boy thanked the miller's boy for allowing him to perform. And as his reward was allowed by the miller's son to search out the dropped oat nuggets in the stable and the Frog Boy fed there just a little but thankfully and happily. And felt blessed. And then dragged his aching body to the great tulip tree on the edge of the hamlet where--unable to climb the tree because of his sore bones--he laid himself among the roots and, in the night, the moles of the town crawled to him, climbed onto the small boy's body and warmed him with a blanket of their hearts and fur. Their eyes blinked in the darkness, as the moles lay on the boy, like so many pink stars. And in the morning the boy was happy and warm.

"And at the tavern there was an old whore who was so ugly and full of bile that no one would lie with her. So she spent her day scraping pots in the tavern's kitchen

38

and cursing the world. The tipplers and idlers of the tavern told the Frog Boy to kiss the old whore in her 'milk pails' and he would receive a reward. The Frog Boy said, 'I shall be pleased', and walked into the kitchen and kissed her there. The old whore swore at the boy, and slapped his ears until they bled. When the boy crawled from the kitchen to seek his reward, they cried with tears of glee then asked the boy to lick the bottoms of the old woman's feet and the boy did and for his reward the Frog Boy was stomped upon by the hag most hurtfully. For this he was given the chicken bones of the tavern idlers to suck on. And the boy was sore but happy that the tipplers were happy and went on his way. And in the branches of the tulip tree that night a great assembly of blue moths alighted on the sleeping boy, covered his frail body, every inch, and softly succored him. And in the morning the Frog Boy was happy and warm and no longer remembered the hurt.

"And the fishermen at the wharf said: 'Frog Boy, jump into the harbor and our bread will be yours to eat.' It was winter at the time and the harbor full of ice but the boy said, 'I shall be pleased', and he jumped among the ice floes and swam about for pieces of the bread they tossed and the men roared when the boy's hair froze and his skin turned a deep hue of blue and his liver and heart were outlined in his chest like a hand held before a candle. And the near-frozen boy then crawled into the branches of the tulip tree and a thousand tiny terns made their nest in every crack and corner of the boy to warm him. And in the morning he was glad.

"And so the boy existed with his tormentors by day. And by night the terns, the moths, and the moles comforted him.

"Now in those days the highest mountain on the Island of Ice to the north rumbled and its crown cracked itself and belched sulphurous fires and lava rivers that ran down to the sea. The villagers gathered in the harbor and looked across the sea to the Island of Ice. They saw great broadening clouds of black smoke. And in the morning the sky over their own island was filled with ash and dust and there was no sun to warm the earth. The village priest told the people that the evil god of the Island of Ice was angry but he did not know why. For three long years the great mountain on the Island of Ice spewed forth rivers of molten fire and the sun no longer shone in the tiny village by the sea. And all the green hills and fields of the island were covered with silt and ash. The sycamore, hawthorn and oaks grew leaves no more and the junipers and yews looked like statues with dusty beards of gray.

"The people and their farm animals were starving. The wild goats, martens, foxes, deer and bears ate the last of the dried currants, the blackberries and the bitter berries of the dying holly and then gnawed the soft branches down to the gray earth.

"The desperate villagers snared the terns and mixed their blood with seeds and dead leaves picked from the ashen snow to form a simple gruel. Or they ate dried brown wood sorrel. Or scratched in the mud for fallen hazelnuts and chestnuts. And boiled the leather of horse harness. Some tried to fill their bellies on the thatch from their roofs. And—such horror!—weeping, starving parents began to meet in the village square at midnight to exchange their children with other parents so as not to eat their own flesh.

"During these terrible times, the Frog Boy walked the by-ways trailed by rags that barely covered his bones, and asked at the doorways: 'How may I please thee?' But the people would not share the little they had and the Frog Boy withered.

"All looked hopeless. Many people were resigned and silently awaited death's certain arrival. Then the old whore from the tavern dragged herself from hovel to hovel, saying: 'The Frog Boy came to us from a land of devils and has cursed us all. If you make a sacrifice of the boy, it is sure that the sun will shine on our land again.' And the hungry townspeople believed the hag and set about building a wicker prison within the branches of the great tulip tree. The townspeople found the Frog Boy and asked him: 'Wilt thy go into the wicker cage of that tree and suffer the torch so that we may live?'

"And the boy said sweetly: 'I shall be pleased.' And even the hardest and cruelest of the village people, in spite of their hunger and suffering, felt pain in their hearts to hear these words of the Frog Boy. But only for a moment as they feared that they themselves would soon perish.

"The boy was placed into the tall wicker cage. The miller's boy was the first to torch the tree but many others also set the straw ablaze.

"As the flames rose to his small feet, the imprisoned boy climbed higher and higher to escape the fire. 'Please,' cried the boy. And the people cheered to hear him and thought that this boy surely had been the cause of their misery. Small boys of the village threw more sticks and hay on the fire and the once mighty tulip tree was ablaze. The flames burned first orange, and then red and finally white, so white that the townspeople cowered in the hot light of the fire.

"The snapping branches covered the sounds of the boy's cry of 'please, please,' and suddenly a great wind came upon them. Then the smell of burning flesh filled the crowd. The people fell quiet as the roar of the fire became a tempest of heat. The tulip tree burned as bright as a hundred suns.

"Then the people fell to the ground seeing a great white bird fly up and away from the blazing tree. As the bird soared over the townspeople, they saw that the bird carried the Frog Boy in its mighty talons. With its beak the great bird lifted and nestled the thin nearly naked boy amongst the feathers of its broad breast. The bird then swooped over the crowd.

"Suddenly the bird was a woman. With hair of gold. Flying over the village she was naked and the boy climbed within her breasts. She comforted him and the two shone as the sun on the brightest day of summer. The golden haired lady with the naked Frog Boy ascended into a bank of billowy clouds and cried to the astonished villagers below: 'This boy pleases me! He is mine! Has always been mine. Always have I loved this child'"

Kevin looked to Patrick. Patrick saw tongues of fire reflected in Kevin's eyes. He continued, but in a whisper:

"Then warmth descended once again upon the people and the place. The sun revealed itself, shone as in the olden days before the belching fires on the Island of Ice, and the land was warmed and the tulip tree stood in the hamlet, great and strong as before. And in the orchards and hedgerows, the fruit tress blossomed and wild strawberries came forth. And everywhere grasses burst from the soil and the starving goats, foxes and lambs left their secret places where they had lain in the hills and romped in the meadows where once again gentian, arnica, and bloody cranesbills released their sweet perfume into the air. The snows melted and carried the ash spewed by the Island of Ice to the streams and then down to the sea. And immense silvery salmon struggled up the river to spawn and the streams were alive with leaping pink-bellied trout and gray sturgeon lazed in pools.

"There was plenty again. The people gave thanks.

"The old whore, afraid because of what she had done to the Frog Boy, became a lizard and tried to scurry from the village. But the lizard was eaten by a rooster and soon hens were laying again and all the people and their children had plenty. At the tavern, ale flowed once more. The villagers were grateful. But sadness was in them now for the false, stupid sacrifice they had made. And so every day in that small village by the sea they remember to give thanks. And the children of the village have been told and retold the story of the goodness of the Frog Boy. That they are to look for the smiling face of the Frog Boy shining in the dew drop that is captured in the spider's web as the morning sun rises. And to seek Frog Boy's face in the corners of the full moon's smile. To gaze deeply into the black waters of the peat bog for there the Frog Boy may be waiting, hiding, and smiling. And small children saying their night prayers spoke of hearing the swish of the Frog Boy's rags as he passed their cottage as the night closed in. Some tell of hearing the Frog Boy whispering his plea just before they give themselves up to dreams: 'Please. *Please.*'"

Kevin asked: "Do you get it? It's like all this suffering, there's a better place. On the other side?"

"Kev, what I don't understand: out here, what the hell kind of estate are you building?"

"When I die, Paddy, I plan to be dead." He closed his eyes, his face colorless.

Patrick emitted a small guffaw. Kevin's head jerked back.

"Something's funny?"

"No. It's just that…you remind me of a guy in Michigan I just fired. He was a dreamer like you."

Kevin slumped forward his tanned face bloodless. He rose from the bench unsteadily: "Let's just say goodnight."

"No," Patrick protested. "Look: I'm no literary critic."

"You know, Paddy, you don't know one goddamned thing about me." This said in sorrow, not anger. "I'm going to bed."

Patrick called after him: "Go. Run away. You been getting good weed, Kev? The mountain boys turn you on to a new clone?" Head down Kevin moved through the knee-high grass to the Emporium. Patrick heard the screen door slam.

Alone in the Idaho night, Patrick was visited with a kind of helpless remorse. He sat on the bench at the river's edge and fell into a reverie. Watched a parade march on the river: guys from eighth grade waved to him: Grimes, Ortiz, Hannigan. He saw Fritz Boyle fellating Jimmy Costello through a handkerchief on a dare in the boy's cloakroom. Saw Sister Mary Benedict slapping her ruler on her palm: thwap, thwap. Then he was at Georgetown and girlfriends beckoned to him with 'come hither' eyes or flipped him the bird but did so smiling. There was Sean Moriarty on the Evans House softball team sliding safe into second on the field across from the Lincoln Memorial. And Annette and Patrick their very first night together. Curious, she touched his sex; explored his squid-like sticky tentacle. Then of Victoria and Patrick, breathless and spent, in a suite at the Plaza Hotel. Patrick sure to the deepest part of his yearning soul that he was born to lie with her for all time.

The night so populated did not allow for sleep. With a full moon throwing so much light that he cast a long, deep shadow, Patrick clacked along the stony bank a half-mile downstream and then slowly back to the tent. Then he meandered along the empty highway away from, and then back to, the emporium over the suspension bridge. The time was almost midnight. In front of the emporium, from the gravel of the parking spaces, he could see Kevin beneath a single suspended bulb sitting at his desk, his bare feet resting on a stack of invoices, pencil in hand with a clipboard before him, working out some mystery. Talking to animals or they to him, his face in a cloud of blue smoke, a joint dangling from his lips. He put the clipboard and pencil down, began to roll another. Red Skelton slept on the desk.

***

Patrick opened his eyes beneath the Aer Lingus blanket. Emerged and looked below. The waters of the Atlantic were obscured by a grey blanket of cumulus. He imagined walking on them far above a heartless earth. He closed his eyes, pulled the blanket and listened to the thump of his heart and the engines drone. Thought of twenty years earlier. And Annette.

VII

Annette

Post Georgetown, Patrick moved to New York where he acquired his dream flat on (a happy accident) Sullivan Street in the west Village. From junk shops, he antiqued twelve gilt mirrors of various dimension to cover the pits and hillocks of the tired plaster walls. He antiqued (from junk shops) a four-poster bed and an overstuffed velvet sofa. At the Met gift shop, he bought a Gustave Courbet print that covered a large measure of the tiny living room wall. Hired by Seagrams, he sold wine and liquor to midtown hotels. To El Mo. To the Rainbow Room. And 21. In a vested three-button suit, a heavily starched Oxford cloth shirt with French cuffs and gold cufflinks in the shape of corkscrews, he went from establishment to establishment. A foot soldier in a town where a car was useless. Between appointments he browsed in Brooks Brothers on Madison Avenue where he acquired a look of Eastern Establishment. *Plaid pants.* On the North Side of Chicago, he would have risked being beaten and bloodied being seen in such. But in New York plaid pants said that you were to the manor born. He bought three pair. No longer Patrick Peter Sullivan of Whipple Street in Chicago, son of Barnaby and Bridget Sullivan of Perfection Cleaners and Dyers. He was Pat Sullivan from Sullivan Street, Seagrams' fair-haired boy, the forever smiling guy in French cuffs.

Patrick, in the executive offices of The Pierre, heard a trilling laugh. Like an exotic bird. The trill emanated from a cubicle. He peeked over the partition: "Did that happiness come from you?"

"People know me by my laugh." The trill again.

Thus did Patrick meet Annette. She was a booker of banquets at the Pierre. "I just contracted my eighth Michael bar mitzvah in two months. Seven Ashley bat mitzvahs this year. Eight Michaels." Trill, trill.

Her shoulders were wide, thrown back; her breasts reached forward: "Have you been told that you have the most perfect posture of any woman anywhere in the world?"

"Thank you."

"Do you love art?"

"Everyone does."

"So we'll go to the Metropolitan."

"Are you always this shy?"

"Actually, most of the time I work. How about Saturday?"

"I have class till twelve."

"Knitting?"

"Dance."

"Which explains the posture. You look like someone out of Degas."

"Merci."

"We'll do lunch first, get to know each other, then hit the Met, sit in the Park, you know tell our stories, then decide about dinner, you know, let's not rush things. I'll pick you up at noon?"

Again the trill. Her glance descended into discretion for only a moment, she searched her papers then she looked up with 'why-not' surrender: "At the dance studio? Seventy-second and Broadway?"

"Exciting. This is very exciting."

She held her index finger in the air as if testing the direction of the wind: "You're Irish?"

"I used to be Chicago Irish. Now Seagram's is my family."

"I am an orphan. Many years."

"A very beautiful orphan."

***

They did all those things. Lunch. The Impressionists at the Met. Talked for several hours seated on the Great Lawn in Central Park. Patrick invited her to see his Courbet.

"A painting?"

"A print. The paintings will come later when I'm CEO."

Holding hands, they walked five miles to the Village.

***

The Courbet portrayed the young artist returning to his village after studying in Paris. Perhaps he had sold a few canvases. In any event, his look shouted both triumph and defiance. He had departed as a boy, this day he was returning as a man. The coach that brought him back can be seen receding in the background. Courbet painted himself tall, his beard knifing horizontally from his chin, a black delta of phallic intent. He stood, in seeming arrogance, self-absorbed and victorious; two burgers show their amazement: 'Could this be the Courbet *fils* who went off to Paris?'

Standing before the print, shaking her head ever so slowly, Annette said dubiously: "I think he's pissed."

Patrick said: *"Ma chère,* he is furious."

They drank wine from his sample bag and ate deli food. "So, how does it hit you, you know, meeting a booze salesman?"

"It's okay. I guess." She stood, collapsed at the waist and grasped her ankles. "Do you mind if I stretch?"

"I don't mind at all."

With her eyes at the level of her knees, she asked: "Would you like to see me dance?"

"I was hoping you would."

In his small living room, she did a Balanchine piece without music. There was only the squeak of her bare feet on the parquet. In a

47

quiet part of the performance he found himself standing. Stroking her. She stopped dancing. They made love through the night.

In the morning over coffee he asked: "Why don't we get married?"

After a moment's thought she said: "Okay. When?"

"I don't know. Next week? Next month?"

"Okay."

***

Annette could not understand Patrick's refusal to get married in Chicago. He said simply: "I like New York. New York is my home. 'The Bronx is up and...'"

"'...the Battery's down'. I know, I know but, Pat, we owe it to ourselves and your family to get married in front of them. Pat, I have nobody. I have nobody but you."

"You will meet—in due time and at times that I will set--all my brothers and sisters. But not Barnaby and Bridget. This must be understood."

"But I'll meet your brothers and sisters here? Not in Chicago?"

"Correct, my love, for my parents, they are little more than beasts. Sorry but that's my reality."

"It cannot possibly be true."

"Too true. And therefore we will get married here."

With a sigh, she acquiesced. It took Patrick nine years to understand that every time Annette sighed, she was murdering a scream.

***

Martin Luther Sullivan was born a year later. Annette did not object to their son's name. Not that Patrick was religious. He would, if pressed, admit to being an atheist; blamed this lack of belief on his Jesuit education, the professors having demanded he follow rigorously every argument to its logical conclusion. (In business he never mentioned his godlessness.) In utter smugness Patrick knew his son's moniker was a high trajectory mortar shell that would land with an ugly but bloodless thud in Chicago.

Matt and Jenny were the first to visit them in Manhattan: he came to buy a skyscraper; she to buy out Bonwit Teller. Jenny's wardrobe was a rainbow of unrelenting pastels: baby blues, suppressed purples, salmon pinks, yellow-greens like spring grass. Her cotton and wool arraignments were intended (never consciously) to soften and even obliterate the social thunderclaps of the day. Daily she drank White Zinfandel, skipped most meals to maintain 105 lbs. and snacked on candy kisses (while watching the soaps) that she had secreted throughout their thirteen room home. She was given over to affirmations, turning any and all problems over to God. Her furniture and walls were pastel too and she had had Matt install a hi-fi system so they could hear throughout the day and night, but barely, monks whose worldly role seemed limited to keeping Gregorian chant alive. Several times as her children disappointed she regretted not having taken the path of the cloister: there was the stashed porn in Seamus's room, empty beer cans in the station wagon, a condom in Brian's sweats. These epiphanies she experienced as stabbing moral failures. At St. Monica's Mass for the Dead each morning she bargained with God on behalf of her children. On her knees she squeezed wooden rosary beads--dimpled like craters on the moon--the beads her cherished souvenir of a visit to Lourdes. "Good morning God, Jennifer here...." The children thought her a bit daft ("Mom's talking to angels again.") but never mocked her directly on the off chance that she was actually being heard. They found her religiosity risible, a family joke. Even Matt could be sucked into the joke. They revered her just the same.

Patrick picked them up at the Waldorf and they taxied to the railroad flat on West End. Riding uptown, Jenny interrogated him: "Honestly, Paddy, you can tell us: why all the rush to get married? Annette is pregnant, right?"

"Actually, Annette's still a virgin. We play Abelard and Heloise each night, sit on facing chairs and say things so steamy that we both come without so much as touching."

"Paddy, I'm serious."

"Annette did want to get married in Chicago."

"But you didn't?"

"I'm a Borough of Manhattan kind of guy. New York has given birth to me so we took ourselves down to City Hall and..."

Matt, who played nose guard at Notre Dame until a knee exploded, preferred yelling to speaking: "Patrick, you're a goddamned atheist!"

"Matt, don't push. I already gave you my sister."

"You want her back?"

"Matt, shut up." Jenny took her older brother's hand. "Marriages have to be sworn before God, for Christ's sake Paddy."

Patrick closed his eyes, was mainly thinking of the wines he'd open that night. "It's about God, is it?"

"Annette was right. You needed to marry before your family, before God and your Church."

The cab sped through Central Park swirling the leaves of autumn.

"And have an old fart priest telling me we couldn't use the pill? I don't think so."

Jenny squeezed her brother's hand: "It's okay to lie a little. The young priests say it's okay if you don't believe in a lot of the old stuff."

Matt barked from the far side of the cab: "Pat, not that you're a total asshole but Jen and I were the ones who had to tell your parents."

"Tell them what?"

"That you got married."

"Somehow I am—actually--not at all bothered."

Jenny asked softly: "And the rest of the family that adores you?"

"Oh I thought about you guys. About everybody."

"And you did nothing about it?"

"Thinking is not nothing."

Matt studied Central Park: "Fucking Jesus Christ Almighty."

During dinner and much wine, Annette heard her first stories of growing up on Whipple Street. Late, at the door, Jenny hugged her, said: "You'll come to Chicago. You'll stay with us."

Annette had one hand in Patrick's back pocket that scratched tenderly: "We will. As soon as I can melt this brother of yours. Pat...?" She squeezed. The promise of things to come in the night.

"Not a chance in hell. And there is no hell."

"We'll come. I can't wait to meet Rosemary. And Douglas. Larry."

Patrick cut her short: "Over my dead body."

Annette sighed.

***

Rosemary journeyed to a banking seminar in Westchester. At twenty-eight, displaying the importance of her expense account, she took a cab from Tarrytown to the Upper West Side. After dinner, she sat on the sofa shaking her head, holding Martin Luther in her arms, saying: "This is stupid, Paddy. So, so stupid."

Patrick took offense: "What's so stupid?"

"Not letting the grandparents enjoy this beautiful child."

"Stupid is how we grew up."

Annette kept an eye on the one true love of her life: Martin Luther: "Spare your breath, Rosemary. You're talking to proud Patrick."

"Paddy is a retard," she said to Annette. "This is nothing new. At home, we talk about it."

"I'm a retard? So tell me, Rosemary, how's your family thing with Tommy Scanlon doing?"

Rosemary had divorced after three years living with Tommy's alcoholism. And after two children. Her face became pasty: "Patrick, you know, you can be a reach-out-and-punch-people bastard."

Annette said, "He is sweeter to his customers than to me."

Patrick ignored Annette: "Rosemary, you married Tommy, you picked him out of a crowd."

"Patrick..." Annette reached for his hand.

"Paddy, you introduced me to him!"

"You were born to boozers and you married a boozer."

Rosemary's lips became bloodless, parallel lines. Martin Luther, just four months, protested with a gagging cry. Rosemary passed the baby to Patrick: "Annette, will you get me my coat?"

At the door, Rosemary and Annette embraced and Rosemary choked on her good-bye: "Martin Luther is so beautiful. As to whether you'll be able to rescue my brother, well…best of luck."

Patrick, with Martin Luther in his lap, watched two hockey players drop their gloves and embrace, throwing punches when able. He shouted to the door without turning: "Rescue yourself, Rosemary! Tommy too!"

Rosemary shouted back: "You are so sick!"

"You found a Barnaby and married him and that makes me sick?!"

There was open weeping from both women. Martin Luther lost all composure. The elevator doors clanked shut. Annette did the dishes without speaking. Martin Luther cried himself to sleep. It was two years before Patrick called Rosemary. To slobber an apology.

Douglas never came. Afraid to fly.

Larry came to Manhattan but, by that time, Annette and Patrick, though nominally still married, rarely spoke. The two brothers took Martin Luther to the Natural History Museum where the six-year-old bounced his voice off the cupola in the Great Hall of Man, said hello to the too real Peking man and cowered before tyrannosaurus rex. At Tavern on the Green, Martin Luther declared the hamburgers the world's most humongous. Uncle Larry was, from that day, memorialized and idealized. Martin Luther was forever saying: "What a great guy, Uncle Larry."

Patrick would say, "Wanna call him?"

Larry's receptionist always recognized Martin Luther's voice, put him through to the boss no matter what: "Hey, Uncle Larry, sold any Camaros today? Any Corvettes? How much money did you make today? A lot? Come on, tell me."

***

Departing LaGuardia Larry got behind Patrick and applied a full Nelson, a wrestling move employed on the unsuspecting frequently on Whipple Street: "Paddy, you can sell whisky in Chicago. Did you know that there are actually people in Chicago who sell whisky like you do here?"

"Lemme go."

"Not till you agree to move back."

"I like it here."

"Paddy! Barnaby would go nuts seeing this kid. MomsaBomb is insane that she doesn't know him."

"Lemme go and I'll…reason with you." Larry released him. Patrick backed off five feet: "Just tell them to stay away. No calls. Things go fine here. I have nothing to say. Not to them."

51

"There's still time to grow up."

"**You** were young, Lar. You missed the funnest days."

***

The marriage to Annette, at the seven-year mark, saw Patrick climbing within the Seagram's organization but married in name only. Annette persisted, even then, in pushing the Chicago connection where nieces and nephews were arriving in obstetrical waves like so many LSTs on Omaha beach. But, in bed, when lust made his skin crawl, a furious resolve demanded he avoid so much as touching her toes. At Seagram's he watched the derrieres of passing secretaries and file clerks. He had a drink with one. She invited him to her place. After, he felt awful, a villain. He shuffled papers whenever she passed. They never spoke again. Later he heard she had quit.

After an hour with Annette's therapist, it was agreed that the marriage was not salvageable. The therapist counseled them to break it gently to Martin Luther.

At the breakfast table, Martin Luther, then six, navigated a butter pat in a wide arc through an   amber pond of maple syrup. Annette said: "Martin Luther, stop a minute. Your Dad has something to say."

Patrick spoke louder than was necessary, his fingers trembling: "You know how we—your Mom and me—how we fight a lot? And how you hate it when we do?"

Martin Luther did not look up: "You're getting a divorce, aren't you."

"Yes."

The boy's face lost all color. He pushed his chair back and ran to his room. Patrick went to the toilet and lost everything. When he came back, Annette was sitting, awash in her own monsoon: "Can't we talk just once more?"

"I'll be late for work."

"Pat, what you're doing—it's all so wrong."

"Honestly, I don't feel a thing."

Martin Luther, at his mother's side, watching his father leave, said: "It's okay, Mom, we can just get a new Dad."

***

Patrick resorted to Comfort Ladies. (Who in turn had resorted to Comfort Men.) Sunday nights it was the Lion's Head for publishing types. Friday nights was owned by P.J. Clarke's for advertising ladies. Custody time, Patrick did an occasional Knicks game with Martin Luther. Martin Luther always brought a book, read despite the roaring of the Garden crowd. Father-son visits became infrequent. Patrick became a sales maven and little else.

***

Then there was Victoria. Victoria was a PR Foodie, a consultant to restaurants, with broad shoulders, lanky arms and hopeful breasts. Their first date was dinner at The Coach House. She expounded on American food to the proprietor, Mr. Leon, who already knew it all but she charmed the old man. She was ten years younger than Patrick and eager to know about wine. The more he revealed, the more she cooed. During the entrée he felt sharp nails on his knee; then she was kneading his thigh. He told the waiter, without looking up from her eyes: "A glass of Discipio Chardonnay for every customer." The other tables stood and toasted the couple who were soon swept by a rutting fury into the street where Patrick hailed a limo to his condo on Second Avenue. A longer ride and they would have known each other, in the Biblical sense, under the twinkle lights and red leather bench of the stretch.

The next morning—sleepless and still pawing each other—they caught a cab to Kennedy and flew to Anguilla where they spent three days on a nude beach, three nights with the verandah door open, within the martial sweetness of hibiscus and bougainvillea. Patrick had an overwhelming sense that he had somehow that they had always been one.

Whether working or making love Victoria was ecstatic, breathless. Bursting. The trade rag Restaurant News gave her a trophy inscribed: "Ms. PR: the East Coast Foodie With Wings on Her Feet." Victoria's beauty was high fashion model stuff without scarecrow gauntness. Walking through a restaurant, every male eye followed her. She rolled her eyes whether eating or making love. Patrick was aroused just being near her. She fed this by constantly touching him. In truth, during their year of heat, Patrick rarely stopped thinking of her: the taste of her, her wet whisper. The games she knew. *Tie me with red silk ribbons. Now bring ice cubes. ...* Patrick believed that Victoria loved him like he had never been loved. That Victoria was twenty-five (untouched, even virginal, despite many encounters) and Patrick was leaning hard against thirty-six, this spread of years, seemed not an obstacle, but a goad to their thing.

On a custody weekend, Patrick introduced her to Martin Luther. Patrick had prepared Martin Luther, revealed that he intended Victoria to be his stepmother. Victoria thought he was cute, Martin Luther said little. Martin Luther, twelve at the time, riding back to Annette, dismissed Victoria as a bimbo.

***

Then, it ended. As suddenly as it had begun. After a six course sold-out dinner at Windows of the World atop a World Trade tower. Victoria had glided from table to table: schmoozing the *Times* writer, passing out press packets, and introducing Rick, her James Beard Rising Star chef. Because of her duties Victoria and Patrick barely exchanged words the entire evening.

Patrick watched from afar. Saw her with the wine writer from *Gourmet*. Five times—he counted—she bent over to chat, each time celebrating the moment by revealing the deep scoop of her breasts. She had begun that way with Patrick. Everything the *Gourmet* writer said seemed to cause her to devolve into helpless laughter. And when she kissed the man, Patrick saw from across the room, it was not polite European bussing. Much more. Late, after Beluga caviar on gray sole in *beurre blanc* and Pinot Noir-marinated breast of Moulard Duck, on the elevator saying goodnight to Rick the chef, she turned down Rick's offer to pick her up the next morning for a TV interview saying: "Thanks but my Dad will drop me off in the morning."

Victoria's father had died many years before.

Rick in his whites disappeared as the brass doors closed. Patrick and Victoria were alone for the first time all evening.

"'My Dad?'"

"I'm sorry, what's that?" she said.

"To Rick. Just now. You called me: 'My Dad'".

"Patrick, don't be stupid. I said no such thing."

"I am not stupid. It happens to be what you just said." Nabokov had pronounced Freud the Viennese Quack and that had been authority enough for Patrick to ignore the primeval bog of introspection. But had he not just witnessed a slip of the tongue in which his twenty-five year-old lover had referred to him as her "Dad"?

Despite the argument, they found their room and after ten minutes the lovemaking—an athletic event--was over. Lying on his back, Patrick felt particularly violated. Used. And—to his great shame--a user too.

It was kill or leave.

As his pulse slowly descended, lying atop cold semen, he addressed her with closed eyes, a flutter of retreat in his belly: "That wine writer, the guy from *Gourmet*, I was watching. You did everything but disrobe him."

"Philip? That silly boy? Don't be stupid, Patrick."

"But I know you, my dear. When you get an itch, you can't wait to scratch it."

"Like I did with you?"

"Exactly."

They laid in the dark without speaking. He listened but could not hear her breathe; decided her quiet was chosen, deliberate, and maintained in silent fury. His biceps stiffened, arms that wanted to strangle and suffocate the one he loved more than his own life.

Staring at the ceiling, he queried: "Victoria, Victoria, my darling, tell me do: Have I become your weekly fuck?" There was not a sound. He had been banished; not worth an answer. But his question sneaked about the quiet room, a counterpoint to the low hum of the mini-bar.

Victoria ended his wait and her silence; "Patrick, when you leave, please don't slam the door?"

***

Martin Luther was not to know his cousins, most of them, until this week—the week of his grandparents' Golden Anniversary--in Dublin.

VIII

Rebecca

Then came the Sunday morning that changed so much.

Patrick was lying poolside at the Bostonian. After a Wine Festival the night before, after Carmine Discipio had signed autographs, spoke of French oak barrels, marine fog, hints of vanilla and buttery toast in his Chardonnay Reserves and then mercifully had, to Patrick's not insignificant relief, boarded the Discipio jet at Logan. With no place to hurry back to except his apartment in Manhattan, Patrick had stayed the night and in the morning, lounging in a hotel robe within a chlorine fog behind frosted windows that revealed random pedestrians struggling against blowing snow, he drank Espresso and read a four-pound edition of the *New York Times*. He turned first to the obits. For several years, he had done this, tried to glean what he could of the parentage of people who had earned themselves an obit in the *Times*. What was their patrimony? Had they been launched with heartfelt support and discipline? Tears and loving sternness? Or had they, like Patrick, fled to make a mark on their own?

He saw it next to the announcements of religious services, a name that jolted him. He read.

Samuel Klein, M.D.

Anesthesiologist

An attending anesthesiologist, Dr. Samuel "Mannie" Klein, 42, died suddenly at St. Luke's-Presbyterian Hospital Wednesday while part of a team performing a multiple heart bypass on a fifty-year-old sheik, a member of the Saudi royal family. Efforts by surgeons on the operating team failed to revive Dr. Klein.

The immediate cause of Dr. Klein's death was said to be cardiac arrest. An autopsy has been scheduled.

The bypass procedure being performed on the sheik was unaffected by Dr. Klein's collapse.

Dr. Klein is survived by his mother Ethel Klein of West Palm Beach, his wife Rebecca, and daughter, Melissa.

***

Mannie had invited Annette and Patrick to dinner. The idea was Rebecca's. She wanted, Mannie said, to meet his handball friend. So on a Saturday evening, having gotten a sitter for Martin Luther, Annette and Patrick walked around the block from West End to Riverside Drive. Mannie let them in. Rebecca, in apron, stirred a pot at the stove. She didn't say a formal hello, just looked up already speaking as one encountering an old friend: "All Mannie does is watch sports on TV and work. Do you like Arab food? Lamb and cous cous? Those people are barbarians, I know, I mean, some are, I guess, but their food compared to Jewish food? Isn't Jewish cuisine an oxymoron? I'm so glad to meet you."

Throughout that evening, Rebecca posed questions. Followed by questions upon her questions. Patrick decided that declarative sentences were, to Rebecca, a caste of grammatical untouchables.

Melissa, aged three, had clung to her father's pant leg or wrapped her arms around his neck with locked fingers when he sat. Mannie seemed unaware of her, opened the Chivas Regal that Patrick had brought, did this with Melissa held within his elbow. He moved to wine when the others drank wine with Melissa sat on his lap. After dinner, when he returned to the Scotch, Melissa fell asleep next to him. He rolled a joint began laughing at jokes he didn't bother to share. Rebecca, Annette and Patrick talked about bringing up children on the West Side.

Mannie said: "I've got an idea: everybody should tell what they want most in life."

Patrick without hesitation said he "wanted to make one helluva a lot of money."

Annette spoke of Westchester. A backyard for Martin Luther. "I am really getting to hate Upper Broadway. Have you seen Mr. Bizarro with the rooster on his head?"

"The one who hangs out in front of the Thalia?" asked Rebecca, "I bring corn for the rooster." Mannie blurted the news that Mr. Bizarro had slit the rooster's throat after a poor performance by said rooster at 72nd and Broadway. Mannie roared.

Rebecca offered her wish: "To read every novel ever written--and then die. I mean, what would be left? A lot of movies, I guess. Mannie?"

Mannie, apparently conceiving an idea, almost choked. His eyes wide, he spit it out: "I want to put a lot of people to sleep." He slapped both thighs. "Get it? The anesthetist's dream." Tears rolled down his cheeks. Rebecca was impassive. Annette rolled her eyes. Things quieted. Rebecca offered that it was late. On the elevator, Annette looked to Patrick: "She's sweet. But him? What do you see in him?"

"Easy. I beat him four out of five games."

***

Patrick dialed information.

"Rebecca, it's Patrick Sullivan."

"Are you calling about Mannie?"

"I just read the *Times*."

"You're divorced?"

"Yes. Actually...it's been eight years."

"Did I know that? My mind--excuse me--is here and there. Everywhere really." He remembered her voice from the dinner in the early Seventies and her voice brought her face into clear focus. Midnight black hair, tall. At the dinner years before, Patrick thought her build could have taken her to athletics however she had the forward shoulders of a reader. Her not insubstantial and very nervous energy was concentrated between brown eyes.

"I picked a terrible time to call."

"Not to worry. My daughter has been trying to stare down her bedroom wall since it happened. Did you ever meet Melissa?"

"When she was a baby. How old is she?"

"Fifteen."

"I understand if you don't feel like talking."

"No. Talking is always good for almost anything. But if I start to scream, feel free to hang up. Just kidding. Maybe not?" The line was silent. Then: "I got the coroner's report yesterday. Guess what: Mannie was stoned. In the operating room. Can you believe it?"

"I can believe it. He always lighted a joint. The second we walked out of the Y."

"The autopsy reads like a cocktail: THC, coke, uppers, downers, barbiturates. Did I know he was doing all that stuff? I mean, where was I?"

"Where'd he get it all?"

"M.D.s write their own scripts."

"'Physician, heal thyself?'"

"'Physician, medicate thyself?'"

They talked for three hours: Patrick in a wet swimsuit and Rebecca (she offered) in the sweats she had worn the past three days. "Patrick, I lived with a lobotomy... I chose him. How sick was I? Now my

59

daughter acts like she's a lobotomy." Rebecca had earned a Ph.D. in philosophy at City College then chucked it, decided that philosophy from Plato forward to the logical positivists was all intellectual gas, "a kind of brain fart", and what really mattered was where you came from. Of late, mothering Melissa notwithstanding, she had begun taking abnormal psych classes at Hunter.

"Melissa is in shock? Mourning, yes?"

"Mourning would be an improvement." Patrick had lived with MomsaBomb who poured forth a daily litany of her suffering with Barnaby. But Rebecca's purging was somehow glorious in its self-indictment, a near-operatic recitative of woes. "She's in her room burning incense. She's got about a hundred pictures of Mannie plastered on her wall. I tried to show her the toxicologist's report. She ripped it to shreds. 'You bitch! You did it to him! You did it.' I'd trade her in on a new model if I didn't love her so much."

***

After that Sunday morning, Patrick and Rebecca took to phoning each other. First once a week. Then more frequently. They did not meet, did not move closer than a telephone receiver as Patrick was flying up and down the eastern seaboard and twice a month to the winery in Napa Valley. In their calls, Rebecca mostly spoke of her angry mourning of Mannie and Patrick related his day's doings: the jerk buyer in Atlanta, the wine bore he wanted to impale on a corkscrew. Or a guy he had just fired. Then after a month of telephone talk, but not so much as a lunch together, he started to reveal stuff to her about whom he was sleeping with--that day, that month. That he hated that he was sleeping with this or that *belle du jour* but also how afraid he was of being alone. Or that he was not sleeping with anybody but had his eye on so and so. Or that he wanted to sleep with someone but the applicant pool was empty and he might as well resign his life to that of the token Irish-American *castrato* in the Discipio *castello*.

Rebecca was nothing if not a great listener. She asked clarifying questions but made few comments. He started to get into the habit of just saying whatever was on his mind: after too long days of meetings and travel, overly long wine dinners on Long Island or Hilton Head. He called her once from Hamburg and it cost a thousand marks which he put on his expense account with the rationalization that Carmine Discipio owed him far, far more than he was paid. No matter what time he called, Rebecca was always ready to talk, even if he woke her. "Patrick, it's never too late to schmooze."

One night, after months of telephone talk, from where he lay upon a hotel bed in Grosse Pointe Farms, Rebecca fell into one of her purging rages: "Don't you think I've moaned enough? Melissa can sequester herself in her private funeral parlor but, Patrick, this girl is ready to live again."

Earlier that evening, an elderly wine geek had cornered Patrick, pulled a computer printout from his pocket, and began to read bottle by bottle, his entire cellar collection, asking Patrick his opinion of each and every wine. Usually, Patrick, hardly a novice at such events, marched out his Ambassador-in-Charge-of-Saying-Nothing who spouted a fountain of ingratiating replies, empty bromides to escape the obsessive-compulsives that populate the wine game, but this night he could only halt the man, halfway through his White Burgundies and demand of his astonished eyeballs that he "stop this assault on my person this very second." Patrick seized the printout, tore it in half. (A week later, the irate collector retaliated with a note of protest to Carmine Discipio which claimed, in short, that there was a madman purporting to represent Discipio Winery. Patrick, when asked, simply countered that the guy was a nut and weren't his sales numbers——Carmine's only measure of life's beauties-- historically very good?) That night of Rebecca rage, Patrick had been on the road for two weeks and nothing lay before him except a flight to LaGuardia and working all weekend on mounds of paper. Moreover, there was the matter of his celibacy: a state that he had caught like a virus not embraced like a virtue, a state which presented him with no woman problems. And no woman. "Listen, old buddy of mine: I am two years without more than two days straight of vacation. Let's get ourselves a cabin somewhere. You bring the novels. I'll bring the food and wine. We can walk. Talk and talk. No telephone service. We can cook for ourselves."

"Where?"

"I dunno. The Berkshires? The Laurentians. Maybe Northern Maine. I've heard that Northern Maine has a billion pines and a million moose. What's the plural of moose? Mooses?"

"Meeses. I can be ready by Saturday."

IX

Mt. Katahdin

They met at Augusta airport. Patrick flew in from Napa, and Rebecca from West Palm where she had deposited Melissa, kicking and screaming, with her grandmother: "Maybe they'll kill each other. Is that too much to hope for? Then I can work for Mother Teresa? You look the same. Not much older, pretty much how I remember you from that dinner."

"You look the same. How do you explain no aging?"

"You sales guys are always quick with the compliments."

"Really you look great."

"Maybe it's because I'm not carrying Mannie on my back any more? All those years I was the reverse of the Morton Salt girl, a nice day outside but under the geedee umbrella I was drowning?"

"You could've just stepped outside the umbrella."

"Easy for you to say."

The baggage carousel gave birth to her bags one after one. There were five. "I'm ready for anything."

"I'm not getting out of jeans."

"But what if we meet people?"

"We are going where few have gone before."

"What about going out to eat?"

"It's cook or starve week. The rental agent tells me that we're beyond the boonies."

They drove four hours through pine forests due north on the Interstate, then crept mile after mile on a logging track in a rented SUV stocked with food and two hundred pounds of ice. It was July and the tree trunks wore subtle green mosses and pine needles carpeted the moist earth. They crawled past rock outcroppings harboring gray ice from the winter past. Rebecca had brought tapes: "Want to hear a Viennese prodigy or a Brooklyn Jew?"

"How's that?"

"Mozart or Streisand?"

"You pick. My mind is on vacation."

They listened to a cast recording of *Funny Girl* and after an hour of slow ascent rolled into a wide clearing of boulders, larches, thin maples and birch saplings where the grassy track petered out. With the engine and music gone, the forest was quiet except for random bird cries and soughing in the pines. The cabin was small: a great room with two small bedrooms with steel-frame beds. The lintel over the plank door was a gray stone slab inscribed: Jeremy Lowe Burke, Trapper and Friend of Jesus, 1796. Only fifty yards from the plank door, there was a ten-acre pond complete with a chorus of croaking bullfrogs. The forest extended above the cabin another thousand feet and after that only boulders and slopes of gray shale loomed higher. A loon called and Patrick's heart raced with a delicious feeling: he was nowhere.

"Walden?" Rebecca asked.

"Xanadu."

The electricity quit on the second day.

***

They hiked the mountain above the tree line. Rebecca looked diligently for arrowheads; she found none but did fill her pockets with obsidian, quartz and stones with off-orange veins which she hoped might be gold. In the evenings they opened tins of *foie gras* and grilled steaks, and sipped red wine from paper cups. Through all the hiking, and noticeably short of breath, Patrick found himself in a place with no phones or faxes and lapsed into long silences as they hiked. On the first evenings he fell asleep not much after dark. Hiking, accompanied by the sound of clicking pebbles and the arrival of light breezes, warming or cooling, he found himself—his mind asserting itself--in places long forgotten. On the third day, resting on a boulder, Rebecca squinted and asked: "Do you feel different?"

"Something's up."

"Does your face...feel soft?"

"I've got some news—I'm soft all over. I don't know what is happening."

"Superman takes a holiday?"

"He doesn't live here anymore."

On the fourth day, they decided to try for the peak. The air grew cooler as they climbed. Loose stones fell away like poker chips. Other hikers could be seen, above the timber line, from time to time but they rarely got close enough for more than a shouted "Hello!" They reached the peak, took pictures of each other celebrating the conquest, and then descended to get out of a blustery cold wind. Lower they entered a birch and pine chapel and Patrick was assaulted by an inchoate tangle of half-thoughts. He started to speak—loudly--without turning to her: "You know when I called last week? I was about to jump out a window."

"You were going to jump?"

"I was on the first floor."

She did not laugh.

They stepped over and through tangles of fallen pines, then crossed a densely flowered meadow of blue and gold. Halting he looked to the forest floor below, a canyon of pine peaks. Facing a warm updraft, he spoke without turning: "Rebecca, you and I are buddies. So I can say anything, right?"

"Like what?"

He walked another fifty yards before he could formulate an answer. "Like...private."

"So?"

"You're not making this easy."

"I'm not?"

"No. You're not."

"But you haven't said anything."

With his head down, he spoke to the trail, the stones: "Okay. In the past I've always been on the hunt. I get worked up about someone and I bed her. Or, in rare cases, she beds me. In the morning, it's 'Adios'. Or I say something vaguely seductive, a total lie that hurts in my throat while coming out, like: 'You are sensational'. And then I sneak off. Like some sort of thief."

He walked another ten yards. Stopped without turning, said in a low bass voice: "What a monster of a liar I am." He turned. Rebecca had halted also, but slightly higher on the slope. "Rebecca, I just can't do it. Not anymore." Before she could reply, he began again the descent, hearing his last words follow pebbles into a narrow ravine: *Not anymore.*

They hiked another half-hour but wordlessly.

Then he stopped, took a deep breath. The stony slope was steep but random sprays of violet nightshade had somehow taken root. Rebecca, too, stopped. The sun, suspended over the upper slope, hung but a few degrees over her head. The sun obscured, in its late day brightness, her face so that he saw only a gray outline that was her shoulder length hair, the bottoms of her khaki shorts and thin ankles disappearing into hiking boots. The warm air eddied with the remains of dry petals.

"Have you been listening to me?"

"Yes. But you haven't said much."

"There's more." He turned, walked. Then called back: "But I can't remember what."

They returned late in the day to the cabin. Over the pond buzzing insects flitted and an occasional trout leapt to feed. They had hiked six or eight miles, the week's longest trek. He lighted charcoal in the grill and took to opening cans and packets for dinner while Rebecca went off to bathe at the spa they had erected, a plastic water bag suspended from a larch where the water got shower-hot hanging in the July sun.

He did not intend to look.

But from where he stood opening a tin, he did: looked through the small rear window of the cabin and saw lines and colors and shapes. Angles. Through a thicket saw outlined the fleshy concavities and convexities of Rebecca. Though this happened in a brief second, he felt

65

shame. Ashamed at his inadvertent glance. He turned away but the vision and the darts of light through the larches remained. He turned to work with his back to the window.

***

They ate at the outside table making only small talk. The sun had already slipped behind the mountain to the west and the early cold of night crept upon them from plinth-like boulders that populated the hillside behind the cabin. He lighted the hurricane lamps and made a fire while Rebecca scraped the pots and plates with sand at the pond. Then, as the sky darkened, they settled on the cabin floor before the fireplace, as on the previous nights, with their respective books.

Patrick repeatedly tried to make sense of the page but could not advance more than a paragraph or two before realizing that the words and letters signified nothing. Words that, the night before, had been a fluid narrative.

Rebecca slapped her forehead, looked up wide-eyed, her cheeks red after the dinner wine. She pointed to a line, shaking her head in disbelief: "Listen to this: 'There is only the present. The past and the future do not exist.' Wow."

Patrick said. "Wow."

"Do you get it?"

"I think so."

"'The past and the future do not exist.' Wow." She returned to her text.

In Patrick there was a stirring with no clear locus. He shut his novel without saving the page, closed his eyes and heard the whipping of the outside wind and wet wood crackling in the fire. Pine cones pelted the roof and the ancient logs of the cabin groaned. His wool-socked toe, he became aware, was touching Rebecca's bare toe where she sat in the lotus position, reading.

He made a conscious decision not to withdraw his toe. Prayed that neither her comfort nor the lack of it, nor some quickening aesthetic moment in her book, would cause her to break their nexus. He started to shiver. Not from cold because the fire if anything was too warm. Feeling kid-scared, he slowly, deliberately, laid his book on the pine plank floor--Rebecca did not look up--and slowly retracted his toe. On hands and knees, not taking a breath, he crawled to her. The book in her hands seemed to hold her rapt. Not until his face was only a few inches from hers did she slowly turn and look at him. She whispered: "Patrick, I don't know."

"What don't you know?"

"I don't know if I want to change everything? Do you?"

"No. Yes."

"Promise not to hurt me."

"Am I that dangerous?"

She lowered her eyes to the open pages and shook her head. "You can be very scary."

Outside, where the forest ended and the barren slope to the peak began, the wind mostly died, softened, and blue smoke curled from the fieldstone chimney then settled, a man-made cloud, upon the clapboard roof. A screech owl in a birch grove sounded softly and a lone pack rat down the rutted car tracks peered through the pebbles, broken glass and tattered cloth that protected its burrow.

***

There was no hiking the next day; rather they lay by the pond and tanned body parts that had not witnessed an affectionate sun for a long, long time. Mostly they mused of from whence they had come. Rebecca wanted to know everything. Everything.

X
Over Iceland

From the 747 port, Patrick peered seven miles below. Through a break in the clouds gray Iceland revealed itself, bright sun dancing upon billowing columns of white mist. Closing his eyes, he returned to Rebecca and her insistent queries. That long day in northern Maine that changed so much.

"There's a lot to tell."

Seated upon the rough woolen blanket high on Mt. Katahdin, he journeyed to a place never forgotten yet unremembered. A place floating in his memory like the cigar smoke that lived in Grandma Powers' damask drapes years after Grandpa Powers' heart had burst. He remembered the Sullivan's first apartment when still a baby where, with the Venetian blinds closed to the postman, the neighbor lady and Fuller Brush, with the radio blaring Sinatra from the living room, Patrick, only two, toddled through the open bedroom door to espy Bridget dancing naked on her bed. Her steps, on the mattress and box spring, were both awkward and beautiful: she hugged her breasts and whispered words he later learned to be vile. Who was she whispering to? And what lay behind that delta of curlicues where she had no puppy dog tail? Tiny Patrick, heated and afraid, climbed crab-like onto the high bed, tried to cling to her bounding legs but she could not--or would not--stop her dance, nor stop touching herself between the legs while doing her dance, a naked lady caressing the naked lady in the mirror above the dresser.

His was a euphoric--even ecstatic--babyhood. A euphoria long forgotten but never disowned.

***

Then he turned to Rebecca and told of a certain December morning in the days leading up to Christmas. A sleepy Jenny and a wide awake Patrick met in the upstairs hall.

"I hear voices," she said.

"Me too."

In pajamas they crept downstairs. To a kitchen full of family. Aunts and uncles smoking a lot of cigarettes and not talking much. Uncle Alex avoided Patrick's eyes like a guilty dog but squeezed him until Patrick had to push away to get air. There were no jokes, no ice cube drinks. Uncle Aloysius asked everyone to kneel while he gave his blessing.

69

They all looked serious, subdued, and even holy. Rosemary sat on Uncle Jerry's lap because she was always his favorite; when she was five, then also on his lap, she had proposed marriage.

Jenny and Patrick roamed the house looking for MomsaBomb but she was nowhere to be found. The babies--Larry and Kevin--woke, began crying in their cribs. Aunt Evie changed their diapers, warmed their bottles, and sang to them. She was a good singer, Aunt Evie was. Dougie thought that perhaps a party was happening, a Holy Day of Obligation he had somehow forgotten. But in this early hour after dawn?

Patrick hung close to the uncles and priests, hoping that a few quarters would be doled out. Barnaby was quiet, talking little. Every seat in the kitchen was taken, the uncles stood, the aunts sat on the chairs. Usually when the uncles and aunts came they would wrestle and argue, clink glasses and tell dirty jokes. Not today. Bishop Quinlan came and all knelt for his blessing, then kissed his ring. He said slowly that it was a sad day. That none were to judge but rather everyone in the family should pray to God and confess their own failings. Rosemary, even on her uncle's lap, was pale, showed no sign that she was happy with the unexpected company. Because Rosemary always seemed to know things first, Patrick whispered: "Where's MomsaBomb?"

"Paddy, you are so, so stupid." She turned as if he was of low caste then cupped a hand over his ear; confided that MomsaBomb had run away during the night. Last night. To Florida. With Bob the Butcher.

Invaded by chills and surrounded by family, Patrick soiled his pajamas. He could not stop the hot stuff that raced out.

Patrick was nine-years-old that day. The day his mother disappeared.

Bob was the nicest butcher at Jewel Tea. Reaching over the glass case, he would give free   liverwurst to the Sullivan kids.

***

Barnaby drove the four oldest children in the delivery van to a place he said was "safe. A place you will like a whole lot." Rosemary, always privileged, sat shotgun. Patrick, Dougie and Jenny sat on the floor atop customers' dirty clothes. None of them spoke. With their clothes in grocery bags, they walked up the stone steps of a large red brick building on Jackson Boulevard. The brass sign on a red brick wall read: Holy Innocents Orphanage for Roman Catholic Boys and Girls.

Rosemary spoke first: "Dad, we're not orphans."

"I should say you're not."

Jenny said: "I'm afraid."

Dougie said: "You're always afraid."

Rosemary said: "Shut up, Dougie."

Patrick said: "He doesn't have to shut up. Especially for you, Rosie-Posie."

Barnaby said: "Ok, listen: I want you to stay here for just for a week or two. Inside these walls, you'll be safe like you're living in Vatican City."

Rosemary said: "I hate it here."

"You better be thankful, Miss, because Bishop Quinlan went through a lot of trouble to get you guys in special." He rang the bell. A nun with a starched collar so tight she appeared to be choking admitted the Sullivans. Barnaby left after five minutes. But before leaving told them that Kevin and Larry were in another Catholic orphanage. One especially for babies. Barnaby said it was for foundlings. Patrick wondered just who had found them to make them foundlings.

***

Some days Patrick saw a distraught Jenny on the girls' side of the playing field where they were separated from the boys by a chain link fence. Jenny's unending tears, and her abrading of her eye sockets, had hidden the blue of her eyes. Her only hope seemed to lay in escaping from the five-year-olds she was domiciled with and seeing Rosemary, Patrick or Dougie somewhere in the orphanage—a chance meeting in a hall, a glimpse at Mass, or on the playing fields. At the chain link fence, Patrick counseled her: "Don't cry, look at Paddy. Is Paddy crying? Be like Paddy, Jenny. Do you think Sister Superior will let you out or something? Don't be a stupe, Jenny, just wait. We'll get out. Barnaby's gonna come to get us. I'll betcha anything."

Rosemary came to the fence with similar words of common sense: "Do you see me crying, Jen? It's crazy to cry. So just don't."

But Jenny was not to be consoled. Some days she wailed so that games stopped on both sides of the fence. Hearing her wail so, the inmates were transported to, and thrown into, the personal hell of their own desperation. Jenny's crying proclaimed and reminded that none could escape the pain of their own abandonment.

Sister Harold threatened Patrick and Dougie with the Whacker if they so much as whispered to Jenny. The Whacker was a piece of wood from a game that English people play. Like a baseball bat but flat. Sister Harold gave the Whacker on the butt to Dougie the very first day and to Patrick on the second. It hurt ten times worse than MomsaBomb ever did. Sister Harold hit hard. And kept on hitting. Because Dougie played dead, and Patrick would not stop smiling.

Dougie adored Patrick, his big brother and protector, at Holy Innocents. (Long before the Sullivans had been admitted, the inmates had shortened the name of the orphanage to HI!) Things were different later on, when Patrick left for Georgetown and started to call Dougie Atkins. Atkins the Terrible. For, by then, Dougie was a crypto-Visigoth roaming the streets and alleys of Albany Park with the Kedzie Bombers and Patrick was a neo-Thomist pursuing both the perfection of intellect and the

71

occasional bedding of a co-ed. Which was no easy trick. Coitus with a Catholic co-ed took skill. One had to trump Maureen or Anne's's superego with a liberal consumption of Scotch or beer, and then after hungry implorations, and even on occasion, a few lines of Andrew Marvell:

> I would Love you ten years before the Flood;
> And you should, if you please, refuse
> Till the conversion of the Jews.

At HI! Dougie was a skinny blond kid afraid of most everything (older boys, strange food, sleeping in the dark) and Sister Harold whacked him again and again for singing and rocking himself to sleep. He learned this lesson quickly, began to hum low and wave his hands fighting demons quietly under the blanket, let his deeds of derring-do be celebrated in quiet song. He hated HI!'s food except the limp white bread, fresh from the baker nun's ovens, thick with melting slabs of government surplus butter. Dougie, who was just seven, wet his bed each and every night at HI! To train him, Sister Harold put him naked in the shower every morning—cold water only--with the yellowed sheets and his wet pajamas over his shoulders. Dougie—drenched--stood without expression, shivering, eyes open but unseeing. When Sister Harold was not there the cottage mates laughed and pointed at his pink butt. Dougie stood stone still focused on the water's vortex in the drain.

At HI! devouring all of one's meal plate was a theological requirement; but Dougie barely ate. When he didn't eat his rhubarb pie, it remained on his plate until the next morning. If he didn't eat it for his breakfast, it was still there at lunch. From meal to meal the rhubarb changed colors. Eventually Sister Harold pushed a two-day-old spoonful of mushy green rhubarb into his mouth. Dougie gagged, spit it onto his shirt along with a thin yellow liquid. Proving again that nobody could make Dougie do anything. MomsaBomb couldn't. Chicago's Finest couldn't. Not until five-foot Constance Axelrod came along did Dougie confront a Higher Power.

The dormitory was high-ceilinged and contained thirty boy-sized cots. After lights out, Sister Harold sat on a chair and guarded her wards while saying her rosary. She herself wasn't permitted to go to sleep until every boy was asleep. Sometimes Patrick would hear her swishing up and down the aisles to rub the back of a kid who was sniffling or crying out in his sleep. Patrick always kept his mouth open when he heard her swishing approach, because he believed that true sleep was done with an open mouth.

Sister Harold stopped each night to check on the boy in the bed next to Patrick's. His name was Abel Garcia. Abel--so the rumor went--did not sleep all night. Because of this, the boys called him Abel No Sleep. Abel was round-shouldered and stocky with brown pupils so enormous that no white could be seen. Only a little over four feet tall, his wiry black hair framed his skull like a helmet. Abel, beginning at nine o'clock each night, would begin whispering to Patrick. Slowly, in laconic wonder, Abel posed questions to Patrick, three years his senior, as if he had withdrawn each question with a bucket retrieved from a deep well, with his head thrust turtle-like into the space between their beds. Patrick whispered in return. But feared that Sister Harold would hear the two of them and pass out demerits that could only be redeemed by cleaning toilets.

"Patrick, psst."
"Go to sleep, you'll get us whacked."
"I can't."
"Can't what?"
"Can't sleep."
"Of course you can."
"I never sleep."
"Never?"
"No. Never."
"Beeswax."
"You can watch me."
"I'm too tired."
"Well if you weren't, you could."

Abel could not fathom how Patrick's mother could simply disappear. "Why would she do that?" he whispered.

"How would I know?"
"Do you think she'll come back?"
"Of course she'll come back. She loves us."
"Then why'd she run away?"
"Because we were brats."
"Were you bad?"
"Sometimes. A lot of times."

Abel revealed in a slow sibilance: "The stupid Rector told me my mother is dead. But she's not. He's lying."

"How do you know?"
"Because she's alive."
"But how do you know?"
"Because she said she was coming for me." He slid from his cot to the floor, knelt at Patrick's bedside, peered up to the older Patrick: "She might be outside this cottage. Right now this second."

"Abel, I doubt it."
"In the bushes by the fountain of the Virgin. She might be."
"Abel, you are nuts."

"You'll see, Patrick. Maybe tomorrow you'll wake up and you'll see that I am gone and it'll be because I'm with her."

"Sure, Abel."

Abel stood over Patrick's head, his face bathed in the red light of the exit signs.

"Patrick?"

"Yeah?"

"Can I get in with you?"

"In my bed?"

"Sister Harold's asleep."

Indeed, Patrick could hear the sonorous flapping of Sister Harold's uvula inside her small bedroom where the door stood open.

"I guess."

***

Sleeping with Abel No Sleep became a regular thing. Patrick didn't mind and they never got caught. In the first light of dawn, as Patrick awoke, always there were Abel's enormous brown pupils examining him. And Patrick had to hiss him back to his own cot.

Barnaby came on visitation day, four weeks after dropping the four older children at Holy Innocents. He came empty-handed. Not even with Baby Ruths which cost a nickel or Mary Janes which cost only a penny. Barnaby, the children agreed when older, never spent a nickel without feeling badly about letting it go. He could still be sore about many things years after MomsaBomb bought them. Like the washing machine with the wringer you had to keep away from or it would grab you by the fingernails and suck in your whole hand and then flatten your arm like a pancake and you would have to get the flattened arm cut off and then you could only sell pencils going door-to-door the rest of your life. When that wringer broke, after six years of use, Barnaby's eyes just about popped out of his head at MomsaBomb, her stupidity for buying it: "I told you, Bridget, that it was a piece of crap."

Barnaby said 'I told you' a lot:

"I told you Studebakers are all crap."

"I told you beer was made from wheat."

Barnaby was the original "I told you" guy.

That first visiting day, the four older Sullivan children and Barnaby sat at a long wooden table. The children listened while Barnaby spoke. He said MomsaBomb was staying with Grandmother Powers.

"Why is she at Grandma's?" Patrick asked.

"She's Grandma's daughter, dummy, you know that."

"When can I live with her at home again?"

"Such questions, Paddy. I don't know when! Maybe sometime. Maybe never."

"Never again I can live with my mother?"

74

"Your mother's on vacation. She's sick and needs rest. The kind of rest where you think a lot. Your mother needs to do a lot of thinking. Sick thinking."

"She's not sick. You can't lie to me 'cause Rosemary told me."

"What did Rosemary say?"

"That MomsaBomb's not sick. That you had a big fight, and she ran away from you and now you won't let her see us."

"Rosemary, you have a big mouth. Paddy, do you believe this blabbermouth here or your own father? Dougie, who do you believe? Me or Rosemary?"

Dougie didn't answer. He was quiet at HI! Someone could point a knife point a quarter-inch from Dougie's wide blue eyes and he would not blink.

Patrick pressed on: "When can we go home?"

"That's up to Bishop Quinlan. Not me. I'm talking to the Bishop. Your mother is talking to him too."

Barnaby faithfully followed the words of Father Aloysius, his brother, and Bishop Quinlan. Patrick thought that if either one told Barnaby to wear an orange wig like Clarabelle the Clown, that Barnaby would do it, no questions asked. When the Bishop and Father Aloysius came to Whipple Street, they would take off their Roman collars and drink Beefeater gin shaken in ice because men of the cloth can cause a lot of Jews and Protestants to whisper if they drink Beefeater gin in a restaurant. That's what a scandal is. Barnaby laughed loudly at the jokes of the men of the cloth and never argued. With anyone else, Barnaby knew it all. But with Father Aloysius and Bishop Quinlan, Barnaby just nodded in total agreement to any and all of their wise, and probably holy, answers.

"Why can't she just come to visit?"

Barnaby pointed his finger at Patrick. "Paddy, that's enough:. Your mother is on a retreat this very moment. With the nuns. Everyone should go on retreat. I should go on retreat too but I have to keep cleaning clothes to keep the money coming in. You know, Patrick, this is a hard time for me. Do you think I'd lie to you."

"Yes! You lie all the time."

Rising from his chair and swinging in the same moment, Barnaby socked Patrick with a closed fist so hard that the boy dropped to the floor. No nun was in the visitor's room at the time. Rosemary, Jenny and Dougie watched. Barnaby stood over Patrick: "Watch your mouth, Paddy." Patrick felt a wandering stream of warm blood curl over his lip and down his chin. Even onto the tiles of the visitation room.

"He hit you? A little kid?" Rebecca was a Jew and Jews were the first to stop hitting kids.

"I pissed him off. Not nice to piss Barnaby off." Patrick, on the mountain in the late afternoon sun, tasted warm blood again; saw his father, a giant with bulging biceps, standing above him with quivering, bloodless lips.

Patrick, from the floor, studied his father's enormous scuffed and unpolished shoes; feared that next a kick would come, after which he'd be beaten until dead. Death, he decided, would be better than HI! Better than no MomsaBomb. Suddenly Patrick's capacity for pain knew no bounds. He spat his words in holy fury, like St. Michael the Archangel's clarion battle cry when driving Satan the Serpent from the Gates of Heaven: "You hate our mother. You're taking her from us."

"Shut up or a nun will come."

"I don't care!"

"Get into that chair."

Patrick, defiant and cowering, clung to the leg of a chair.

Barnaby counted to three. Then, breathing heavily and with a grunt, lifted the boy, threw Patrick into the wooden chair. Patrick's head screamed pain but he would not let tears come. Barnaby, catching his wind, turned to make his case to Rosemary, Jenny and Dougie. His voice was unusually meek: "Things are not so easy. You kids don't know."

Patrick's demeanor dissolved, through tears and snot he shouted: "This whole thing is your fault. Your fault!" Barnaby, visibly shaken, declined to come after him again. Stared at Patrick for a full minute. Then walked out of the visiting room with his head down. Not another word. No candy. No quarters for the canteen. No kisses or hugs goodbye. Dougie was impassive. Jenny squeezed her face till it was crimson trying to keep back tears. Rosemary, always first with rules and ethics, said they should return to their cottages.

They walked to their cottages in the gray of the late February morning. On the slushy path, Jenny said: "We are going to be here forever, aren't we?"

Rosemary said, "No, of course not. And don't start crying, it is just too stupid."

Patrick put a hand on Jenny's shoulder and lied: "He didn't hurt me. Honest. He just has a lot on his mind."

Patrick held Dougie's hand and walked with purpose. All the while fearing that Jenny was right, that he would have to remain at HI! until high school was over. Then the nuns and the Rector would force him to take a job in their greenhouse growing flowers to decorate the altars of the archdiocese in order to pay HI! back for all the orphanage had done for him.

***

As the Chicago winter gave way to spring, things got better. Dougie stopped wetting the bed and HI!'s daily repetition of mandatory rituals—from morning prayers to classes to playground to night prayers-- made life close to tolerable, or at least comforting in the lack of the up and down dramas that Whipple Street was full of. Sister Harold nominated Patrick to be thurifer at Solemn High Mass. He was named the altar boy who held the incense pot until the Rector's signal. Then the Rector would swing the incense pot directing its scent to all the nuns and children of the orphanage. Patrick, in his own mind, soared in self-importance. Holiness, he thought, would certainly come from his breathing deeply the incense made in Italy by privileged monks and blessed by Pope Pius himself, incense mailed all the way to Jackson Boulevard on the West Side of Chicago where North Side people were better and richer than the people on the South Side and West Side both of which had become jigaboo jungles, and all but the poorest Catholics had moved to Oak Park, but the Sullivan children were not part of the Negro jungle because they were with the nuns and priests behind high walls. They were as safe as the Vatican was safe, the world's smallest country where Pope Pius was like a president, even an emperor, the holy man chosen by God the Father.

Patrick wrote to MomsaBomb to tell her he had become a thurifer. He printed in block letters his Latin responses from memory. Wrote the priest's part too. Wrote her in that dead language that made the Mass secret and holy, certainly nothing the Protestants or the Jews had. He began to write MomsaBomb nightly and Sister Harold never asked him for stamp money. MomsaBomb did not write back. He feared that her not writing back was a punishment from Bishop Quinlan. Because she went away on the Florida train with Bob the Butcher from Jewel Tea. He guessed that she was getting his letters but that they made her cry and she hated to cry. She was like that.

He composed a long letter on rainbow-colored note paper while Sister Harold and his cottage mates were gathered at the tiny gray oval of TV screen watching a princess of England get the crown of her father who had died. After this night she was to be Queen. Sister Harold said the crown's jewels cost more than the entire city of Chicago. Patrick could see from his table at the back of the common room that there were millions and millions of Englanders standing in the streets where the police kept them behind ropes. The Englanders all cried out "Hooray" and waved tiny flags as the new Queen's horse carriage rolled by. Sister Harold said that the Englanders do have some cars and trucks but most of the people still have to ride horses and that they were very poor since the terrible war with bad Germany. MomsaBomb had already taught the Sullivan kids about the poverty of Europe holding that the English were so poor that they used newspaper for toilet paper and she would never go there in a million years for that very reason.

With his cottage mates busy watching the Queen get her crown, Patrick wrote this letter:

Dear MomsaBomb,

You can't believe how awful it is here. First the food is really terrible. Everything else is terrible too. When I remember your fried chicken, mashed potatoes and the way you boil frozen corn in a plastic bag I could cry and you know how I hate to cry. Sister Harold makes us scrub the floors every Saturday. And then we have to wax them once a month too, which means polishing with rags while we kneel on the floor. Sometimes Sister Harold lets Dougie put his hands on the rags and then I push him by the ankles like a wheelbarrow but there are no wheels just the waxy rags and Dougie slides on them. Sister Harold lets us do the wheelbarrow as long as we don't yell a lot or crash when we're racing other kids. It's about the only single one time she has been nice to us. And the nun who teaches sciences keeps a giant dead moth in a glass box and lets its babies eat the body of the mother. It's really enough to make me puke. I dreamed about the mother moth and woke up sweating one night. It was really terrible. And nothing like this could happen at St. Monica's if only I was at home with you and things were normal like the good old days when we were all together. When can I come home? Jenny is really lonely. She cried a lot at first but now she doesn't talk too much. You should come for her first if you can't get me right away. But Dougie and Rosemary and I want to come back also. I didn't ask Rosemary but I am sure she would say the same things I am writing in this letter. If this letter doesn't get to you, you should make a complaint because that means that Sister Harold tore it up because the nuns only let good mail get out of here because you see they read everything just like they do in prisons. Anyway I know Barnaby doesn't want the family to get back together. He told me you were sick which I know is not true BUT NO MATTER WHAT THE REASON IS IT'S OKAY WITH ME. I know you really didn't do anything really bad and if you did then it was because you couldn't help it. And I know you might sometimes be mad at us when we're not good but I for one am going to be totally good all the time as soon as you come and get me. I will bring you coffee— very very hot the way you like it--in bed and that is a promise. And it's Barnaby's fault too, you are right when you always say that, because I know he never helps you but always leaves us kids (I just erased 'brats' ha ha) with you all alone and the 6 of us are I know are a big problem but I'll never be bad again. Come for us tomorrow or the day after. Or next week for sure. I will be waiting for you. Or I will be playing baseball. I love you, your loving son, honestly and truly yours,

Patrick Peter Sullivan

Then Jenny disappeared from the girl's side.

Rosemary whispered to Patrick through the fence, that Jenny had been put into a special orphanage for crying too much. That Jenny was "mental". Patrick knew "mental" meant something serious having to do with brains. But he also knew that moving her was probably totally justified because all the time at HI! Jenny had been gushing tears like the Blessed Virgin, a perpetual outpouring for all the sins of the children and big people of the world.

Patrick wished, at times, that he too could cry like Jenny did.

He could not.

***

On a late Friday afternoon, before dinner in the Refectory, Sister Harold took Patrick and Dougie aside, instructed them to run, not to walk, to the Rector's office: "We never keep the Rector waiting. Never, do you hear?"

Rosemary was already there when Patrick and Dougie—breathless and afraid--arrived. Monsignor Timothy Hettinger, the Rector, who sat behind a huge desk with piles and piles of papers, pointed them to chairs without so much as a word. Patrick prepared himself for terrible news. Someone had died. Or Barnaby hadn't paid their tuition and now they were being put out on Jackson Boulevard to fend for themselves.

The Rector put a paper aside and began speaking in soft, kind tones. Patrick had held the Missal three times during High Mass for Monsignor Hettinger but, in the sacristy, before and after Mass, the Monsignor had never said a word to him. "You know, you three, that your parents have been given a great challenge by God." The three Sullivans nodded yes without knowing why. "Your parents love each deeply and God has challenged them, laid before them a rocky road. Now the three of you do have parents, parents who are both alive, unlike so many of your cottage mates. So you'll be good to them, won't you now?" They all nodded their silent promise. "So tomorrow morning, after morning prayers, come here to my office. At eight."

Rosemary, Patrick and Dougie exchanged glances, all three equally perplexed. Patrick asked: "Why, Monsignor?"

"Because you are going home."

***

Sister Harold told the cottage that Patrick and Douglas were leaving in the morning. And that she would miss them like her own children. Patrick, alive with imaginings of his old room on Whipple Street, said a last good night to Abel No Sleep. But Abel insisted that he wanted to leave with Patrick, to live with the Sullivans on Whipple Street. Patrick was unable to stanch his pleas which continued, in Patrick's bed, until the church tower bell sounded twelve times. Patrick fell asleep. He awoke to Sister Harold shaking him by the shoulders.

"Where is Abel Garcia?"

"I don't know."

Sister Harold made every kid in the dorm stand along the wall. Then she got on her hands and knees and crawled through the dormitory peeking under every bed. Only then did she face the ugly mortification that she had lost a boy. With her back to the whispering boys, all in slippers and pajamas, she rang the alarm.

***

Barnaby arrived and drove them to Whipple Street. Rosemary got to sit next to Barnaby, while Patrick and Dougie rode in the back with the dirty sweaters, drapes and dresses. Patrick hardly believed that she would really be there. He tried to remember what MomsaBomb looked like. Her smell of Pall Malls and face cream. He tried to imagine what exactly his first words should be.

Then there she was: on a warm June morning, sitting on the front stoop of Whipple Street in a pink summer dress. MomsaBomb ran to the van. As beautiful as ever, with the beauty of a young girl. Rosemary, Patrick and Dougie were out of the van and themselves running. Patrick got his face into her dress and smelled perfume and it was like HI! had never happened.

Inside the house, Kevin and Larry were together in the playpen. Jenny, sitting on the sofa as if planted there, was calmer than at HI! but still cried to see them. Patrick hugged Barnaby while trying to ignore the memory of his being socked onto the visitation room floor. Barnaby was stiff with muscles. Croaked something to the effect that "everything'll be good like it used to be." MomsaBomb sat on Barnaby's lap that night in the living room and the six children sat at their feet. Barnaby announced that from now on MomsaBomb was going to work every day with him at Perfection Dry Cleaners. MomsaBomb was going to work with him side by side so they could have more money. So Barnaby did not have to hire a girl to wait on customers while he was in the back taking food spots out of neckties.

"Honestly, kids, cleaning house all the time, it's enough to drive any Saint to drink," said MomsaBomb. She told Patrick that, from that night forward, he was to be Kevin's after-school keeper. His mother said he had to be "more than a brother now; be like another father." Kevin was three. Bessie Mae would watch Kevin and Larry during the day and then it

80

was up to Patrick. Rosemary was to be in charge of Larry who was almost two.

Kevin sat that night on Patrick's lap. The one great night of no fighting. Barnaby splurged and sent out for pizza, more pizza pies than even the Sullivan kids could eat. Happiness happened. One great night of bliss. For six months they had eaten no pizza. Barnaby let Patrick and Dougie, but not Kevin and Larry, sip from his beer. More than just the foam.

***

Before sending them to bed, Barnaby made a long speech about how nosey everyone in the neighborhood was (especially the hooknoses, the Moskowitz's) and what to say when people asked where they had been. The children were just to say no more than that their mother had been sick, that they had stayed at an aunt's house a long way from St. Monica's. "That's all. Not even to the nuns. Not a single other word, ok?"

"It's none of their beeswax," said Bridget.

There was unanimous, easy agreement. That night, the Sullivan children, the six of them, would have agreed to become Zoroastrians.

Patrick's thoughts, at odd times over the following years, went to Abel No Sleep. Wondered whether he was ever found.

***

The nightmare that was HI! now over, life on Whipple Street began again much as before. One night MomsaBomb and Barnaby were dancing together. Barnaby wore the kind of hat people in Panama wear, a hat left two years ago at the cleaners by a customer. Patrick tended bar and Dougie carried a tray with toothpick-pierced cheese squares and tiny sausages wrapped in bacon. Douglas giggled when MomsaBomb danced close and romantic with a man he'd never seen before. Barnaby was in the kitchen retelling the jokes of Fat Callaghan. Most of the guests were strangers. But friends. A guy called Piggy was a drummer in a band. He wore a grass skirt and a brassiere made out of coconut shells. The children saw him fumble in the grass skirt where he caught a black rubber snake thing that he caressed and shook. His fat belly shook so hard that he bit through his cigar and his lady breasts slipped out of the coconut shells. The big people were as dirty as some of the boys at St. Monica's. But much funnier. Jenny peeked through the banister from upstairs; wide-eyed she stared at Piggy's black thing. She was supposed to be asleep. Piggy made the snake speak, "Hi, I'm Big Blackie, want to play with me?" Barnaby called to MomsaBomb that "If old bag Schroeder next door can't hear this party, she'd better get her ears fixed." Patrick made six dollars in tips.

Two of Chicago's Finest came to the door because of the loud music. Barnaby invited them in and they stayed for a couple of hours. They liked the drinks that Patrick made. They were nice guys. They said how cold it was outside and their guns were bigger than cap pistols. They let Patrick and Dougie count their blue-gray bullets but they would not let them touch their guns which were so powerful that one bullet in the chest of a bad guy would drop him. They had never had to kill anyone but might some day.

***

Patrick's eyes were suddenly wide. Noises outside his room. Saw MomsaBomb pressed against the closet door, held there by Ben, a guy at the party who gave Patrick two dollars. Ben pulled at her dress until Patrick saw her garters at the top of her nylons. Ben hugged her while her hands pushed him away but their lips were together. "Bridget," he whispered through kissing lips, "come on, come on..." Patrick's throat locked. Fear raced up his legs to his chest and locked his throat. He could neither breathe nor scream. He squeezed his eyes shut. Screamed inside rapid Hail Marys. He sweated but it was a cold sweat that made him shiver. Tried not to shiver too loud or Ben and MomsaBomb would know that Patrick knew and then Patrick was in for a terrible punishment. Barnaby was probably sleeping on the sofa. Patrick willed himself to a secret place at the bottom of a deep well. No one else knew this place. In the morning, Patrick awoke with a pain in his stomach. Peered out his bedroom door. The hallway was empty.

***

Bridget and Barnaby went each night after work at the cleaners to The Play Pen. To have a Martoonie and a hamburger before they came home. Jenny, her face peering through the parted drapes, waited each night for their safe return, held her breath until the van arrived at the curb. Anxious, she called The Play Pen on the half-hour. But the waitress would say: "Oh, Jennifer, I saw the van. It just left the parking lot. They'll be home in just a few minutes." At times, Barnaby and Bridget did return early--by nine or ten—and the Sullivan children charged them, kissed MomsaBomb and tried to ascend Barnaby whose coat smelled of Chesterfields which were Patrick's first cigarettes.

Barnaby didn't like his kids to hang on him. "Ok! I've got to read my paper. I'm beat, beat." He'd disappear behind the Daily News complaining about "Jewsevelt and Truman!" About what they had done to the country. Senator Joe McCarthy was a good Catholic, he went to Marquette Law, a man after Barnaby's own heart: "He'll catch all those Commies spies in the White House." Soon Barnaby was asleep in his chair and MomsaBomb had to shake him, "Barnaby, Barnaby, go to bed, go to bed now" and MomsaBomb turned on the television for her nightly movie. She knew and loved all the old Hollywood stars, the stars of her youth. Patrick sat next to her watching Carole Lombard and Humphrey Bogart. Or Ginger Rogers who had married Harry James because they were around each other a lot making movies and singing at night clubs. When Bridget told Patrick to go to bed he knew she didn't mean it. Because when her

82

glass was empty, she'd say: "Patrick, honey, make me a Martoonie and then go to bed." And after he brought the drink, she took his hand, and they watched the movie together until midnight when the Star Spangled Banner came on and the Marines implanted Old Glory atop a low mountain on Iwo Jima. Patrick whispered that he was going to be a priest. MomsaBomb said: "That's my big boy."

In the morning, MomsaBomb made no mention of the vocation he had discovered. Patrick said it again, loudly, clearly, as she and Barnaby hurriedly sipped hot coffee. MomsaBomb heard him this time, stopped; became teary eyed, kissed him. Barnaby too was touched. Said that the day Patrick became a priest would be the happiest day "of this Dad's life".

Patrick walking alone to school—he the Chosen one--pictured his ordination day: the Cardinal consecrating his thumb and index finger. Barnaby would be all smiles when MomsaBomb presented her newly ordained son with a silver chalice embedded with rubies and garnets.

There was only one thing wrong with this lofty vision: Patrick had begun touching himself two or three times a day. Jesus Christ never touched his privates. Patrick never mentioned a vocation again.
***

At age fourteen, Patrick was drafted by Barnaby to work at Sullivan's Perfection Dry Cleaners. Barnaby told him he was keeping score of his hours and would pay him when he got to college. This was okay with Patrick. This drafting accompanied a feeling of some importance. He was in the family business.

Late on a Saturday, after mopping the floors and cleaning the bathroom, MomsaBomb and Barnaby took him to The Play Pen. The three of them seated at the bar, with Patrick in the middle, MomsaBomb announced that Patrick "serves 6:30 Mass every morning of the week." She kissed him. "And he speaks Latin and Greek."

"'Omnis Gallia'", said Mr. Herndon, the insurance agent: "Patrick: is good old Gaul still divided in three parts?" He slapped his thigh.

Patrick was not sure why a tri-partite Gaul was so very funny but laughed along to show he was somehow in the know: "Still in three parts. Yes."

Across the bar, Curly Herlihy, the postman, said: "Six children, Bridget, and you still look like somebody's bride. Won't you give us a song tonight?" MomsaBomb from her stool accompanied, in a small sweet voice, Ella Fitzgerald on the jukebox:
I'm wild again, beguiled again...

All were charmed. She stood. Held an imaginary microphone. Played the crowd.
Those ants that invaded my pants-finis

The lyric brought the house down. Such a community! The patrons seemed to have known Patrick a long, long time. He felt them as so many new aunts and uncles. Fat Callaghan spared him a Shirley Temple and gave him a Coke. Miss Billie Fogarty, MomsaBomb's hairdresser, let Patrick sip her Martini when MomsaBomb went to the ladies room and Barnaby was shooting pool; the gin made his brow bead. He prayed he would not to throw up.

MomsaBomb cried out: "One more Martoonie, Mr. Barman, puh-leese. Make it wodka this time." Fat Callaghan, within the mahogany horseshoe that was his bar, dipped his corpulent mitt into a rack of bottles, raised it high over head and let loose a stream of vodka into the cocktail shaker held at his thigh. Billie Fogarty was amazed each time as the vodka cascaded with only a few drops hitting the floor boards. Billie Fogarty gave Patrick a quarter: "Play J-2,.Pat, J-2 is the song I need to hear."

***

As the hour grew late, Patrick, to stay awake, roamed the bar and wished he had every one of Fat Callaghan's beer mirrors on the walls of his bedroom. Fat Callaghan told a risqué joke every five or ten minutes. The regulars roared each and every time, even if they had heard it five other nights. Jenny called The Play Pen three times that night but each time the waitress told Jenny that the Sullivans had just left. Barnaby, with only a few dollars on the bar in front of him, said: "Bridget, get me out of here." MomsaBomb in reply stuck out her tongue. Barnaby and Patrick, in gloves and jackets, warmed the van for fifteen minutes while MomsaBomb said her farewells.

Toward midnight, creeping in the ice channels of Whipple Street, Patrick saw Jenny's nine-year-old outline in the front window. She cried when they came in. Because they had promised to be home early.

"No such thing, you big baby," said Barnaby.

"I never promised, Jen," said MomsaBomb. "God, what a baby you are!"

They repeated to her five times she could not sleep with them. But, as soon as they fell asleep, she crawled between them. In the morning, they called her: "Our darling."

***

Mr. Terry Curtis, the Oldsmobile dealer in Rodgers Park, was a regular customer. Mr. Curtis never picked up his dry cleaning and laundry without saying something to Patrick. Not just about the Cubs or the weather, but something about Patrick. "How's school? Who are you reading?" Patrick would carry the boxes of shirts while Mr. Curtis carried the dry cleaning to the car. Walking behind him, he saw no wrinkles in the stiff cotton shirt. Mr. Curtis wore his shirts with heavy starch, French cuffs and gold links. The uniform needed, Patrick thought, to meet people with the means to buy a Rocket 98 Olds. The car loaded, Patrick hoped Mr. Curtis would say something more. More about anything.

Mr. Curtis, climbing into the driver's seat, almost as an afterthought, said: "Patrick, you caddy, don't you?"

"No." Patrick, for once, told the truth. He had never so much as put a foot upon a putting green or a fairway. Normally he'd say yes to such a question. And, then, to the next question he would lie again, thus building——or sinking--upon the prior lie.

"How about four tomorrow? At Tam O'Shanter?"

"I don't know how."

"I'll be very pleased to show you." Mr. Curtis smiled. Always when he smiled Patrick would kind of shiver. Shivered upon hearing kindness from that man.

Patrick caddied for Mr. Curtis several afternoons after his day at the dealership ended and before he went home to Mrs. Curtis. Just the two of them walked the links as he worked on his drives, his bunker shots and his putts. Mr. Curtis talked about the president's heavy choices and Russia and the Race to Outer Space while he gave pointers on the art of caddying. After the first few outings, Patrick acquired a sense of which iron or wood Mr. Curtis would reach for next. Patrick made fifteen dollars each time. He began cheering Mr. Curtis's shots.

Then, late one afternoon, after putting out on eighteen, Mr. Curtis introduced Patrick to the caddy master, said a lot of exaggerated things about Patrick. How "Pat" had caddied many, many times. How good he would be for the other members at Tam O'Shanter, and the caddy master said: "Welcome, Pat, we need another good man here."

Patrick was immediately listed among the A caddies, the top level of experience, and got twelve dollars for eighteen holes, not six like the D class caddies got.

Some days he made forty dollars with tips included, a sum that staggered him. To earn that much, he had to carry two bags at the same time while touring eighteen holes twice. This was far superior to Barnaby's promise to pay Patrick for working at the dry cleaners at some indefinite day in a halcyon future when Patrick had enrolled at some college not yet known. After thirty-six holes, Patrick slept ten hours and was up again at five, hitchhiking to Tam O'Shanter, to get a bag with the first foursome off the tee. If Mr. Curtis was golfing that day, the caddy master kept Patrick on reserve until he arrived. Seeing himself on the request list, Patrick swelled with importance. That he was chosen made him feel complete and utterly well placed in a just world. He would sit on a bench far from the poker game and read a novel until Mr. Curtis's foursome was called on the intercom.

The caddy shack was mostly teenagers and a few skinny alcoholics in their thirties and forties. The latter would make their twelve dollars carrying a bag, twenty bucks double, and then drink pints of Old Crow in the Cook County Forest Preserve where they also slept. When it rained they slept off the bourbon under a railroad trestle. Patrick imagined, though he was never sure, that none of the adult caddies had real homes. Mornings, they would arrive in silence, strip naked in the washroom and splash water on their white lean bodies and tanned leathery arms and faces, creating puddles of soapy grey water the young caddies were forced to wade through. Within the crew there were three or four teen sharks who passed the day playing poker, skinning greener caddies of their earnings, only packing up the cards when the caddy master threatened to throw them off the course if they didn't take a bag.

The members were mostly male and women weren't allowed on the course except on Wednesdays. It was a Catholic club meaning there were no Jews or Negroes. Patrick imagined that the Jews wanted their own club anyway. And no Negro had ever played golf to his knowledge. Mr. Curtis bought Patrick Cokes which the cheap members did not. When he played in a foursome, Mr. Curtis always introduced Patrick to the other men. Patrick, despite being red-faced, always shook hands, and said that he was very pleased to meet them.

Patrick almost never lost a ball. Just the ones Mr. Curtis dumped in the water at six, ten and fourteen. Years later, Patrick could still hear Terry Curtis' urgent cry from the tee: "Got it, Pat? Got it?" And Patrick would wave from seventy yards down the fairway that he had it, had the spot in the rough or the woods marked indelibly in his mind, no matter where Mr. Curtis had shanked it.

Mr. Curtis spoke with pride of his daughter who lived in New York City where she was an actress. Patrick got the idea, though nothing was ever said, that he missed not having a son. He did not work day and night like Barnaby but was relaxed, and had about eighty people working at the Oldsmobile agency. He never drank beer on the links, only water on the hot days, and waited until he was in the clubhouse to order a gin and tonic. He worked at his golf. It didn't get better but, to Patrick, it didn't seem to worsen either. Mr. Curtis did not jump up and down when he dumped a ball in a pond like some of the members. He just smiled, shook his head and hit another. Mr. Curtis, to Patrick's eyes, walked like a prince without a crown, tall and majestic wearing yellow, orange, or red golf slacks that were perfectly tailored.

Barnaby let it be known that Patrick's caddying was a wee traitorous. There was an occasional dig about his parents having to do it all, no help from the big ones. (Little was expected of Dougie, for some reason.) But Barnaby could not argue with the money Patrick brought home, even offered to bank it for Patrick. But Patrick demurred--perhaps from a developing sense of propriety, perhaps from a suspicion that

Barnaby would spend it--and secreted his earnings in a metal box in the attic.

At the end of the summer, Mr. Curtis told Patrick about a scholarship--the Chick Evans scholarship--that Tam O'Shanter gave each year, a four-year ride to the college of the student's choice. "For an excellent student and sterling fellow like you, Pat, it's a great opportunity." He put his hand on the boy's shoulder and said slowly: "I want you to win that scholarship, Pat."

Patrick instantly committed to winning the scholarship. To Georgetown University, Mr. Curtis' alma mater. Through sophomore and junior years at De La Salle's, he got nothing but A's. If the Christian Brother asked for a five-page report, Patrick gave him ten. If there was an extra credit assignment, he did extra over the extra. He became known as an egregious brown nose which bothered him not at all. Saw himself as that freight train full of Sherman tanks like the one he once saw rolling to Korea on the Irving Park Road overpass. He wrote for the school newspaper and covered football, basketball and track. He envisioned himself in college as a totally different person. No one at Georgetown would know that he was one of the lowly Sullivans who lived on Whipple Street. Nor that he slept in a musk-laden lair with a brother who rarely bathed. Patrick envisioned himself on campus wearing pressed khakis and button-down baby blue Oxford cloth dress shirts, dirty bucks and navy-blue cardigans. He would date girls who'd know nothing about him except what he told them. On the map, he measured the District of Columbia as being eight hundred and thirty two miles from Chicago. Safe. Removed. Indeed in another world. He was to be anonymous. Boys from De La Salle graduated to become members of Chicago's Finest. Or joined the fire department. Became chauffeurs. No one from De La Salle's ever went to Georgetown University in the shadows of the White House.

In the first month of his senior year, Patrick received a letter from the Tam O'Shanter scholarship committee congratulating him. Patrick knew that Mr. Curtis had put in a fix. That the scholarship committee probably had all gotten together over drinks and Mr. Curtis had said: "Patrick Sullivan is a good kid. He's smart and I want him in." Conversation over. Patrick had an idea that things worked that way at the top. That there was a seriousness when someone solid like Mr. Curtis spoke, a force in the room no one would counter. Barnaby also admired such men. But from an inarticulate distance. Barnaby was forever in awe of the money other men made.

The October of his senior year, on a Saturday morning after the first frost, Indian summer had arrived. Mr. Curtis' foursome walked and talked beneath an azure sky dimpled with high white clouds while red and gold maple leaves eddied on the fairways. Patrick watched as Mr. Curtis, addressing the ball, absently dropped his driver, and began squeezing himself under the armpits. He collapsed, his mouth wide but soundless. Dr. Flanagan, a pediatrician, pounded his fist on Mr. Curtis's chest while Patrick ran to the clubhouse. Only the toes of his sneakers touched the grass but by the time the ambulance with its siren screaming had crossed four fairways and rolled onto the tee, Mr. Terence Curtis, the proprietor of Curtis Oldsmobile, was no more.

Patrick absented himself from school to go to the funeral at St. Mary's in Evanston. There he saw Mr. Curtis' daughter for the first time. She was lithe and moved with a sullen sad grace. She stood with head bowed next to her mother. Mrs. Curtis wore a black lace mantilla so the other mourners couldn't see her hollowed eyes. Patrick saw those eyes when she lifted her veil to kiss him. He hid his face as Mr. Curtis' golf friends carried the bronze casket down the steps of the church to Philip Monaghan's hearse. Patrick did not make the trip to the cemetery; the courage to beg a ride failed him. Back at Whipple Street, all that day and night, he cried in his room. The kind of colicky bawling that babies do.

XI

Georgetown University

On Mt. Katahdin, Rebecca's curiosity continued: "Your Terry Curtis must have been wonderful." Rebecca sat up on the blanket. "But I know you went to Georgetown. You got the scholarship?"

"I did but life was complicated." Patrick's eyes took in her nakedness, a concave belly despite childbirth, her limbs supple and gaining a tan even as they sat on the blanket they borrowed from a cabin wall. "You are so beautiful...let's, you know, adjourn..."

"Later. Tell me first. About Georgetown."

"You want me to tell all my secrets?"

"When you are not wearing clothes, the rules of privacy sort of change?"

Patrick studied his fingers than looked across the vast valley of stubby pine and crooked oak. The scholarship was tuition, all books and a room and meals at the Evans House. There was a stipend each semester. Most of that went to beer. The first Thanksgiving he went back to Whipple Street and had a terrible time of it. He had fallen into a hot hated for everything and all he had come from. So in December he called MomsaBomb collect at the Dry Cleaners and told her about the several term papers he had to complete and would not be home for break. That the had to stay and study or lose the scholarship. "Ma, you just can't know how unbelievably difficult Georgetown is."

The Evans House was officially closed over Christmas break but Bridget didn't know that. Patrick had a key. His bet was that his fraternity mates would never know he had stayed through the holiday. The first few days, he ate peanut butter from a five pound tin. There was no bread or jelly. He could not eat in restaurants or buy at the grocery store because his stipend was long gone and his next check not due until January. The first five days and nights, he spent reading, cover to cover, *The Rise and Fall of the Third Reich,* finishing on Christmas night. Then his utter isolation struck like a thunder clap. He was in a massive brick house with thirty rooms and nary a soul to speak to. The start of classes in early January seemed a lifetime away instead of nine days. Also, he had eaten the Evans pantry bare. Christmas morning, he ate the last stale crackers, some olives, and an institutional size can of crushed tomatoes. The can of tomatoes revisited him two hours later with a violent case of skitters.

Late on Christmas night, having read of Eva and Adolph's last days in the bunker, Patrick set to walking the streets of the capital city.

Terminally lonely and ravenous for anything caloric, he strolled the capital's empty streets.

Suddenly, crossing the great lawn in front of the Washington Monument, he hit upon the idea of robbery. Not actual robbery but rather petty theft which was sure to have few consequences. He decided in an epiphanous moment that his answer to surviving the holiday was to hit-and-run a hamburger shop. For food not money. The D.C. cops would be busy with murders and rapes and a few dollars worth of hamburgers and fries was not going to get him investigated, arrested and hauled off to jail. Tasting the burgers and fries already, he started off at a slow run, to a White Castle where the burgers were tiny and sizzled in onions that had been dried and then made fluffy with water. The hamburgers were not among the world's best. But the shakes were good. The fries too were good and which he tasted them from memory as he ran. With food so very ordinary, and it being Christmas night, White Castle, he guessed, would be fairly empty.

Through the window of the white turreted building, Patrick from the sidewalk watched a customer leave then entered. The counter worker was high school age and offered a bright "Merry Christmas". With a sandy throat unaccustomed the past several days to words, Patrick wished the boy "Merry Christmas" in return. This he did with the thought that robbers, in general, were not of the social class that would make much out of Christmas. His teeth, however, began to chatter uncontrollably. He stammered an order for eight of the tiny hamburgers, four fries and two shakes. While the boy packed the bag, Patrick made a stabbing attempt at small talk, asked the boy what college he was going to. The boy said he didn't know but he definitely wanted to go away to Texas or California, anything to get out of D.C. His mother was a nag and he didn't live with his father. He was saving his money. He was the kind of kid who smiled no matter what the subject. Even if he said, 'My mother just threw me out of the house' or, 'My dog died this morning', he would say it with the same broad smile with which he now announced proudly: "That'll be three thirty-five, sir."

Patrick searched his pockets then slapped his forehead: "I think...you know this sounds silly...but I left my money. In my Corvette." With the bag in hand, he backed toward the door: "How could I forget? Silly me. I left my money with my girlfriend!"

Into the cold night he ran across the parking lot and down a side street, made right angle turns at several intersections to confuse any agents of Justice, ran easily for a mile, amazed at his speed, and thought that when faced with necessity--and some degree of danger--his running could take him to the Olympics. He imagined that the counter kid, out to protect the fortune of White Castle, was close behind him. That Patrick would be forced to fight him for the hamburger bag. He imagined the D.C. cops

91

cornering him in an alley, slamming him to the ground, cuffing him. Quickly, there was Barnaby darting into the D.C. holding tank wielding his wide leather belt with the coiled cobra and its fangs to prove once and for all what a coward his son truly was.

Breathless Patrick took refuge in a doorway. He listened. No sounds. No footsteps. No sirens. His legs were cramping, his lungs were on fire and a dagger was piercing his groin. Unable to run further, he decided it was foolish to assume that a dragnet had been put in place over a few hamburgers. Somewhat comforted by this thought, he walked--in a roundabout way—back to the Evans House with the bag under his jacket on the off-chance that the Capitol police were on the lookout for White Castle's hit-and-run thief.

In the cold kitchen of the Evans House, he found that the milk shakes had leaked onto, and made sodden, the hamburgers and fries. Despite this, Patrick devoured the blended meal while skimming Joyce's *Ulysses*. He got lost in the prose and could not decipher, for the most part, precisely what was happening but he did not care: the prose was supremely beautiful and his stomach was beginning to fill.

In bed at midnight, wrapped in blankets from four other beds, he was obsessed with the fear that the D.C. cops would, in the next minute, ring the bell of the Evans House. "You, you in there. We know you're in there... Get out here!" This night's theft, he resolved, was to be his last. Though the caper had come off as planned, a life of crime was not worth the anxiety he now suffered. Patrick felt sick in the heart. Sick, he thought, in the chest cavity where a heart should reside. Shivering, despite the borrowed blankets, at three in the morning he bolted to the bathroom and vomited the White Castle dinner. Shaking over the toilet bowl, he conceded that he could not last another week.

Not alone.

***

Thumbing rides, Patrick cleared suburban Maryland by dawn, Pennsylvania by noon, then got a lucky ride from a salesman through all of Ohio and Indiana. The guy called on hardware stores in small towns in three states. Patrick was both thankful and held hostage by the man's glib conversation. In a friendly but seemingly unending monologue the salesman painted pictures of what Patrick could expect of life: not much in the way of happiness, maybe a cold beer just before bed. In Toledo, he continued his avuncular warnings while Patrick engorged himself--the salesman's treat--to two Bob's Big Boys burgers and fries. On the Indiana Turnpike, the salesman tearfully admitted the failure of his lifelong dream: to marry and have kids. Needing the ride, Patrick, smiling sympathetically, said to himself: *Self, don't ever get this bad off because this poor slob looks like he's about to cry.*

92

The last ride got him deep into Chicago's North Side before the driver leaned to Patrick and suggested Patrick owed him fellatio. "I would, sir, but as a Catholic I cannot." Holding his duffel bag between them, Patrick jumped from the car, crossed empty Western Avenue and walked past Riverview Park on black ice. "Grand Opening May 25!" was painted in screaming red letters on the high white wooden fence. Beyond the barbed wire, Patrick saw the massive structure of wooden struts that supported the roller coaster. The parachute drop was hung with stalactites of ice and there was an eerie stillness to the park which in the summer was a cacophony of screams, barkers, and an organist playing polkas in the beer garden. With his duffel over his shoulder, he walked the last two miles to Whipple Street not having a quarter for the bus. He felt oddly bold, even touched with nobility as he walked through the quiet cold city in the salted slush, hungry again, fatigued but alert. *Hog butcher to the world, give me a pound of your bacon...* Up the middle of quiet Whipple Street he approached home. Only the Sullivan bungalow still had lighted windows. Tiny shards of ice blew from the black sycamore branches stinging his face. The delivery van was not at the curb; Patrick guessed that Barnaby and MomsaBomb were still at The Play Pen. The front door was unlocked. Kevin and Larry had fallen asleep watching TV covered in their blankets in the living room. Jenny was asleep between them, her thumb in her mouth. Dougie wasn't there. Patrick assumed he was celebrating the holiday season with the Kedzie Bombers. Rosemary would be with her paraplegics. An empty pizza box lay on the floor; a chitinous beetle darted among the crusts.

Kevin and Larry awoke first, gave Patrick a hero's welcome. Then Jenny wept for a full hour, delirious to see him. A small Christmas tree was shedding needles and tinsel. Under it, he found two unopened gifts, both for him: a tie and wool gloves. He stuffed them into his duffel lest they somehow be taken back.

The memory of many Christmases past settled upon him. The furniture was threadbare, worse than the Evans House common room where ten or twenty of the brothers played football each night after dinner despite house rules. He was hungry again and wanted to eat but Jenny said there were water bugs in the pantry because the toilet upstairs had been leaking. Barnaby said he was going to fix the problem the past couple of weeks but hadn't gotten around to it. Tired, Patrick didn't want to lie down in his old bedroom for fear that it would smell like Dougie who bathed seemingly in rhythm with the lunar cycle. He squeezed onto the sofa with Jenny, Kevin and Larry while a new movie began. They draped their arms around his shoulders while he picked at the cold pizza crusts and watched John Wayne take back one South Pacific island after another. Larry and Kevin were bug-eyed as the Japanese defenders poked their heads out of dugouts in the jungle floor, their helmets featuring a spray of tropical grasses. Or they sniped at the Marines from where their ankles had been cuffed high in the palm trees by their officers. Jenny wanted to turn on something else--anything else--but was outvoted three-to-one. She stayed anyway. Kevin laid his cheek on Patrick's chest.

They awoke to loud cursing as Barnaby and MomsaBomb arrived at two in the morning. The TV was all dots and a steady buzz. Seeing Patrick, MomsaBomb got sloppy and tearful. Despite getting kissed with alcohol breath, Patrick felt that his earlier life was a bad dream, a nightmare now obliterated by her excitement to see him. She was, she said, the happiest woman in the world. Barnaby asked if he would come to the Dry Cleaners with them this week because business approaching New Year's Eve would be madness. Patrick readily agreed. Remembered that he had *carte blanche* when working to take money from the cash register and buy hamburgers at the Greek's.

On Friday, New Year's Eve, the entire clientele seemed to be picking up their party clothes. For the big night. Barnaby and MomsaBomb went to The Play Pen for lunch at noon telling Patrick that they'd be quick about it. He had qualms about being left alone on such a major business day but, just having had two hamburgers from the diner, he felt the expansiveness of the season and told them to have a great lunch. And that they deserved it.

Wave upon wave of customers flooded in and he, hanger by hanger, gave out hundreds of dollars in clean clothes, while amassing piles upon piles of dropped-off dirty garments which he positioned on the floor. Soon the piles mounted like a semicircle of woolen burial mounds that hemmed him into an increasingly narrow valley where he took money at the cash register.

At half past four, he decided the luncheon must have been on its eighth or tenth course or more likely his parents were crooning *auld lang zyme* with a gang of acquaintances and had moved on to liqueurs. He called the restaurant twice. Each time the waitress said they had just left. Patrick was quietly enraged, smiled at the customers through gritted teeth. The 'they just left' trick they could pull on Jenny but not Patrick Peter Sullivan. What a fool he was! He wondered which of his parents was glued to the barstool. Decided it was probably both.

A lucid moment came upon him. A moment after which his life would be forever changed. The next moment the store was clear of customers, he put the "Closed" sign in the window and locked the front door, withdrew a hundred dollars from the till. A draw on all he was owed. For services rendered over too many years. Walking to the rear, Patrick stopped, returned to the cash register and took another hundred. And with a bug-eyed woman pounding indignantly on the glass door, scribbled in an oversized, jagged script, this note:

94

MomsaBomb & Barnaby,

I hope your New Years Eve 'lunch' was a gourmet treat. I also hope you both rot in hell. I for one have decided to have a wonderful New Year. All year long. Have a Happy and prosperous New Year. I am gone forever. Thanks for nothing.

Patrick

He taped it to the wall next to the phone where they couldn't miss it. Passing J.C., the presser, he whispered: "Later, baby". J.C., who had been singing softly while pulling on a pint throughout day, waved in return. Patrick exited the back door, and caught a bus to the Loop and Union Station. Waiting for the train to pull out, he called Rosemary at the rehab institute.

"I'm never coming back."

"Paddy, I didn't even get to see you."

"Come to Georgetown. You can stay at a women's dorm."

"Will you—you know—introduce me to guys?"

"I'm thinking of one right now. Sure."

Flush with the two hundred dollars he had separated from the till, Patrick spent thirty-five of it on a sleeping berth. All that night the train rocked and he listened to the clacking rails and the warning bells at crossings. Red lights flooded and then disappeared in the cocoon of the pull-down berth. He dreamed on and off of Jenny. Of Kevin and Larry asleep on the sofa among the pizza crusts. He dreamed that he stood on a barren isolated sidewalk with no houses in sight anywhere. Patrick tried to run. Each time he did, he slipped and fell. The broad sidewalk turned to sand and lard like a mix of the muddy sands of Montrose Beach and offal from the Stockyards.

"This is the part when you never went back."

"You're a good listener."

XII
Chez Antoine

Summers Patrick worked at Chez Antoine in St. Michael's on the Eastern Shore of Maryland. Antoine, a chef/owner with rheumy eyes and long cheeks that sagged like over-ripe pears, took a liking to Patrick: if ten lobsters were dying in the tank, Antoine counted on Patrick to sell them: "*Bon! Très bien,* Pa-treek," Antoine cried loudly in the kitchen where he stood in a nimbus of fish stock sipping Champagne: "Good boy, Pa-treek."

If Antoine got drunk and erupted into one of his rages, 'Pa-treek' was never the one to get axed.

Those summers Whipple Street existed for Patrick only in a few dog-eared and wrinkled photos in a sweat-beaten leather billfold: Rosemary cradling a paraplegic in a therapy pool; Larry, at thirteen, selling ice cream from a cart in Hollywood Park; Dougie, still in the sweetness of youth, his junior varsity football photo; and Kevin, aged three, trying to jump into the camera.

Patrick bunked in Antoine's back cottage with five other waiters and worked ten hour days. His back pocket slowly filled with fifties and hundreds, the summer's take. Late each night waitstaff from the tourist restaurants gathered around a driftwood bonfire on Dead Man's Beach where the red lights of Annapolis blinked to the northwest. They drank beer and bragged of fifty per cent tips or complained about stiffs. Most nights, twosomes would form. A he and a she would begin by holding hands or rubbing each other's back and then, arm in arm, disappear into the reeds. One of Patrick's late night couplings showed up at Antoine's for lunch still glowing with the embrace of the previous night. Patrick was nonplussed as she greeted him with a hug and kiss. In truth, he did not remember her nor the performance, an amnesia resulting from a surfeit of beer. To the co-ed he murmured his apologies for not recognizing her whereupon she slapped him, then stomped through the luncheon crowd upsetting, at the door, the hostess' menu stand. Antoine, who witnessed the scene, thereafter thought even better of Patrick.

***

"I got a job from a Seagram's recruiter just before graduation. Moved to the Apple and here I am. Now you know everything."

"I doubt it."

"No, really, you do."

She sat up, looked him in the eye, crossed her arms cradling her breasts then flicked an ant from her shoulder. "If my prying gets too much you can stop but I really want to hear more."

"Okay. You asked."

***

Back at Georgetown, after turning New Year's Eve into his personal Declaration of Independence, Patrick fell into a funk. For three months, he barely got out of bed. His frat mates reasoned with him but Patrick just said, "Leave me alone." By mid-term, he was failing every class. With a three week beard, the only one he ever grew, he limped into the office of the Jesuit who had taught him Composition the first semester. Father McAvoy had a frank way of speaking, while always smiling, that had kept Patrick from openly denouncing the Church of Rome.

"Father, I don't believe in anything."

"Okay, Pat, this is the walk you are walking."

96

"It's not right, father. Every guy in the Evans House believes in things."

"Pat, you are not everyone else."

"There are guys——-Brannan, my roommate, he is so in love with his girlfriend! Father, I hope you can understand this, but I *only want to get laid.*"

"I've been that way."

"Really?" Patrick suspected a trick.

"Hey, what am I, Pat, a eunuch?"

Patrick lifted his eyes to the white-polled Jesuit: "Father, I hate myself. I do."

"I have been that way too."

"I feel sick unto death."

"You look dead."

"Usually I can smile through anything."

"I used to do that. Smiled all the time." Father McAvoy rocked, found great humor in a memory, then leaned forward: "*Lumen Gloriae,* Pat. The Light is the Word and it will come to you but you cannot cause it to come. When it does, you will be in it and of it."

"Father, I don't know what you're talking about."

"Pat: the Light of Glory and the Word will come to you."
***

"And you never went back to Chicago?"

"Never."

XIII

Life with Father

Cradling Patrick's cheek on her thigh, Rebecca asked: "How did you ever survive?"

"I'm okay."

"How could you be okay?"

"I just am." His lips grazed her thigh. North. "Back in the cabin, I have a present for you?"

"What?"

"Me."

"Later. I want to hear more."

"I'm down to vignettes."

"I like vignettes."

***

On a Saturday morning, at half past six, Patrick rose before the rest of the family, peed but did not flush, sneaked out the front door and hid in the rear of the van. Hid under suits and dresses that smelled of perfume and the bathroom, held perfectly still and tried to will away the tickle of worsted wool.

Not long after the driver door opened and Barnaby got in. The van crept from stoplight to stoplight. Barnaby was silent. Patrick peeked once only to see the back of his father's head and the blue curls of the morning's first cigarette. The motor stopped. Patrick heard the driver door open and shut. Upon opening the van's rear, Barnaby gasped—trousers with a third leg.

Patrick, afraid he had made a terrible calculation, threw back the dirty garments, and began a desperate explanation and apology. Told his father that he really wanted to work with him. To make money. To be with him. Alone. Because MomsaBomb did not got to the cleaning store on Saturdays.

Barnaby listened. Thought. Then laughed. "Why not?"

He gave Patrick thirty cents to get him coffee from the Greek's. Then Patrick spent three hours sweeping the floor and washing the sink and toilet. The presser, J.C., listened to jazz on the Negro station and smiled at Patrick whenever he passed. Patrick felt more than special: he was the son of the owner. The son of the man who was the boss of workers. Late in the morning a buddy from Barnaby's high school days came by. Harry. Harry said hello by punching Patrick in the arm. Not once but several times. Harry laughed. Patrick laughed too, despite the pain.

Barnaby took Patrick by the shoulders: "I've got a job for you, Paddy: turn every pocket. If a lipstick or a ballpoint pen goes in with the clothes, it'll cost me a thousand bucks. Jesus, we might even have to sell the house on Whipple Street! You wouldn't want that...so no mistakes, ok?"

Patrick agreed with apostolic zeal. After thirty minutes of turning pockets, he had found four dollars in nickels, dimes and quarters. Patrick thought he must be some sort of a born genius to do the job so well. Barnaby and Harry could not believe Patrick's luck: "I've never found that much," exclaimed Harry.

"You don't work as hard as Paddy, you dummy!" said Barnaby.

The luck continued. Patrick could do no wrong. Barnaby and Harry continued to throw compliments along with the next garment. In almost every pair of pants, Patrick harvested a quarter or several dimes.

Then Patrick saw Harry reach into a trouser pocket. Before he threw the pants to Patrick.

Patrick realized himself as a fool. "You're doing it, Harry, aren't you?"

"Doing what?"

"Putting money in the pants," Patrick said. Harry almost threw up he laughed so hard. Barnaby took back the money back and gave it to Harry, sent him for beer. After that, Barnaby told Patrick to "just watch" because Barnaby didn't want him to get hurt near the steam where J.C. was pressing. "Also because he's funny. If you know what I mean."

"Dad, what do you mean?"

"J.C. is...." Barnaby looked back to where J.C. existed in billows of rising steam: "J.C. is one of those kind."

"Really?"

"I don't want you near bad influences, you know?"

So Barnaby waited on people and Harry turned pockets and they drank beer after beer. When things got busy, Harry too waited on customers. But Harry's math was bad and he had difficulty making change. Barnaby didn't say anything. Patrick, taking a page from Dougie, played dead. All the while that Saturday, Harry and Barnaby traded stories. Barnaby told about a Negro who rented a board over a bathtub for a place to sleep. But the guy could only use the board eight hours a day before the next renter's turn to use it.

Harry was not amazed: "I can believe it."

"The guy is saving up for a Cadillac. It's true, I swear it," said Barnaby.

"Of course, it's true."

"The more things stay the same," Barnaby assured Harry, "the more they're going to change."

Harry said, "You're right about that, Barney."

Barnaby showed Harry a black silk suit he took in the day before: "This guy is Mafia. I know it. See how the lapels are stiff? It's blood. This guy, Andy, he says to me, like he'd been a bad, bad boy: 'Mr. Sullivan, I must have missed a stair because I fell down.' Harry, feel this blood. Can you imagine what the other guy looked like?"

Harry laughed and coughed so hard he had to put his cigarette out. His face was squeezed until his pupils became black shiny balls in overflowing pools: "'I must have missed a stair, Mr. Sullivan.' My rear end!" Harry laughed so hard he had to run to the bathroom but before he got there he threw up. Barnaby told Patrick to get the mop. Patrick did but it made him feel like he too had to vomit. After he tried to nap atop a pile of dirty clothes. With his eyes closed, he heard the two men resume telling jokes at the counter, and Patrick wished, even prayed to God that Harry was dead. Barnaby too. That everyone in the entire world was dead except him.

Patrick awoke to Harry's loud snoring. He lay close to Patrick, wrapped in dirty drapes.

***

Sunday morning, just past dawn: Barnaby and MomsaBomb arrived home having closed the last blind pig. Patrick heard them come up the stoop stomping snow from their boots then heard the front door open. Barnaby called from the bottom of the stairs: "Ok, you sleepyheads, my little darlings and sweethearts, here he is: the biggest dope of a Dad in the whole round world! Who wants breakfast? Come and get it!"

Patrick and Dougie were first down the stairs followed by Kevin and Larry to a chorus of, "Yea, Daddy! Yea, Daddy!" MomsaBomb, plodded up the staircase, her lipstick reduced to red flecks. She moved in a halation of gin, perfume and Pall Malls. In passing, she pecked each child wetly: "My little darling, hi sweetheart, your Mom's so tired..." Barnaby, in the kitchen with a cold beer in hand, began his Sunday morning gift to his bride: making breakfast for his "six monkeys". In blue gingham apron, he raised his Pilsner glass in regal proclamation: "Hair of the puppy dog!"

"Hair of the puppy dog!" Dougie and Patrick cried in return.

His eyelids drooping, Barnaby wagged a minatory pinkie: "Don't wake your Mom."

100

Dougie and Patrick repeated themselves, but in a whisper: "Hair of the puppy dog, hair of the puppy dog". Each got to bite at the foam in the frosted glass while Barnaby at the stove—a sailor on the deck of a listing vessel--fried two pounds of bacon and toasted raisin bread, a half-loaf at a time, in the broiler.

Then Patrick discovered--when sent to the van to retrieve groceries—that the eggs were stiff as hockey pucks. Frozen in the ten below temperature of the night before as Barnaby and Bridget migrated from one blind pig to the next.

"So no eggs---but bacon we got lots of." He cooked with one hand and a glass of beer in the other. "Eat! And then I'm sleeping till noon."

Dougie snatched a strip of bacon from Patrick's plate. Patrick slapped his hand away, yelled: "That's mine!"

Dougie whined, "Paddy's hogging!"

"Jesus!" Barnaby cried. "One more peep out of you two and I'm closing the restaurant, you hear? Jesus Horatio Christ, my *nerves*."

With Barnaby's attention focused on the spit and sizzle on the stovetop, Patrick appropriated a strip of Dougie's bacon but Dougie, always the quick one, pinned the strip to his plate with his fork. It shredded. Two glasses of orange juice spilled, one was Rosemary's. She screamed. Barnaby wheeled, pan in hand, and struck Patrick across the face: "Paddy, it's always you, always the older one that's making the trouble." But the frying pan tilted and slid, spilled bubbling grease onto Jenny's ankle. She screeched and screamed, fell to the floor, rolled and rolled till she hit the wall. Patrick saw grease on the ankle, grease on the floor. Jenny was wild-eyed as bacon fat ate into her.

The scream produced a clatter from upstairs; MomsaBomb was downstairs in seconds. Barnaby spilled his beer onto the floor while bending over, then kneeling over, Jenny, who now lay in a marsh of beer and fat. MomsaBomb crashed upon the scene. Demanded to know "exactly" what Barnaby had done. Barnaby, weeping, explained that "the boys did it" while he tried, with trembling fingers, to convince a flap of skin to cover once more the red meat of Jenny's ankle.

"No! You did it, you terrible drunk!" She pushed Barnaby aside to minister to Jenny.

Barnaby turned on Patrick and Dougie and with spitting rage pummeled them. They cowered in a corner. Barnaby flailed. Patrick did not smile; Dougie did not play dead. Patrick, through a web of fingers while sliding down the wall, saw MomsaBomb kissing Jenny; he protected his mouth while waiting for Barnaby's arms to tire.

MomsaBomb told Barnaby to stop, that Patrick had to drive to the hospital. Because "you are too damned drunk." MomsaBomb carried Jenny to the van; his little sister's cries of pain stabbed at Patrick as he turned the ignition key. Patrick, at thirteen, had never driven a car. For the past two years, he had watched Barnaby's every move while coordinating movement of the clutch and the shift column. The still-warm engine turned over and the delivery van lurched from the curb, MomsaBomb screamed: "Goddamnit, Paddy, put the gas to the floor! What kind of pig shit car is this for a family to have, my pig shit husband...poor Jen, my poor baby, Jen, don't cry!"

The van bounced in and out of the ruts. Jenny wailed with every lurch. MomsaBomb slapped Patrick's hand from the floor shift: "Paddy, I'll shift. You work the gas and the clutch! My poor, poor Jenny! Now, Paddy, *now*...the clutch!"

***

Returning from the Emergency Room, Patrick's jerk of the steering wheel to get the van out of Whipple Street's icy channels caused a front tire to jump the curb. "Leave it, Paddy. You did fine." Patrick turned off the motor. Then realized that he had missed Sunday Mass for the very first time. He remembered Religion class, knew that he had not sinned. Because he had been engaged in an act of mercy. He lifted Jenny from MomsaBomb's arms while she gave steady praise to his courage, his driving: "You're a wonderful boy, Paddy. Never, never be like your damned drunk of a father, do you hear?"

"Okay, Mom."

"You saved our Jenny, you know that?"

Patrick carried Jenny up the icy stairs and through the front door with caution so that her foot--now swathed in soft, white gauze--did not graze the jamb. Larry and Kevin looked at their big brother with eyes wide. Rosemary kissed Jenny and cried. Jenny, who had quieted down with medicine, cried with Rosemary. Barnaby was snoring on the sofa while on the television the Bears were dancing with the Green Bay Packers. MomsaBomb looked him over and then struggled to get him onto his feet: "Go up and sleep, Barnaby." She shook him lightly. "Go get some sleep, honey. Barnaby, sweetie."

***

Father Carolan, the young assistant at St. Monica's, was assigned the parish's morning round of delivering Communion to the infirm. And training a corps of altar boys. He held a drawing to give away two tickets to the Golden Gloves. At the Chicago Stadium. In the meeting, while Father Ryan swished names in a bowl, Patrick, one of twenty boys all hoping to win, made a vow to utter a thousand Hail Marys and five hundred Our Fathers if God would cause his name to be picked. Father Carolan unfolded a scrap: "It's Patrick Sullivan."

Patrick never said the Hail Marys or Our Fathers.

Patrick did not pester Barnaby for things as Rosemary and Jenny did relentlessly but on this occasion with tickets to the manliest sport of all, Patrick implored his father to commit to just one night together, a night they would spend at the Golden Gloves. After a week's pleading and no answer beyond a one-two to Patrick's ribs, Barnaby agreed.

On fight day, a Sunday in early December, Barnaby spent the afternoon watching the Bears on television and drinking beers with Harry. Patrick fretted—without saying anything--that his father would drink too many beers and fall asleep. But at five o'clock, with darkness descending upon Whipple Street, Barnaby said: "Paddy, we don't want to be late."

***

Barnaby drove with caution, a one vehicle cortege down Western Avenue, into the bowels of Chicago to the housing projects west of the Loop. The van crept with implacable gravity straddling two lanes. Patrick for once sat in the front seat while Barnaby revealed many truths: that Heeb promoters fix all the pro boxing matches but that the Golden Gloves were above corruption; that amateurs were unspoiled and honest; that professional boxers were all crooks. ("Not Rocky Marciano. That man, maybe the only one out there, is a Saint, believe me.") That the young boxers, even the Negro ones, are just trying to get ahead in life and the sheeny kikes and Mafia bozos had not yet gotten to the Golden Glovers who were innocent and incorruptible. Barnaby whispered: "Dives, Paddy: they pay the pros to fake getting knocked out. You didn't know that, did you?"

"No, Dad."

"Never, never gamble, Paddy. You won't, will you?"

"No, Dad, never. I will never be so stupid!"

They parked on Lake Street under the El along side Cabrini Green; parked on the street because the guarded parking lots charged "an arm and a leg". At the curb, a hassle of a project kids, none older than nine or ten, surrounded the van with boastful promises to protect the delivery van with their lives.

"Mister, gib me a nickel."

"Is safe wif me."

"Me, Mistuh, me."

Barnaby, weaving somewhat, giggled. He dispensed his entire pocketful of change—three or four dollars—which made Patrick vaguely sick, the feeling before vomiting, as his father dispensed more money than he would ever give to him or Dougie. Patrick thought how rich Barnaby must seem to the Cabrini Green kids despite the dents and chipped paint of the vintage van. Patrick saw himself as the son of a rich man.

Having appointed eight or nine guardians, they walked to the stadium through an icy wind that sliced and whipped through the monolithic gray buildings with concrete lawns of. Patrick's eyes welled wet, the tears turned to crystals on his cheeks.

"You were smart to pay for protection."

103

"You bet."

"Very smart, Dad."

Their seats were high in the second balcony. The long climb challenged Barnaby. Twice he called to Patrick to "slow down". Seated, Barnaby picked up that Patrick might feel bad about their location and said: "We can see better than any of those jokers at ringside. Sure we can. What an angle! We're on top of it all!"

Barnaby bought a Coke for Patrick, a beer for himself, and hot dogs for both of them. "Fifty cents," he whispered, "*fifty cents* for a lousy hot dog. You can bet, Paddy, that Mayor Richard J. Daley gets a nickel for himself out of every hot dog. What a town."

Patrick ate the hot dog and, although he was still hungry, did not ask for another. It was thrill enough to be part of a great screaming crowd of men. With his father. In the Chicago Stadium. In the middle of the greatest city in the world. In the middle of the greatest country in the world. How lucky to have been born Catholic, a Catholic who stands a chance at eternal paradise while hundreds of millions of Jews, Moslems and Protestants were destined to die in eternal flames. High in the balcony with his father Patrick felt blessed. Thanked Jesus and reminded himself that he had not yet said the   penance prayers he had fervently promised God.

The first two bouts were "dancing lessons". Barnaby's judgment. The cigar chewing men surrounding them agreed. The stogie chewers booed. Barnaby booed, Patrick too. Patrick was afraid that Barnaby's boredom was his fault but then came a bout between two bantamweights. They didn't dance. They were both throwing punches like their lives depended upon it. A Mexican kid hit his teen opponent with an uppercut right and the opponent went down like a floppy doll. Patrick was electrified. The thin young man lay on the canvas not even writhing. That one uppercut was total destruction. The winner bounded with elation, his gloves over his head, while the ref counted the unconscious pugilist out. The crowd, on its feet, roared its approval. Patrick stood on his seat to see over the heads in front of him. The victor was the happiest guy in the world. With his face alive with excitement, Patrick turned to Barnaby. But Barnaby was out cold too. Asleep with the rest every working man needs.

After the last bout, Patrick shook his father's shoulder to waken him and Barnaby drove slowly back to Whipple Street, saying what a fine night it had been, and how lucky Patrick had been to win those seats.

XIV

GRASS LAKE

The afternoon had become perfectly still. No bird cries, no breeze; only the pale resonance of Patrick's words. The sun shone but thinly through a nimbus of cirrus clouds. Patrick turned to her. Raised his eyebrows as if to say 'that's how it was'.

"Pat. Full disclosure? I think it will be better then."

Patrick fixed upon the pine forest below. Then hit upon yet another day.

***

On a Sunday in July, the Sullivan family rose at six, went to seven o'clock Mass, then drove north to Grass Lake, one of the hundreds of lakes that dot the northern Illinois landscape of low hills and dairy farms with red barns and steel silos.

Dougie and Patrick kept their faces in the two small rear windows watching where the van had been, witnessed mile after mile of disappearing corn fields. Each time a car was stuck behind the slow van, they giggled and gave the driver the finger. Rosemary said "both of you are stupid, you don't even know what that means." Patrick told Rosemary that giving the finger meant, "Go to hell". Rosemary was bored to be in their company. She had been born to Commoners. "No, ignoramus puss, it means something so dirty that I can't say it." She closed her eyes to shut herself off from their puerile world.

When Dougie started singing a "hundred bottles of beer on the wall" all the Sullivan children joined. Even Rosemary. Kevin (still the baby, in the weeks before Larry was born) tried to sing despite the thumb in his mouth. Wire clothes hangers swayed above their heads on horizontal poles. At eighty-three bottles, Barnaby demanded that they quit.

Patrick rode with closed eyes with his nose pressed against clothes that seduced him with the intoxication of naphtha solvent. Impatient and thrilled at the same moment, Patrick dreamed of what would come next: the compact he had elicited with Barnaby--they were to rent a sailboat. The two of them--alone--would navigate the great Grass Lake.

At Shade's Shady Cove, they were the first customers. They had their pick from a flotilla of ten small sailboats. Shade's son was perhaps only thirteen but already close to six feet tall. His arms dangled at his sides and boasted biceps thick enough to drag a boat off the sand and up to their house when a storm was blowing up. Patrick wished he had biceps like Shade's son. He wondered if Shade's son ever went sailing with his own father. As Patrick was going to today. He wondered if Shade's son was smart. Whether he had ever won a spelling bee or a multiplication tables quiz. Probably not, he decided. But Shade's son did live on Grass Lake and did not have put up with the snoopy neighbors of Whipple Street. And there were muskrats in these lakes. Maybe beaver too. If Patrick lived in the country, he thought, he could trap muskrats, skin them and sell the pelts. There were no jobs for kids like that in Chicago. Just paper routes. He wondered if the Shade son ever talked to Shade the father. Whether his father told him jokes. And secrets about what he hated most about Mrs. Shade. But Shade's son was not the talkative kind, all business. He arranged the ropes and lines of the chosen boat while Patrick wondered if he could spell "recommend" or "fairy", words that had gained Patrick a gold-embossed blue ribbon. Patrick wondered if Mr. Shade was mean and left his son to do all the work while he set out alone to fish for perch, wide-mouth bass and northern pike. Patrick had heard men of northern Illinois, Grandpa Powers' workers, speak of how they fished year round. Even through three feet of ice. Patrick asked Shade's son where his father was.

Shade's son looked to Patrick like he was Canadian money, worth something but not locally: "Why you wanna know?"

"I guess to ask if he ever goes fishing."

"Course he goes fishing. He's fishing now."

Patrick asked no more questions of Shade's son.

Barnaby and Patrick, barefooted and in swimming trunks, pushed the boat from the shore, walked it until the water was over Barnaby's knees. Barnaby hoisted Patrick over the thick gray gunwale, pointed the small craft toward the middle of the lake, and clambered aboard. The canvas flapped in the light wind and Patrick thrilled at the sound. They glided noiselessly, the breeze their friend. Patrick, in the bow, looked back to his father at the tiller, and further to Shade's beach, the fleet of gray boats with tall masts and lowered sails, as the marina steadily became smaller. He basked in the smells of seaweed and fish, and reached for the elusive seeds of milkweed which filled the air.

The day was already hot. Even at ten in the morning, Barnaby's shirt was plastered to his stomach and back. He took it off. "No need for this, huh, Paddy? You keep yours on. Or your mother'll murder me." A posse of horseflies buzzed Patrick's hair and face; one hitched a ride on an oarlock. Two dragonflies, one perched atop the other, alighted on a pulley at the spit of the bow. Patrick, at nine, knew there was something sexual going on, but not the sort of thing he could ask his mother. He asked Barnaby if they were "doing it" and Barnaby said, "What a stupid question, of course. Just like dogs."

107

Patrick, feeling somewhat rebuffed—yet now wiser--let his hand trail in the water leaving a wake of bursting bubbles. *Feeling a little stupid is the cost paid on the road to wisdom.* The warm lake waters and darting schools of minnows just below the surface transfixed him: he was alive, in a morning sun growing hotter, while the sounds of the irregular flapping of the canvas and the bow breaking the blue water transported him into a world of nature's perfect order.

They heard music. At first, it was broken and erratic with only tinny strains reaching the sailboat as it neared the middle of the lake. Barnaby pointed to the far shore: "There's a Rooskie campground there, Paddy. Don't turn your head, Paddy. Those Rooskies have binoculars on us this very second." Patrick, who got under his desk every Tuesday at noon to wait out the air raid signal, knew that the Russians wanted to drop an atom bomb. If they dropped it on Chicago, the children had to hide under their desk to avoid pieces of glass, the blinding light of a thousand suns, and strong winds to shame any tornado. "You can bet Mr. J. Edgar Hoover is watching these guys, watching them real good. Don't look, Paddy!"

Patrick held still. From the corner of his eye, not daring to turn his head, he was able to see the Communists, heads bobbing, white sunlight on wet arms and a red, white and blue beach ball lofted high. Patrick thrilled to know he was safe and on the right side of things, sailing on Grass Lake. There they were, Communists posing as innocent bathers, people so stupid and evil that they did not believe in the existence of God, nor that the Pope was His living representative.

After an hour, they neared the far side of the mile-wide lake and glided into a shallow sedge of brown felt bulrushes and green willowy reeds. Patrick saw carp sunning themselves, their serrated fins reaching above the lake level. Weeds brushed against the hull. The wind in the sail barely moved them forward. To sail back, they needed to turn around. Barnaby turned the tiller repeatedly to the left and the right to no effect. Barnaby began to swear, at the boat, at the tiller, at the horseflies biting his back.

Patrick had seen his Uncle Tony set the sail to catch the wind. But he had only seen it once. If he could remember that trick, they would be saved. Uncle Tony just moved something, and then the canvas and the mast swung (he remembered ducking) turning the boat. Now gray-green weeds beckoned just below the surface, slithered and whooshed against the hull. The bulrushes were so high he could no longer see shore. Toads croaked dumbly "Hello" or "Keep away" and a red-winged blackbird perched on the mast kept an unblinking eye on the two sailors. The water now gained a covering of green slime. The rudder stuck in the mud. The sailboat was idle.

There were no oars or paddles. Barnaby had refused them: "In a sailboat?" he said to Shade's son: "Boy, we are going *sailing*. Not *rowing*." Now Barnaby barked at Patrick: "Paddy, get out of the boat. You have to push us out of here." His face was red, his voice gruff, final. Grandma Powers had told Patrick about the quicksand that lurked in these lakes, about boys sucked into the bottomless mud, the devil's talons grasping their ankles, their screams stifled as their lungs filled with water, boys who were then forever gone. "I can't, Daddy. I'm afraid."

"*Get into the water!*"

Barnaby walked to the bow on unsteady legs, the boat rocking violently. He steadied himself, then lifted Patrick over the gunnel, and, with his hands in the boy's armpits, lowered him into the slimy water. The depth was only eighteen inches but Patrick's fright was total as his bare toes touched the fine cold silt.

"Take me in, it's quicksand." Patrick pleaded but Barnaby, without speaking, lowered the boy further, to mid-calf whereupon the boy began screaming. The wild look in his father's eyes made Patrick fear that he was about to be hit in addition to disappearing into the quicksand.

"I'm going to let you go now," Barnaby hissed, "So stop your goddamned blubbering."

Patrick's throat locked. He tried to kick at the knee-deep water as if to climb a liquid ladder but the silt had seized one foot. His scream finally came from his belly, a boy soprano sang out to Northern Illinois, a craven shriek.

Barnaby surrendered.

Without a word, he elevated Patrick and then dropped him on the floorboards, his legs brown with mud to the knees. Everywhere around them were fish floating belly up. The smell of rot. Patrick began to shiver even as the midday sun blazed. Barnaby too was shivering and shaking. He stared into the water for a full minute then lowered himself slowly over the transom. With his face contorted into ugly winces, he slowly pushed the boat out of the reeds. Patrick saw swirls of muddy clouds in the wake behind. Patrick cheered: "Good going, Dad." Barnaby, the furls of his face twisted and contorted, said nothing.

Once out of the thick sedge, Barnaby remained in the water, unwilling to relinquish his destiny again to canvas and a fickle wind. Instead, he pushed the small craft in the shallows along the shoreline. He could not avoid wading through the immigrant bathers; but he kept his head down, ignored their accented greetings which were largely lost in the music from loudspeakers beyond the beach. When past the Russians, Barnaby moved to the bow and towed the boat with a short rope. This towing took the better part of three hours. During this time, neither father nor son spoke a single word. Barnaby's shirtless back, so white when they had set out from Shade's, was broiled lobster.

Shade's son wanted to charge the full day rate. Barnaby argued that the boat was defective. Both were adamant, both loud. Shade's son was not beyond firmness with his customer. Patrick thought they would fight but Mr. Shade came down to the pier. Barnaby complained again about the quality of his "lousy sailboats" but Mr. Shade, in the end, collected for the full day.

Returning to the picnic grounds, Barnaby kept Patrick in front of him, cuffed the back of the boy's head repeatedly to make him walk faster. Barefooted, Patrick skipped gingerly on flaky pebbles that stung his soles.

"Pissy sissy."

Patrick buried his head in MomsaBomb's lap where she sat in the sun and gave himself up to bawling. Barnaby sat alone under a tree, talked to no one, and drank beers until he fell asleep on a blanket. MomsaBomb spent all day talking and drinking with the next picnic table and Dougie got robbed of his baseball game with his father because Patrick had gotten Barnaby lost on the other side of the lake in a defective sailboat and Dougie had no option but to play catch with Patrick. Later, Barnaby woke from his nap and took the family to dinner at a hot dog stand. Announced that the kids could eat till they "throw up, Bridget, what do I care. Let 'em be pigs for once."

Dougie swallowed six hot dogs and Patrick five. Riding back to the city, with night closing in, the children fell asleep on the floor of the van. There was a jolt and a metallic grating. Patrick opened his eyes to see Jenny roll out the back door as Barnaby navigated a wide turn. Rosemary, too, saw Jenny disappear. She screamed. Jenny, then four-years-old, rolled like a runaway tire on the asphalt, then stopped, flopped silently to the ground. She picked herself up and, not completely awake, ran to the rear of the van. Rosemary and Patrick snatched her up. She began hiccoughing violently, unable to cry. Passed forward to MomsaBomb, Jenny clung to her shoulder, looked back at her siblings while sucking her thumb. Barnaby put the van into gear. Drove slowly. Barnaby called back, asked repeatedly who "the dummy" was that closed the van door last; no one could remember. MomsaBomb warned: "This story never leaves the family. Does not get told to your grandmother, not to your aunts or uncles. If it does, I will personally pull out the tongue of the blabber. Have you got it?"

One by one, each child was required to assure her that the legend would not spread. Never leave the family.

Of course, it did.

***

Rebecca shifted on the blanket. Embraced his shoulders as he toyed with his toes. "You should have joined the circus."

"Want more? I'm on a roll."

XV
The Runaway

Rosemary was forever running out of sanitary pads and asking Patrick to get them at the drugstore because she was embarrassed to buy them herself from the teen clerk who would surely smirk. Patrick hated to cook but it was his job to cook for the six of them each night. And all hell broke loose nightly when Barnaby and MomsaBomb rolled in.

One night, while Dougie was getting beaten because he had done less than a less-than-ideal cleanup of the kitchen, Patrick, now fourteen, was suddenly possessed by a totally new idea. That he did not have to endure Whipple Street a second longer. He was amazed that such a decision had eluded him. He could be off on adventures of his own. He'd start his own family some day. All would be different. He would be kind and never think of hitting.

He slipped unnoticed into the boot room and out to the dark, empty alley then walked aimlessly until he found himself on a cul de sac of bungalows that abutted the Chicago River. At the edge of the roiling black river, under the Mercury arc lights, he watched unfurled condoms swim by, latex worms. The October night was bone chilling with the promise of the winter yet to come. The maples and sycamores had already dropped most of their leaves. The river wafted excrement. His teeth chattered. He only had taken a light jacket. Where to go? He had sixteen dollars in his pocket. He thought of St. Louis for no particular reason. Imagined washing dishes in a restaurant where truck drivers and kindly old women drank coffee. He'd make just enough money to have a room of his own. He could graduate high school in St. Louis. Somehow. Or, perhaps, he would continue down the river to New Orleans where it was always warm and steamy and music flooded the streets every night. People in New Orleans laugh a lot and like each other, even strangers. No longer would he sleep in the same room with Dougie whose sweat left a locker room stench and a gray outline on the sheet like the Shroud of Turin. No more Rosemary always on the phone gossiping with her door closed. No more Larry and Kevin watching television even while they ate their dinner. Two months prior, rats had invaded the basement. Barnaby had baited the coal bin and within two weeks Patrick had lost his safe study hall, his private retreat, to the stench of carrion.

In a lighted, frosted window of a two-flat, he saw the silhouette of a girl. She brushed out her hair in a dreamy fashion, one stroke after another, without hurry. Patrick wondered what she was like, bet millions upon millions of play dollars that she was very gentle and sweet and never yelled. The silhouette disappeared. Might she have intuited his presence and needs, the fact of his isolation, and be even that very second hurrying to the street to take him in? To hold him and keep him safe forever? But the street, save for scudding leaves on the tarmac, was quiet. He looked for an open car door, climbed into the rear seat of a Hudson. In the corduroy fabric, he breathed the smoke of a thousand cigarettes, pulled his legs into himself for warmth and planned a story should the owner discover him. In no event, he swore, would he ever return to Whipple Street.

He awakened to a tapping on the roof of the car. Thought for sure he had been caught. Police. No. Sleet. He blew into his cupped fists. Outside the car, he jumped up and down and swatted at his sides. Thought that he should have, as MomsaBomb always reminded him, worn a hat. He walked to Whipple Street. The house was dark. The back door was not locked. The kitchen clock showed three in the morning. He climbed to his attic lair, the house still as a graveyard save for Barnaby's fluttering snore.

***

A sudden warm gust from the valley below flared Rebecca's sable hair. She drew close to his ear, whispered. "Let's go inside. Little boy."

XVI
The Rutherford Bench
Rebecca, like Annette twenty-odd years before, wanted to get married in Chicago. "To be with your family, Pat, to share our joy?"

"Not until I am smitten on the road to Damascus."

Rebecca was slow to accept but, mollified nightly with Patrick's aged Chardonnays, did capitulate and agree on nuptials in the Discipio *chai* dug from base of the Mayacamas.

His siblings came with spouses and a few vintners: the Cakebreads, the Essers, the Shafers, the Rodenos. Kevin confirmed but then failed to show. Martin Luther had no interest in the wedding or a stepmother; he refused a ticket. Melissa wore a wide smirk and a shroud-like black cape. Rebecca's mother Ethel was aghast witnessing the volume of alcohol the Sullivans consumed.

Vows were exchanged in candlelight, the air thick with the perfume of hundreds of calla lilies and the yeasty breath of red wine seeping through barrel staves. The ceremony, as scripted by Patrick and Rebecca, was witnessed by Miss Julie, the Healing Mother of the Northern California Church of Total Oneness.

"I choose to take you, Rebecca, as witness and companion to my journey, the end of which I know not."

"And I choose to take you, Patrick, as witness and companion to my own future of which I know nothing."

"I know somehow in my heart, Rebecca, that my best chance for the next days and years is at your side."

"And no matter the sorrows I have faced nor the mistakes that I have made, Patrick, I give my hand to you. I trust you will help me find the peace my heart cries for."

"And though my heart may wish to close, Rebecca, yet will I walk with you."

Miss Julie made it legal: "This is so utterly over the top awesome! I now pronounce you..."

Then a squishing of wheelchair tires was heard on the clammy concrete of the cellar floor. A sixty-something nurse with gourd breasts and body builder biceps wheeled the stroke victim patriarch of the winery, August Discipio, to the nuptial couple. Patrick took Discipio's hand.

"He pressed my palm."

"No, Mr. Sullivan, he cannot," the nurse corrected him.

"He did. I felt it."

"He might as well be back in the womb. That's his level."

"Is that all bad?" Patrick turned to his bride: "Kiss him, Rebecca. This is the man who has loved me more than my own father." Rebecca kissed August, tried to hug him. August, old and failing but still a *gallo*, cupped the breast nearer to his face. Later, Patrick whispered that her kiss and his touch may have added a month or two to August's life.

The wedding feast went on till midnight. Patrick and Rebecca heard Ethel tell tales of Cracow, how she and her Max slipped past the Nazi net to Haifa and then Brooklyn and then Florida and they made plans for her to visit New York. Patrick's peripheral vision could see Rosemary and Jenny using a thief to taste cabernet from barrel. Matt arm wrestled B.J. and then Seamus. Just a few feet away, Larry was explaining fuel injection to a nodding, but certainly uncomprehending, August Discipio. Patrick was happy. Happy in every auricle and each testicle. Happy having come in from the alone.

After many hugs and kisses Patrick and Rebecca sneaked through the kitchen to a limo which took them to Napa airport and the waiting Discipio jet for the short flight down the coast to Monterey. Forty-five minutes after landing they had checked in at The Highlands Inn. Carmel by the Sea. Patrick dragged a futon alongside their private pool where beneath the Northern sky, his blood coursing still with purple wine, he reminisced: "Kevin and I used to lie in the backyard like this and imagine that gravity didn't exist. That we could fall into the universe forever."

"Like reverse falling."

"He swore he would come."

"It hurts?"

"Of course it hurts."

"We'll invite him to New York."

"I'm done with him. Doing for him." This he said though he longed for the opposite. A ghostly fog crept up the imperious bluff then rolled over the entwined couple.

XVII

Dublin

Patrick sat upright. He tasted a retch wanting to happen. He leaned, looked behind him where a stewardess was emerging from under a blanket. He pressed his forehead to the cold plastic port. The jet descended through feathery clouds and there below emerged the savage green of the Irish coast. Turbines whined and the landing gear locked with a terminal clank. With a shudder the wheels touched the earth, the plane lurched airborne briefly, then settled on the runway. The engines reversed and he, propelled forward, wet with the sweat of a long night's dreaming, threw aside the blanket. Atop a far terminal, a sign: *Aerfort Bhaile Átha Cliath.* Dublin International Airport.

***

Patrick saw Dougie's head high over the Customs queue; Constance, all five foot of her, stood beside.

"Atkins!"

"Yo, bro! Connie, lookie here, a gen-you-wine intellectual."

Constance stood on tiptoes to accept Patrick's buss. "This is such a wonderful surprise, Patrick."

Patrick said: "I'm surprised myself."

Dougie bear hugged Patrick, raised him off his feet: "This means you love us?"

"Don't start." Patrick searched the passport line. "Where are the boys?"

Constance offered an apology: "The attorney made us take separate planes. Estate issues."

Dougie's eyes danced: "Just like Whipple Street, hey Paddy?"

***

In a cab entering the ancient city, the traffic crept slowly through a light but steady rain in the gray morning hours. Constance was sandwiched between the brothers. She held Patrick's hand. She asked if anyone knew Patrick had decided to come. Dougie barked: "They're not expecting him. Why would they?" Douglas spoke in aggressive jabs like a cagey boxer.

"I wasn't expecting me."

"So why our good fortune?"

Patrick looked to the rain outside the cab. "Back to the scene of the crime?"

Constance asked: "Where's Rebecca?"

"New York."

"Why didn't you bring her?

117

"Long story. You guys didn't come to our wedding."

"You didn't come to ours. Professor."

"So why no Rebecca?"

"I can't think of a good answer."

"And that means exactly what?"

"Things between us have not been working."

Dougie, peering around his wife, faked that he was choking: "After how many lousy years?"

"It seems like ten. But it's been four."

"Professor, it takes about ten years just to find out what a woman is really about. *Jerk!*"

"Douglas, you're yelling." Constance turned from her husband: "Pat, you can work it out, the two of you, can't you?"

"Connie, Paddy just runs from everything."

"Things look bad, Connie."

Dougie barked at the cab driver's cap: "Don't waste words on a stone!"

"Douglass, you're *yelling.*"

"Yeah, Atkins."

"Nobody calls me that but you."

Constance asked: "Why do you call him Atkins?"

Patrick squinted, peered into the steady drizzle. "It started Thanksgiving Day? My freshman year. I was back from Georgetown."

***

Uncle Aloysius came on Thanksgiving Day. His Roman collar and jacket off for the day, Uncle Al sported a black shirt of Italian silk. MomsaBomb sat on the armrest of his chair, her fingers covering the gold Swiss watch given the young priest by his brothers and sisters at his ordination. Jenny, Kevin and Larry sat on the floor. Father Aloysius had with understandable diffidence forgiven his sister-in-law her infidelity with the butcher. He told himself that he was forced to forgive by the example of Christ forgiving Mary Magdalene. Now Bridget had become, after his own mother had died, his comfort and refuge from life in the Rectory, life free from the gossip of the widow O'Brien who cooked and cleaned for the pastor and his three assistants. Patrick was glad to see his uncle, a literate man, schooled by the archdiocese. His visit promised a day where discussion could rise above Barnaby's barks and Bridget's nostrums. ("Here's to you, binkie." "All aboard that's going aboard." "Cheers and more cheers!") While the turkey was in the oven, the family watched the Bears battle the Lions. His uncle, a born debater, began a slow interrogation of Patrick, while nominally following the football game: "And what do the Jesuits say of the Swedish experiment?"

Patrick replied: "I don't know the Swedish experiment."

"Oh, please: you frat boys don't talk about free love?"

"Free love? No. None of my professors."

"Well there *is* a group of lunatic theologians--Catholics joining up with Protestants--talking up the Swedish experiment." Father Aloysius lifted his eyes to his brother and sister-in-law: "There's talk of a major powwow at the Vatican. All the red hats. Celibacy is going to be on the table." He sipped his Martini, winced: "I'll become a Buddhist if they drop the celibacy thing. Not after all I've missed."

Barnaby shook with glee: "*You?* A Buddhist? Mom is turning over in her grave."

"Hush," said MomsaBomb. She tapped her brother-in-law's wrist: "Don't talk naughty in front of the children."

"We *do* talk about a free society," Patrick interjected.

Father Aloysius turned to Patrick, his eyes dancing: "'A free society' that does *what*?"

"Anything the citizens want. So long as it doesn't hurt anyone else."

"So, Patrick, you're saying: if it feels good, it's okay?"

"Now the horseshit starts," said Barnaby.

Uncle Aloysius waved off his brother with his free hand: "Barney, let him speak. I love to hear college boys."

"It's okay. Sure." Patrick's head was swimming. In class, and at the Evans House, theory was one thing. All agreed on most everything. Now in Chicago he felt himself swimming in quite a foreign lake. "So long as you don't hurt anyone."

"This is sick, Buster. Do the Jebbies really say that?"

"They talk about freedom. Yes."

"You've been there three months? Barnaby, is this the right school for him?"

MomsaBomb said: "This is just a stage, Allie. All kids go through stages."

Barnaby guffawed: "Paddy, we know already you're a genius." MomsaBomb laughed lightly.

Patrick saw himself, a wild windmill of retribution, socking them Hollywood style, launching them through the swinging bar doors of a Western saloon one by one while the piano player played on. But he did nothing. He became a statue with a faint grin.

His uncle pointed with his cigarette: "Get this straight, Paddy: freedom is not the liberty to do any damned thing that pleases you."

"The Popes in the Fifteenth Century had freedom," said Patrick. "Freedom to have their orgies."

"That never happened."

"Of course it happened."

"Don't be a smart mouth."

119

Patrick's voice began to tremble, his stomach rose and fell but he continued: "I read it. You read it. Pope Alexander. I think the Sixth?"

"Shut up, Paddy," Barnaby said.

Bridget joined in: "Don't lie, Paddy. That's not nice."

His uncle now gave Patrick, at the expense of the Bears, his entire attention: "Where'd you get this?"

"A book. A library book."

One of the Evans Scholars had liberated--from a locked-off section of Georgetown's library--a book reserved for certain theologians with prior permission from Rome. Six frat brothers including Patrick had spent two long nights poring over the text. "Uncle Aloysius, the Popes back then, as you know, spent their nights making little bastards."

"What do you mean—'as you know'?"

"My theology teacher told me. All priests are let in on these little secrets. You read books from the Index. You know all about the Pope's poking the Vatican ladies, so don't pretend you don't."

Uncle Aloysius bolted from his chair knocking MomsaBomb's Manhattan whiskey and ice cubes onto the carpet. Reaching Patrick's chair, he swung. A closed-fist roundhouse to the chin.

Father Aloysius stood over Patrick shaking with rage. Barnaby was slack-jawed. MomsaBomb cried: "You two! Spoiling Thanksgiving..." She ushered Patrick into the bathroom where she dabbed at his bleeding lip. Patrick held his tears until the door was closed: "He's a shit. He's a shit, Mom."

"He's a priest. And your uncle."

"He's a bastard."

"Father Aloysius, Paddy, loves you."

Back in the living room, Barnaby and Father Aloysius had gone back to watching the TV where on both sides of the fifty yard line Lion's Stadium was devoid of turf, a morass of pasty mud. Patrick sat in silence. Sore but unbent. For a full quarter hour of no talk and no cheering, he was an invisible presence until Father Aloysius said, without taking his eyes off the screen: "Talk to me again next year about freedom. Buster."

Though his jaw ached, Patrick was able to emit—slowly--the words he wished: "Did the story get here from two weeks ago? The Georgetown Jesuit who destroyed his office and then jumped from the eighth floor and splatted himself on the sidewalk. Did that little item make the Tribune? Couldn't take the lies any more. He left a note."

"More malarkey," said Father Aloysius, rubbing his fist where Patrick's incisor had broken the skin.

"Not malarkey. Scattered his files onto the street, dumped every book, then jumped. Splat-squish onto Constitution Avenue."

Barnaby hit his fist on his overstuffed chair: "That's it, Paddy. Watch football or get out."

120

"Give me the keys. I'll watch Dougie's game."

"What Dougie does is not football." Barnaby's heart belonged to the Bears and Notre Dame. Georgetown did not have a football team which was confounding.

"I'll tell you after I see him play."

"Don't leave, Paddy. I never see you," Bridget implored. "Help me with the turkey."

"It's just a couple of hours. Can I have the keys to the van?"

Barnaby did not look up from the game: "The van needs a rest."

"It's a mile each way."

"Walk. At your age, your uncle and I walked everywhere."

"Thanks, Dad, a *lot*."

Barnaby sipped deep from his Manhattan, then grimaced: "The van needs a rest. Like me."

"Barnaby let him take it."

"It's a question of freedom, Bridget. I'm free to say no and Paddy is free to walk."

From the garage, I lumber to the house with two five-gallon cans of gasoline, Barnaby's reserves against Rooskie invasion. I empty both cans into the casement windows, throw a match and then, from behind a tree on the far curb of Whipple Street, see the house explode in flames and black smoke, see Uncle Aloysius and Barnaby propel their fireball bodies through windows. MomsaBomb's apron, dress and hair a Roman candle. They roll on the brown lawn, madly try to extinguish the purifying flames. Smelling their roasting flesh, I am both terrified and full of glee.

The taxi inched slowly. "You haven't said why it is you call him Atkins."

"Patience my sister-in-law."

That Thanksgiving was a Great Lakes day with gray low clouds and a wet wind that bit Patrick's face where he stood alone on the sidelines. He stood apart from the Kedzie Bombers' girlfriends and a few substitutes, the smaller guys who hoped to get some minutes. Dougie was a lineman and played both offense and defense. The Bombers, a brotherhood devoid of a coach, yelled commands, criticism and plays at each other. Patrick watched with his collar turned up and his knit cap pulled over his ears. The opponents were the Cicero Studs from St. Charles Borromeo, a team, for the most part, of Italian extraction. The Kedzie Bombers were, for the most part, of Irish descent.

The opposing sides resembled not so much athletic teams as goons with pads and helmets. Winning took second place to causing pain to the opponents. Patrick saw Dougie trip a couple of guys he was unable to tackle. Twice saw him kick an opponent who was trying to untangle himself from a pile. Patrick tried to be generous, assumed that the guy Dougie kicked was only getting his just desserts. Then Dougie got into a fistfight with an opposing lineman, an obese six-footer whose uniform shirt stretched over a belly of that shook like Jell-O. Others from both teams joined and, as fists began to fly, the ref, displaying more discretion than valor, turned his back and busied himself shaking spittle from his whistle.

That Thanksgiving Day, watching Dougie, Patrick renamed him: Atkins. Doug Atkins was a six foot eight inch defensive end for the Bears who screamed bellicose oaths while crossing the line of scrimmage, screams to rival a Mongol warrior assaulting a Slavic village. Atkins' screams tended, and were intended, to unnerve the opponents. Dougie screamed at the line before the snap also. His screaming, however, had not begun with football. Rather he had, from his earliest crib days, screamed and sung himself to sleep. As a child, he had rocked his head, poured forth bold narratives of his invincible self dominating cowardly armies. Patrick recalled five-year-old Douglas Sullivan refusing to let his older brother into the Sullivan's only bathroom where, perched upon the porcelain throne, Dougie sang of a successful letting-go: "Dougie's done it, folks! Dougie's done it again! Bombs over Tokyo! Dougie's dropped his bombs..."

Dougie's Kedzie Bombers, winning by a large margin early in the fourth quarter, began chugging beers during timeouts. They upped their level of taunts toward the boys from Cicero, the taunts for the most part concerned certain sexual proclivities of the opponents' mothers.

The last minutes of the game devolved into an ugly slog. After a play in which the ball had been advanced not even a yard, Patrick saw Atkins, inside a pile, struggling to punch the obese Cicero Stud he had fought earlier. The opponent, who had been dubbed Stuffed Sausage by the Bombers as early as the second quarter, now extricated Dougie from the pile-up like a longish log with flailing branches and threw him to the ground, then jumped on Dougie's middle. Dougie clawed as best he could, however, Stuffed Sausage, atop him, was winning on leverage alone. The Bomber Brothers came to Dougie's rescue, dived atop, screaming retribution. The ref walked to the sidelines. The game was, regardless of the clock, *de facto* over. Through the tangle, Patrick could see Stuffed Sausage trying to unscrew Dougie's lower leg from his knee. Suddenly Stuffed Sausage bellowed horrifyingly, piteously. Everyone in the park, adjacent playing fields included, craned their necks, were transfixed by the sound of feral agony. Patrick's skin crawled. The mêlée ceased. Bombers and Studs, friend and foe, separated, all stared at Stuffed Sausage who, still screaming, rocked violently on the playing field, holding his blood-stained crotch. "He bit me," he howled. "The bastard bit my balls!"

Indeed Dougie-now-Atkins had bitten Stuffed Sausage: through his canvas britches, through his jock strap and underwear, and penetrated the Cicero Stud's scrotal sac. Stuffed Sausage's crotch was, as he was borne from the field, a crimson Rorschach suggesting a post-modernist asterisk. In retreat the Studs threatened mayhem and revenge while loading Stuffed Sausage into a car. Dougie and the Kedzie Bombers gathered their equipment without special haste but with a clear sense that there had been enough war for the day.

The mood of open warfare lightened. The Bombers, along with Patrick, and their consorts set off for their club house, marched on the wide median of Irving Park Road chanting: "Dougie bites balls! Dougie is a Bomber! Bombers bite Balls! Dougie! Dougie!"

***

They drank victory beers at the Bombers' clubhouse where the members showed an ecumenical welcome to Patrick as case after case of beer was consumed. After all Patrick was Dougie the Ball Biter's brother. Each Bomber made it a point to tell Patrick how great Dougie was, how they usually didn't take guys not yet twenty-one but Dougie (now Atkins) was an exception to their rule. The girls asked Patrick about Washington, D.C., and about college life. Carlotta, in tight jeans and with beer bottle in hand, a five-footer of Sicilian extraction, pulled Patrick's face close to hers, whispered, shyly but forthrightly, that she had never "done" a college boy before.

"Well…why don't you do me?"

"Yeah. Okay." Patrick glanced about for a private place in the— for the most part--bare open room of the clubhouse. The furnishings were discarded sofas rescued from the alleys of Albany Park; the windows, broken long ago, were boarded up with plywood. Electricity had been obtained by knocking through a brick wall in the dark of night and splicing into an outlet of the adjacent grocery. "But where?"

"In there, college boy." She led him by a pinkie finger into an empty closet.

"There's no bed," Patrick said.

"It's okay standing. You never done it standing?"

Not until that Thanksgiving Day. And not since.

"I want to go to college myself," Carlotta said *in acto coitus*. "To better myself."

"Ambition is good," Patrick panted.

"But am I good enough to go to college?"

"You couldn't get much better, Carlotta. But, listen--college girls don't talk, not at a time like this!"

"I can talk through anything."

"Carlotta, *please* shut up."

"All right already!"

The Bombers all cheered when Carlotta and Patrick emerged from the closet. Patrick had joined a second fraternity within a scant three months.

123

Walking home to Whipple Street, Dougie, still in uniform and cleats, was touched that Patrick had dubbed him Atkins. They walked arm in arm while Dougie limped. "Bro," said Dougie, "Excuse me but for the last few years I've thought you were a total asshole playing like you are some sort of an intellectual freak."

"Dougie, with many fratricidal thoughts directed toward you, I probably was indeed a bung hole."

"There you go again. Why can't you talk plain?"

Because of the longish victory party, the two brothers missed the turkey and the cylinder of cranberries pushed from the can open at both ends. For which they had to withstand from MomsaBomb's laments while devouring turkey sandwiches. Barnaby was out cold and Father Aloysius long gone. Patrick, before the turkey sandwiches, had locked himself in the bathroom and, using an old toothbrush, scrubbed his privates until they were red, raw and hopefully free of any microbial trace of Carlotta.

Late that night MomsaBomb and Patrick drank together. She carried on about what a drunk Barnaby was becoming, how he never really talked to her or took her to the movies.

"Fucking A, Ma," Patrick said, using the expletive that preceded most sentences at the Evans House, "Why don't you just leave him?"

She admonished him for his foul mouth and then poured forth sorrow from a deep well. Patrick sat silent, wished himself a stone, or a mummy, listened for an hour while she, in maudlin self-pity, delineated a life that had never delivered upon the dreams of her youth.

   ***

In Dublin, Dougie observed: "My brother, the great intellectual, has parked his penis behind his forehead."

Connie wanted peace: "Douglas, there you go."

"And you Atkins never read a book that wasn't all telephone numbers. How's business?"

"Tush warmers," Atkins winked, "in the bathrooms of every house. Our new marketing thing."

Covering Dougie's hand, Constance said with a proud smile: "We try to give them something the other builders don't."

"We've got eighteen foundations dug. If Bush or the Arabs don't butt fuck the economy, we're looking pretty good."

Constance stared into and through her husband: "You know, Douglas, that the driver can hear your every word." Admonished, Dougie turned to view the passing city. Connie rotated to Patrick, spoke sweetly: "Dougie had his men put the tush warmers in our house too. In all our bathrooms. They're…nice."

"I remember Chicago and cold mornings, sitting on the throne."

Atkins leaned forward with an accusative smile: "You should come and visit once in a while. Professor."

"I haven't seen your new house."

"We've been in our 'new' house, Pat," she said gently, "for five years."

"That long?"

"You could stop by," Douglas shot the words, "when you bop in and out of Chi-town and don't call any of us because you're afraid Barnaby might be there. Right?"

"That's hardly it."

"Not nice to tell lies." Dougie leaned back and studied passing Georgian doors.

"I've been gone a long time but…you guys, you're the American dream. Look what you've done."

"Douglas is a worker, you know that, Patrick."

Dougie leaned around Constance. "I was just saying to Connie: what I owe to the Chicago cops."

"You jest."

"They turned me around."

"By beating on you?"

"Some did. Some just yelled. Nice guys doing what Barnaby and Bridget didn't or wouldn't. And we know where Barnaby and Bridget were, right?"

"Customer development!"

"At The Pig Pen!"

"No." Patrick shook his head like a Jesuit amused at his student's ignorance. "*The Play Pen.*"

"The *Pig* Pen."

"Pulaski Road. I was there many times. Fat Callaghan was the bartender."

"They never took me. You were always their favorite."

"I'm surprised you remember anything."

"Douglas was wild then."

"I still get wild. Not often enough." He squeezed her knee.

Dougie impregnated Constance when he was eighteen and she just sixteen. His first job was as a hod carrier transporting 150 lb. forms from one tract house foundation to another. Constance issued five sons on an annual basis.

"Connie, however did you get the brave boy to fly today?"

"I can answer for myself, thank you. Three Martinis in twenty minutes."

Constance allowed the faintest of smiles. "He snored. Most of the way over." The cab, in traffic thick with smallish cars, was advancing a hundred yards or so every three or four minutes. The rain was light but steady. Constance asked, with narrowed, prayerful eyes: "Have you and Rebecca thought about counseling?"

125

"I don't talk to strangers."

Atkins, without removing his gaze from the street scene, shook his head, barked: "Hand Job, you don't talk to your own family."

The cab inched past Trinity College. Connie was moved, teary: "I'm so sorry."

Patrick tried some optimism: "How long are you married? Twenty-five years? Twenty-six?"

"You were invited to our twenty-fifth."

"I...was in Germany"

"Thanks for the wine you sent." Dougie peered around Constance: "Fart head."

"Really, *Douglas,* you can do better...."

Douglas looked into the roof of the cab: "Paddy, I have not been to a great university which is probably why I don't understand something," Atkins tapped a fist against his forehead, got louder with each word: "You are married, so why not just stay married?"

"Because, Dougie, *I don't want to.*"

Dougie's head swiveled like a cannon on a turret, "You're running just like you ran away on us way back when."

"That was an *escape.* And I'm surprised you remember what with all you were putting up your schnozzola back then."

"I'm talking about you, Paddy, not the asshole I used to be." Only Constance, a smallish but impenetrable barrier, kept Dougie on his side of the cab.

"Both of you." Constance shouted with raised arms: "S*hut up!*" The driver's head jerked back. *"Two infants! Douglas!"*

The cab slowed to a mincing crawl at the Bank of Ireland which stood placidly, lighted a violent white in the grey damp. The bank's porticoes were flanked by ancient cannon, the massive lintels crowned with gleaming statues of Celt ancients in flowing robes. On the street, in the light rain, student couples rushed along the sidewalks speaking as of a great moment. Atkins quieted, folded his arms and closed his eyes: "Barnaby's not the same-old-same-old. But I still might, some night, slit MomsaBomb's throat. How much time would I get, Professor?"

"Two years. If you really bawled your brains out to the judge. But your bawling would have to be the Oscar-award level. Could you do that?"

"Maybe."

Constance tsk-tsked.

The air was thick with light mist and diesel haze. Plashing tires disturbed the glisten of oily puddles in the roadway. The cab dropped them at the Shelburne Hotel on St. Stephen's Green where Larry, the family's *ex officio* travel consultant, had booked an entire wing. Entering through oaken double doors, they beheld ten Sullivans—nephews, nieces and sons--playing football in the center hall. Patrick's heart stopped, all life suspended as he saw Martin Luther circumnavigate a table and its high floral display to run a deep pass pattern with Jenny's daughter, Shannon, defending. The trajectory of her brother Seamus' spiral was contained easily within the twenty-foot ceiling. Except for an aging waiter ambling with a tray of Champagne flutes held high, Martin Luther might have caught the ball. However, he and the waiter collided. The poor waiter, locked in unwanted embrace with Martin Luther, spun in horror, while golden streams of bubbly ascended, hung gloriously illuminated by the chandelier, and the stems--slaves to gravity--shattered upon the oaken floor.

Atkins, in a manner every bit as bellicose as Barnaby's, boomed to the footballers: "Okay, every one of you, *outside!* On the count of three! One, two..."

Red-faced, Martin Luther attempted to make amends with the waiter by delicately picking at the thousand shards. Patrick crossed to and then stood over his stooped son. Blushing with contrition through his Caribbean tan, Martin Luther was slow to look up, and, when he did, could only gape: "What...are you doing here?"

"A last minute decision."

Patrick had paid Martin Luther's bills at Bard without so much as a note accompanying the checks. Annette was kind enough to pass his grades on. It had been four years since Patrick had spoken to Martin Luther.

He gave a twenty punt note to the waiter and suggested to Martin Luther that they find a pub. Martin Luther, staring at the shards of Waterford, agreed with a "whatever" toss of the head.

XVIII

The Plough

Wordlessly they walked. Patrick tried to formulate darting thoughts into sentences but could not. Rebecca would say endlessly: *He might look twenty-one, but he's only eight or nine. Take the hit. You need to take the hit.*

A small procession, both political and religious, inched along O'Connell Street, halting father and son's progress: two stalwart gray-haired men led the parade with an effigy of the Virgin balanced on their shoulders. These men were followed by eighty or so elderly women who, fingering rosary beads, recited Hail Mary's as they shuffled slowly. A few bore posters:

Peace in the North.

Bring us Together, O Lord.

The Legion of Mary Prays for Peace.

A Honda with a loudspeaker on its roof passed last. In the rear seat, a diminutive priest led the women in prayer through a loudspeaker.

Blessed art thou amongst women

And blessed is the fruit of thy womb…

***

At The Plough, they found a table along a back wall. Moaning fiddles, bodhran drums, penny whistles and flutes filled the place, a working man's pub. At the center of the music players, a humpback woman, with empty black sockets instead of eyes, fiddled. The angle of the chairs of the other players, if nothing else, acknowledged her lead. When the music stopped, she drank deeply from her mug of black Irish wine, then smiled deeply but modestly, and wiped her upper lip with her cuff. The players, without a word or direction, began anew.

"I apologize for showing up like this." Patrick had to shout to be heard. Since graduating Bard, Martin Luther had crewed on a catamaran out of St. Maarten. His head bore sun-bleached curls that cascaded like the golden locks of Absalom. Patrick, through ribbons of smoke, saw Martin Luther's cobalt pupils. A Sullivan gene. He swelled that his son's Caribbean bronze was singular in a pub of pale Dubliners. Stout arrived, Martin Luther's only words had been to the barmaid."

Martin Luther asked: "So why are you here?"

"I got fired yesterday. In New York. Or quit. I'm not sure which."

"I don't believe it."

"It's a fact."

130

"Weren't you their star?"

"Well, thanks, but old August had a stroke and Carmine's taken over."

"The family brat?"

"First son in an Italian family is a big deal. I don't care. I do care. To tell the truth, I'm a bit up in the air. What's with you? How are the island girls?"

He rolled his eyes and smiled, whispered: *"Incroyable."* He straightened, announced: "But I'm leaving the Caribbean. I've decided to make movies. A crew shooting on the island hired me as an extra for three days. Forty dollars a day. Then they gave me a walk-on. I got to tend bar in a Dutch dive. All I did was wipe glasses and stare at the star, nod a couple of times. No lines. The movie will play in the States but only if it does well in France. Movies are...well I can't think of a more exciting life."

"Selling's been good to me."

"Selling." He expectorated the word.

Patrick kept his tone muted while having to project loudly: "It's not all that bad. I have..."

Martin Luther cut him off. "I've been wasting my life sucking up tips from rich tourists. I have to make my move now." He took a breath of resolve. "I'm moving to Montreal. The Canadians give tax breaks for movie companies. You probably hate movies."

"I don't hate movies. I just don't go much." Patrick sat forward, spoke loudly to be heard: "Listen: other news. Sad news."

"How sad?"

"Sad. Bad. Rebecca and I...we're splitting."

Martin Luther pursed his lips: "My mother said it wouldn't last."

"Your mother was right. And she ought to stay in her own backyard."

"I don't want to talk about my mother."

"Ok. There is something I want to say." *How am I supposed to say it? Rebecca coached me non-stop.* "I'm sorry. Sorry that we're so far apart."

Martin Luther replied with icy measure: "You're a little late, aren't you?"

"Ok, it's late. But I want to say it. I've been an extraordinary failure as a father."

"That's about the first honest thing I've ever heard you say. You're a 'fuck and flee'. There's a whole bunch of you out there."

"Martin, don't smart mouth me." Patrick felt choked; in the past words had forever exploded from him like rabid bats from a cave. This day he held his tongue.

131

"Patrick, I'm what you made me. Okay?" His fingers tapped on carvings in the varnished table. Glyphs from prior times: Sean Loves Francoise June 1934. Eineach + Julietta 4-ever. "The only good thing that has ever happened to me has been my mother. Now I need you to stay out of my life. Do you think you can do that?" The rapid clacks of the bodhran drum made a reply impossible. Patrick, avoiding his son's glower, focused on the opaque pint, every muscle locked like a suit of chain mail. "You have fucked my life, you did your worst to..."

Patrick roundhoused him. Swung across the table with closed fist. Martin Luther, knocked to the sawdust, gathered himself. In pain and terror, got to his feet then backed away. His face drained except for a circle of red where Patrick had socked him. With a hand on the offended cheek, perhaps fearing another blow, he turned, pushed his way through the tipplers who had turned to the father and son when they heard Martin Luther's chair clattering across the floor.

Patrick watched the blond locks of his scion disappear.
***

He walked Dublin for several hours, still wearing the suit that had flown the Atlantic. He walked until his gait was more stumble than strut. At reception, he was given a note.

Patrick,

Yet another lie: that you wouldn't be here.

Believe it forever that I don't want you in my life. I am out

of here. Don't ever call.

M.L.

Entering his room, Patrick smelled cannabis. He turned on the light to find Kevin Sullivan stretched across the bed, the worm merchant wearing a black T-shirt with Day-Glo lettering:
Snakeskin, Idaho
Totally out of this World
With reddish locks framing his shoulders Kevin blew a smoke ring to the chandelier.

"Have you seen them yet?"

"No. I got in early this morning."

"I think this idea, your idea, really is not a good idea."

"Larry says they've changed."

"I doubt it." Kevin swung his legs off the bed. "Paddy, I'm really scared."

Though his cheeks were cratered, and his lanky arms indolent appendages, Patrick recognized the fleeting imp's grin; the grin that Kevin sported then and now for Patrick, in honor of the thousand intimate times they had shared. Patrick tugged at his tie, unbuttoned his collar. "How'd you get in here?"

"Told the desk I was you." His grin widened, but only slightly, with his cleverness. "When you sent me the ticket, I felt like a prostitute. Then like a total failure. I came anyways. Really because of you. No one else."

Patrick sat in the room's only chair, started to reach out, to touch something of Kevin, even his booted foot. He stopped himself: "Been a long time, Bro. Not since that night you set me up in that tent on the river?"

"Almost nine years."

Kevin's face was tan, weathered but glowing: "Paddy, you look like cow plop."

Crossing a pasture to the Fox River, Grandma Powers had taken Patrick and Kevin on a picnic. Patrick was twelve, Kevin six. Kevin high stepped to avoid buffalo chips while booming a youthful version of a bass admonition:

>Cow plop cow plop

>Watch out gumdrop

>Cow plop cow plop

"I quit the winery."

"You're kidding."

"Really I stopped believing in the whole Discipio thing a couple of years ago. It probably showed. Now I don't believe in anything."

"You're welcome anytime in Snakeskin, Bro."

"I might take you up on that." He leaned back, spoke with eyes closed: "Martin Luther. He just gave me what-for, then walked out. Probably because I socked him."

"You *socked* him?"

"He wise-assed me. Barnaby would have done the same thing."

"You're not Barnaby."

"I used to think that. You missed my wedding."

"I was going to go and then I was all mucked up."

"Everyone else came. Not Dougie."

"So I'm guilty, ok?"

"It's good you didn't come. There's a divorce in the wings."

"White man you lie."

"I'm best alone. Always have been."

"No. Your alone thing, it started with Georgetown."

"Why with Georgetown?"

"Because you never came back."

"I'm here now. Irish whiskey?"

They shared a bottle. Kevin stumbled off down the hall. Patrick stripped and slept the day away.

XIX

The Bridal Suite

"I baptize thee in the name of the Father, the Son and the Holy Ghost."

Choking, and attacked by daylight, Patrick awoke to see Larry, Chicagoland's highest volume Chevrolet dealer, drip cold water onto his face. Paulette, Larry's wife, stood cheeping at his side sounding like a mixed aviary; her position in the Sullivan family, which she had never completely joined, was more bemused audience than in-law. Larry leaned over the bed so that his face was mere inches from Patrick's wide-eyed sudden break from sleep. "Good morning! I mean...Good afternoon!" Paulette giggled. "Paddy, we are back where it all began. Ireland, Paddy. Isn't every bone in you thrilled?"

Patrick dried his face with a corner of dry sheet. Blinked. "What time is it?"

"Going on five."

"Morning or night?"

"Afternoon. We started calling you at twelve but you wouldn't pick up. The anniversary dinner starts at nine." Larry was wearing a green golf shirt with the Chevrolet logo. Under the logo the embroidery read: See Sully for Your Chevy! He sat next to where Patrick lay. "So tell me: where's your wife? And why does your son hate you? I sent him a ticket and then I find out that he's checked out. And where's Rebecca?"

"Rebecca's not coming. Jewish holiday." Patrick's head throbbed. "Whatever tales Martin Luther tells of me, they're all true. And something else: I am unemployed"

"Not a cork sniffer anymore? You're better off with a real job. For the first and last time: do you want to sell Chevies or not?"

Paulette fiddled with the television: "Larry, I know we can't get any Chicago stations this far away. But why not New York? We're closer to New York."

"Paulie, you do remember the puddle we crossed yesterday? That was the Atlantic Ocean."

"Paulette, throw me that bathrobe?"

***

Patrick squinted under the bathroom's single light, peered into the mirror, saw a whiskered face and matted hair. He poured three glasses of cold water over his head in slow succession and then drank three. Reentering the room, Larry sat in the only chair as Paulette switched from channel to channel.

"So where *is* Rebecca?"

"Manhattan."

"Why?"

"Because I have the frequent urge to kill her."

"I feel that way a lot toward Paulie."

"Watch your mouth, Larry." Paulette clucked softly but her most urgent worry remained the channel knob: "They *have* CNN. I can get CNN."

"Paulie, the man is in trouble with his wife. Please."

"We're splitting."

"You're what?"

"I'm bailing is what it is."

"And Martin Luther?"

"He's pissed. He's been pissed forever. Everyone recovered from the divorce but Martin Luther. And I'm the geedee jerk who caused the whole mess."

"He told me the same thing."

"And against this background, at your bloody insistence, I have come to celebrate. Family joy? Is that what we're doing?"

"The all-time greatest week possible. Barnaby's a born again leprechaun and MomsaBomb Queen for a Day."

"Lar. Really. There's nothing here for me."

"Paddy, in fact, if you don't mind my saying, you've gotten back just about exactly what you've put in. Jerk."

***

Barnaby, after failing to connect with his first sons--Patrick, Dougie and Kevin--decided he would improve, do better with Larry. A son to carry on the name. Larry, the last available, was Chosen. Two buddies weekly in the Upper Deck at Wrigley Field. Summer it was the Cubs; in the fall, the Bears. The two of them hugging and jumping up and down, celebrating Gale Sayers with cries of "Super Nigger!" In December, when blasts off Lake Michigan froze the drip of their nostrils, they imbibed Scotch in the name of staying warm, always from the same bottle.

***

Larry stood, crossed to Patrick, took him by the wrists: "They're in the Bridal Suite. It's at the end of the hall. I want you to go make it up with them. I am asking you to show a little kindness to two very special people. Our parents."

"My gut tells me it's too late."

"We've all had our problems. We've had our successes."

"You've had all the success."

"Bull. You've been my idol."

"Don't throw roses, please."

"You and Rebecca are so sweet to each other." Paulette, who had hit upon an American sitcom, spoke without turning. "I like Rebecca *so much.*"

"Paddy?" Larry turned his brother's name into a plea. "Here's the deal: they're going to die one of these days." *He's selling, he's always selling: Buy my Chevy. Love thy parents.* "She's had stroke after stroke. We stopped counting after fourteen."

Paulette looked up from the black and white television. "Larry thinks she is set some sort of medical record."

"While we're here, really, I'm calling the Guinness people. I read the Guinness book cover to cover and there's no record for number of strokes."

"Only book I've ever seen him with." Paulette did not turn from the television, "Is Guinness the book the same people as Guinness the beer?"

"Maybe."

"Lar. Call me for their wakes. I will enjoy seeing you guys like never before."

"Listen: get on board: I've got a guy coming tomorrow afternoon to give a lecture on our *entire genealogy.* Back into the *fifteenth century,* for God's sake."

"We go back that far?"

"Maybe further."

Paulette said without turning. "Of course further."

"We're a dynasty, Paddy."

"I don't feel dynastic."

"Patrick?" Paulette pointed at last night's Bushmills bottle now empty as his stomach. "Did you have company? Or did you do this—it's not possible--by your lonesome?"

"Paulie! May I?" Larry reached at an arm around Patrick's shoulder, spoke softly: "They feel like you hate them."

"I don't *hate* them." Patrick looked into Larry's smiling face. "Maybe I do. No. I'm indifferent."

"They asked about you again this morning." He tweaked Patrick's cheek. "Go. Go make it up."

"I'm in Dublin. That's enough."

"No. Go and say you're sorry."

"I'm not sorry."

"Even if you're not--go"

"This is so stupid."

"Maybe. Just go and say something stupid, like--you're 'glad to be here'."

137

"But I'm not."

"You should be."

Patrick had known, driving to JFK, that the scene now being proposed was inevitable. Had indeed been inevitable for parts of three decades. "Ok. I'll have dinner with them. But I fly to New York first thing tomorrow. My bank accounts are wide open for Rebecca to plunder."

"I'm sure she's at the bank this minute. You are such a flamer."

"Ok, I'm a flamer. Now take your fucking arm off me."

"*Paddy:* I'm telling you: *give it up.*" Larry reached to fully embrace his brother even as Patrick tried to escape. With both palms Patrick shoved Larry. Not as hard as he might have. Larry reached, pinned Patrick's arms so that he could not do it again. Their faces were kissing close.

"Fuck you."

"Fuck *you*."

***

"Fuck you" fights at Chez Antoine between the *sous-chef* and the *poisonnier*. They'd suck down beer after beer while pushing out platters of soft shell crabs. Three, sometimes four, "fuck you" fights in an average week. Patrick learned early that no one ever gets hurt. Not in a French "fuck you" fight.

***

"Listen. Lar. I don't want to fight you. And I think I'm going to throw up."

"You're fine. Mom and Dad, they're waiting down the hall."

"I'm not dressed."

"You're fine just as you are in the robe. They're waiting."

"They're sober?"

"They're having a Twelve Step meeting. *Let's go.*" They sat eyeball to eyeball. "They talk about you, Paddy, eight times a day. Their hearts go pitter-patter because of you. Don't you know that?"

"And what do you expect when I go down there? *If* I go."

"That you make it up."

Patrick studied a palm. Larry held his breath.

"Ok."

"Really?"

"Really."

"You'll go?"

"In the robe."

"Now?"

"Now."

"Why I love you." Larry kissed Patrick's forehead, walked to the phone: "By the way, Rebecca is the only thing stopping you from ending up a lonely dickhead."

"That I am a dickhead is hardly news."

Paulette turned from the television: "Listen to Larry, Pat. Listen. My friend Hermione, she was an orphan, says it's never, never too late to be born all over again. Really. Somehow."

"Hi, Dad. Hey, good news. Paddy's coming down to visit. Is Mom ready? Are *you* decent?" Larry's long-faced smirk. "Well it's *about time*." He put the phone down, displaying the seraphic smile that had launched ten thousand Chevrolets: "They're waiting."

"You are an amazing prick."

"I cop to that gladly. Now go."

"Asswipe."

"Jerk."

Paulette clucked. And chuckled.

Patrick lurched down the corridor of the Shelburne wing, his land legs not yet secure, while thoughts shouted: *If they don't like the way I am, I'll just walk out. If they give me any crap about anything, I'll turn and walk. Unless he tries to cold cock me. Or gets stupid and wants his two hundred bucks back. She's an aging lounge lady but he's a vicious old bastard. Ethical problem: if an old man socks you, do you sock him back? No, definitely not. Just walk out. How hard can an old drunk hit?* To Patrick's right and left, doors disappeared. He slowed his stride to postpone an arrival never prepared for: *I must watch his hands: if he feints to hit me, watch for the sucker punch. I will not let him hit me. Those times are over. Goddamnit all to hell. And by the way, fuck you, Larry.*

He stepped through an open door. Stopped. Sure that he had the wrong suite.

"Excuse me. I'm sorry." An elderly couple together on the settee. Holding hands. She: with blue rinse do and thick make-up attempting to hide wrinkles. He: white-haired and elfin in a bright green blazer. His shoes barely reached the carpet; hers did not.

"Paddy? That's you?" Her voice like a rusty hinge. They had called three times in twenty-eight years. Once each decade. Each time the words were slurred. "Paddy? *Paddy:* it's your Mom. Please won't you pick up? *Please*, Patrick. Paddy? Damn it, Barney, *I told you* he'd be out." Once Patrick answered not knowing who was on the other end. Hearing from ancient times his father's cigarette rasp he panicked. Hung up without a word.

Tiny points danced on her sequined dress. A Sullivan Chevrolet logo on the breast of Barnaby's jacket. He wore a painted necktie with a leprechaun clicking his heels. Both parents rounder than he remembered. Bridget beckoned: "Paddy, *oh Paddy,* come here to us."

Barnaby shuffled in his seat but did not try to rise, croaked through mucous: "Paddy, you can't know all the times I have been thinking of you." Patrick heard a rising tremolo in his father's words, an

139

ascension. While all those early years, there had only been a mordant falling. Patrick stepped before them. They offered their free hands; he stooped to take them. Hers rubbery with gnarled joints; his, freckled with stubby fingers, the paw that had broken Patrick's nose.

Patrick dropped to one knee.

"How are you, son?" Barnaby squeezed Patrick's palm; Bridget pinched his fingertips with staccato nervousness.

Patrick, too, croaked a little: "Not so good. Not lately."

"We met your Martin. He's so handsome! Like you, Paddy. Calling him after a Lutheran! You rascal, give us a kiss, Paddy." Bridget, grasping the hotel robe, tugged him closer: "Oh how I've missed my Paddy boy." She mussed his hair, pulled on the nape of his neck so that his head lay in her lap. With closed eyes, he felt her tiny fingers move on his face, like a toddler's fingers exploring a dog's muzzle.

"Give me a hug, son," Barnaby said while patting Patrick's shoulder. Patrick hardened to his touch. Barnaby, however, spoke from a well of pride: "Every neighbor up and down Whipple Street, Paddy, they're all drinking your Discipio stuff. I won't let 'em buy anything else."

Patrick looked through Bridget's exploring fingers at the father who peered with rheumy eyes, his neck a wattle where stubbly whiskers struggled in clefts and folds. "I know I wasn't the best father." His words full of phlegm. "Will you...forgive me?"

"Dad, I...I was so....*angry*. So long. So *goddamned long*."

"Don't swear, Paddy," said Bridget rubbing his ears while her free hand reached through the robe's neck, tugged at the hairs of his back.

"What church do you go to, son?"

"St. Agnostica's."

"I don't know that Saint."

MomsaBomb, taking his measure, squeezed his biceps, a way of knowing: "Bishop Quinlan--he's eighty-four if you can believe it--says it's not a mortal sin any more to miss Sunday Mass. Can you imagine that?"

"Everywhere, Ma, it's a new ballgame."

She asks: "How much do you weigh, Paddy?"

But Patrick, fighting a soft weeping, could speak no more. There was movement. Soft steps behind him, shuffling. Many feet entering the carpeted suite. One someone knelt at his side, reached an arm across his back. Others stood behind, placed hands on his head and neck, fingers touched his face. His sibs. The in-law mates. The grandchildren. Tricked and trapped. Everything orchestrated. *Fucking Larry*. Patrick stiffened against a powerful welling in the silent room when, of a sudden moment, the strokes stopped. As did the soft cooing of his mother.

"Hey, you! Get out!" Barnaby, whose rasp, thirty years ago and this day, sounded like a bass fart, broke the quiet: "We don't want any!"

140

Larry hissed: "Dad, for Christ's sake, just this once, *shut up.*" The past several years, Larry's embarrassments with his father had metastasized.

Patrick lifted his head from MomsaBomb's lap. Barnaby and Bridget were fixed on the door of the suite: he with scowling chin raised; she with squinty eyes, a mother reaching, reviewing an era now cobwebbed, dusty. Through leg wickets, Patrick saw the other prodigal; there, propping the door jamb, blue eyes peering through wire-rims past his golden mane.

Barnaby croaked: "Larry, goddamnit I won't shut up. Not for you or anybody. You! This is a private party."

Larry hissed: "Dad, it's Kevin."

"Kevin...the mountain man? The hippie's here?"

***

Kevin's dream of becoming a writer had grown into a percolating passion. Most of his stories were about animals. He tried to read to the family but got little response. Then junior year of high school his English teacher told him of a Creative Writing scholarship at an Eastern college. He scrupulously and honestly filled out the application, included as samples of his talent a box of his forty best stories. But never heard back. With no tuition support from the family, and needing to be enrolled in college to avoid Vietnam, he took classes at a two-year college on the West Side. Wright Junior College. Living on Whipple Street, Kevin got many, many phone calls from many different voices at all hours of the day and night. "When do I get to sleep?" Barnaby would cry out when the phone rang at two in the morning. But MomsaBomb would just hush Barnaby, reminding Barnaby that he should be proud that Kevin had so many friends, friends that are made in college are friends to last a lifetime. Bridget continued to defend Kevin in this way until two of Chicago's Finest pounded rudely on the door one midnight with a search warrant and proceeded to find six pounds of cannabis under Kevin's bed. Barnaby called Bishop Quinlan who spoke to the judge and by noon Kevin was released to Barnaby and Bridget at Cook County jail, the arrest record having been quickly expunged.

Riding back to Whipple Street, Barnaby harangued Kevin who sat in the seat beside him, punched Kevin's bicep to punctuate each moral pointer. Bridget in back was quiet except for occasional sniffling: she held a hankie, mumbled to herself and watched the hotels and townhouses of the Gold Coast pass. Barnaby was indignant: "What is it with my sons? First, Patrick robs me and disappears. Then with Douglas I have a petty hoodlum. And now you, Kevin, have become a drug addict and a dealer to boot. What did your mother and I do to deserve such treatment?"

"Dad, everybody in Chicago does pot. I am just a....do you know what a scapegoat is?"

141

"Listen Joe College, don't talk down to me. You are a criminal so don't talk about scapegoat."

"Dad, those buddy-buddy cops you were talking to--they use it, they sell it."

"They do not!"

"They take it off the dealer and hold back half from the evidence room."

"Don't bullshit me."

"You'd trust the fucking Chicago police over your own son?"

"You're damned right I do."

Bridget from the rear said: "Kevin, don't swear, honey."

Barnaby snorted: "Kevin, I expect you to lie about the police."

"Dad, you are so *fucking dumb*. I...."

Barnaby slammed on the brakes and pulled the car into the breakdown lane, bounced over the curb and began pummeling Kevin on the head and shoulders like an enraged drummer. "Dumb? Dumb? *Dumb am I?*"

Kevin was six foot by this time; Barnaby five foot six. MomsaBomb screamed at Barnaby to stop. But Barnaby beat Kevin to manifest his fury. Kevin cowered against the door protecting his face and head with his forearms. Barnaby's curses became unintelligible, more spittle than syllables. Spent finally, or because his fists were sore, Barnaby got back behind the steering wheel, put the car in gear and they rode in silence save for Kevin's sobs. MomsaBomb reached over the seat, tried to swipe at Kevin's tears with tissue through his web of fingers.

"Kevin, my darling. You should be out east right this minute. Away from all this. That was your scholarship, Kevin, you won it and you should be out east." She dabbed. Then stopped. Said no more. Withdrew deep into the upholstery of the back seat, made herself small. Kevin's sobs slowed. He dropped his hands, looked back at Bridget, whose gaze was now lost on the choppy waters of the lake.

"What scholarship?" Kevin's last tears continued their erratic tumble down scarlet cheeks to a weakened chin.

Bridget said nothing further, only studied the cold gray waves where they lapped at the white ridges of January ice that blanketed Oak Street beach. Barnaby remained engrossed in the steering of the car on a near empty Lake Shore Drive.

"Ma, what scholarship?"

Bridget spoke to the waves: "I told your father that you won that scholarship. That it was not his place to be a buttinski."

"Shut your blabbing mouth, Bridget. He won nothing."

Kevin looked to Barnaby whose white lips were parallel bars of resolution as he drove. Kevin was incredulous, thrown back in time, than outraged. "You did *what* with my scholarship?"

Without looking at Kevin, Barnaby defended himself, spoke with assumed innocence not to Kevin but rather pleaded to a jury of invisible peers: "Here in Chicago, the Windy City, the greatest city in the world, you have De Paul and Loyola and my son wants to go to a Jew school? Why doesn't he want to be a devout Catholic? Isn't that what we have worked and prayed for? I ask you, Kevin: what kind of a Catholic father would I be if I sent my boy to a kike school? To school with a bunch of sheenies?"

"What kike school?"

"Brandeis. You know damn well."

"No! The school I applied to was Bowdoin. In Maine."

Kevin now realized how vilely he had been betrayed. Perhaps had always known it in some cellular fashion. But now, riding on Lake Shore Drive, on that post-holding tank morning, the car was suddenly a coffin of traitorous revelation: "You fucked me out of a ride to Bowdoin?"

Barnaby, exposed in his perfidy, let Kevin's question pass without retort. The car now contained another felon: Barnaby himself. Sweetening his tones, he assumed a pleading tack: "Those kids at Brandeis, Bowdoin, what's the difference? They're probably trying to lose the war, son. I got a good feeling about this one. It's a good thing you stayed home and went to junior college. Wright brothers. First flight. Wright is a great Junior College. And you and Larry have the house almost to yourselves. Someday, Kev, you'll be thankful."

***

Kevin disappeared two days later having said goodbye only to Larry.

143

XX

The Wolfe Tone Suite

After the reunion with the parents--after Kevin had retreated without entering the room, without so much as an innocent rejoinder to Barnaby's scorn--Patrick sat in a wing chair in Matt and Jenny's suite. The couple, now married twenty-odd years, sat on the bed holding hands. Patrick watched them. Holding hands like teenage sweethearts.

Matt grilled when he talked, had some prosecuting attorney in his interrogatories: "You didn't make it with Annette. Now Rebecca too?"

Jenny said: "I'll call her. She must be sick with worry."

Patrick waved a hand at his sister. "Don't call."

"Two bad marriages, you got to look in the mirror."

"I'm sure you're right but..."

"But what?"

"I don't know but what." He bent, kissed his sister, punched Matt's shoulder lightly. Turned and left.

***

Passing Kevin's room, the Wolfe Tone suite, the door was open. Patrick stopped. Perhaps it was whiffs of pot clinging to carpet. Perhaps he saw through the wall. In any event he stepped in. The room was eerily still. Except that Kevin had hung himself. With his belt. His kid brother rotated ever so slowly, dangled from the light fixture. A silver buckle gleamed at his throat, the cobra's fangs snarling still. *He took the buckle when he left Chicago?* Patrick thought: *He's turning clockwise. Why? Lunar drift? The tide of death?* Patrick could do that. Disappear into nothingness. Rebecca called it his *"quotidian trance."*

Then the trance was no more. Patrick began screaming. Hot, painful throaty cries of "Kevin! Oh no! No!" The cries filled the corridor. The Shelburne's walls contracted in shared horror. The clan came running, a thunderous pounding. The family, young and old, entered the room and found Patrick standing on the bed bawling and bellowing while suspending Kevin, trying to reverse a deed that gravity had already performed.

The grandchildren were stunned more than sorrowed; none had known Kevin except as legend. Matt and Patrick commiserated with a Garda detective then called a mortuary. Some hours later the siblings and the in-law mates convened in the Bridal Suite. The subject: the impact of Kevin's death on the parents' festivities.

They began as a silent bunch. Looked at the anonymous floor, shifted in their seats and squeezed palms amidst neutral exhalations.

145

Barnaby cleared his throat: "I know you kids see it as a brother lost. I see it as a son who failed us. All of us."

MomsaBomb cajoled: "We came a long way to celebrate. We can't let Kevin poop our party. "

"Ma, Dad!" Rosemary stood to speak. "I just can't go to a fun dinner and celebrate."

"Maybe, Rosie," Larry spoke softly, "we let them have their party."

"All my life it's been just like this." Rosemary, as if at the bank, shook an index finger at a class of green cashiers. "When do we get our way?"

Larry answered his standing sister: "When they're gone? It'll all be different when they're gone."

"Larry, shut up!" Barnaby's croak. "I'm not going anywhere. You just want my money."

Matt turned to his father-in-law, said flatly. "Barney, what money? You haven't got bupkis, never did."

"This is about money." Paulette, the outsider, the Cassandra, rarely missed a chance to speak her mind. "This family is forever all about money. This is about not wasting the money spent on the trip. Right, Bridget?"

"That, Paulette, is a terrible, terrible thing to say." MomsaBomb dabbed her cheek with a tissue.

Rosemary, a wobbly tower of emotion, erupted in wide-eyed disgust: "You have hit the truth, Paulie. Never, never say the truth. Not in this family." Patrick rose to her, embraced her and as he did she could no longer contain a well of sorrow. Just as quickly tried to stuff it. Holding his big sister, Patrick, rubbing her back, looked down upon Barnaby, and comforted his big sister: "It's okay. Go ahead and bawl. I can't believe we're even discussing this."

Douglas declaimed: "Paddy, strangers don't get to vote, okay? You gave up your friggin' place in the clan a long time ago."

In the hall, out of earshot, the siblings agreed—after loud debate-- to go forward with the opening dinner.

XXI

The Golden Anniversary (continued)

Patrick wandered the corridor till he found the loo whilst the squeaking whine of the piper in the banquet room followed. He used a towel to dab at the white wine Rosemary had used to chasten him, patted his hair and shoulders dry, then retreated from the bleak image the mirror reflected, and enthroned himself within a stall. His hangover had not, despite repeated hydration, begun to lift. Closing his eyes, visitors arrived. Carmine Discipio with his pompous grin. Rebecca irrigating the windowsill begonias with the green cliffs of New Jersey beyond. Into the ER, Patrick on the run with ninety-pounds of limp and naked Melissa over his shoulder.

Kevin was no more. Rebecca was to be relegated to a legal conversation; he would only have to agree to a final dollar amount. Now he was among nagging family and all held him wrong. In the closed-in walls of the stall, he knew his safety would be brief. Before long a search party would be dispatched. To obviate being dragged back to the dinner, he returned of his own volition.

***

"Matt." Jenny grabbed her husband's arm. "He's got a bottle."

"Who's got a bottle?"

"Your son."

"Seamus? I told him beer only."

"Well he's got a bottle. Under the table."

"Jenny, he's twenty."

"And how old are you?"

"Jen, let it lie. He hasn't got a car. He'll be alright."

Jenny neither agreed nor disagreed. Glowered at her oblivious son two tables away.

Patrick returned, spiffed only a little. Jenny reached, took his hand. She drew him to her, bussed him, asked: "Do you remember that poem?"

"Poem?"

"I made you recite it a million times. About another Jenny?"

The poem emerged within Patrick like an errant puppy coaxed from under the porch. He recited it haltingly:" 'Jenny kissed me...When we met...Jumping from the chair she sat in...' "That's all I can remember.' "

Jenny looked back over many decades: "Wasn't it something about 'Time you are a thief...'?

***

Rosemary took Patrick's measure, tilted her head back. *J'accuse.* "So where-oh-where is Rebecca?"

"The entire family has already worked me over."

Rosemary pressed on: "B.J. is interested in Melissa. He only met her at your wedding but he's swears he is going to Manhattan. To find out what she's about."

"When he finds out, he needs to tell me."

"He's a bit smitten, I'd say."

At surrounding tables, several of the grandsons wore white jackets with Kelly green bow ties. The granddaughters reminded Patrick of Bridget in her prime: the promise of her generous bosom, her hourglass figure at parties gliding from person to person. Patrick sipped the first wine of the day and shuddered.

"I know!" Jenny grabbed Patrick's hand. "Let's call Rebecca! The waiter will bring a phone to the table! In Europe, they do that."

"Don't."

Jenny bit her lip. Patrick saw—recalled from long ago--the endless tears of St. Monica in the grotto of the parish church beseeching her wayward son, St. Augustine. Cold winter rains and melting snow had for decades cascaded upon the stone statue's head, had slowly etched gray rivulets in Monica's piteous smile.

Jenny took Patrick's chin, turned him to her, said meekly: "Rebecca tells me that you travel four nights out of five. Is that true?"

"Sometimes five out of six. Her daughter hates me. Don't ever become a step anything." Patrick sipped his white wine, saw Melissa on the gurney. An express package for delivery to Bellevue. Thorazine in the O.J. makes for a malleable ward. *Dr. Rangsnathan: "What is best vintage?"*

Rosemary said, "Paddy, goddammit: You ran away from us. Then from Wife One. And now Wife Two?"

Jenny added quickly: "Don't forget Martin Luther."

Patrick turned in retreat, looked to the head table. There, Barnaby, his head cocked toward Dougie in apparent audition, was nodding slowly. Patrick dropped through several decades to hear his father say that, of all his kids, only he--Patrick Peter--was capable of making the perfect Martini.

"Ow! Who the...?"

Larry with a jack-o-lantern grin was behind him pinching shoulder skin: "Bro, aren't you just goose-bumps-glad that you came?"

"About as many goose bumps as Kevin." Patrick watched the patriarch crane, tap the base of his Martini's stem to coax a last drop.

149

Jenny said: "He agreed to drink no more."

Matt said: "I'd say that as dry periods go, this one doesn't make the history books."

Jenny grasped Patrick's hand: "On United Dad grabbed the stewardess by both boobs. Said he wanted to fly her plane."

"Lovely."

"The captain wanted to put him off in Halifax, have him arrested. Matt sweet talked the captain."

Matt leaned in: "I could've been the next Mayor. Except for Daley's son."

B.J. Scanlon visited their table, asked over the piper's continuing wail: "Uncle Patrick, I bought this book. The fucking English, do you know…?"

Rosemary snapped: "B.J! Your language? You are me you know."

"I don't think so but sorry, mother. Uncle Pat, do you know what the lovely English did to fuck the Irish?" B.J. looked to his mother then back to his uncle. "I found this book. For nine hundred years the Brits cut off Irish balls. Not real balls, you know, cultural balls. National balls."

"I read about Ireland. In college."

"And Cromwell? You know the great English statesman?"

"Only the name."

"He was a *butcher*. Quartered his horses in the cathedral and then deported tens of thousands to Barbados. All for the crime of being Catholic men? And Dublin? The name of the city in Gaelic means 'black pool'. What a book. You have got to read it."

The piper exited the hall; the ardent, sad squealing receded down the corridor. At the honorees' table, Barnaby held high a finger, making some symbolic point. Then drank deeply a refreshed Martini while holding a locked yet floating gaze upon the family.

Patrick recognized the 'finger high' salute as originated by Rosemary's husband, Tommy Scanlon, who died in the wee hours, when B.J. was two, after last call at O'Brien's Terminal Tap, the night he became meaningless tissue under the wheels of a CTA bus. Rosemary, then pregnant with Shannon, called Brian Joseph B.J., as in "By Jesus"; her effort to discount Tommy's sperm. Patrick knew Tommy from De La Salle where they sat in the same classes; even then Tommy was an alcoholic in training. Patrick introduced Tommy to Rosemary at a St. Monica sock hop.

"Leave the book, B.J. I'll read it. I promise."

On the small stage, a three-piece band, elderly gentlemen in shiny black suits--drums, piano and clarinet--began to play. GrandmomsaBomb left the head table, pulled Seamus, Matt and Jenny's oldest, to his feet. Embarrassed but game, Seamus slow danced with his grandmother. Turning Seamus' backside to the family, Bridget lowered her hand from the small of her grandson's back and squeezed a buttock, then shrieked: "Oops! I am so *sorry!*"

The grandsons thought this droll. The granddaughters blushed in unison. Two booed. Barnaby clapped, then sipping his Martini dribbled onto his jacket. Smiled in mock horror at his clumsiness. Inserted a pinkie in the corner of his mouth. If no one's hero, then why not the clown?

In Kelly green jacket and white shoes, Larry advanced to the stage, took the microphone and proclaimed with a sense of moment: "I have a few announcements to open the week..."

None took notice. He waited, tapped on the lectern. Tapped on the mic. Ten seconds. Twenty seconds. Then shouted into the mike: *"You Sullivans..."* His amplified voice boomed off the high ceiling, and echoed dully before coming to rest in the window treatments. The family, at one table after another, turned to him. With mouths gaping and not a few titters. Larry played them like a fisherman who'd hooked a big one. He cried again: *"You Sullivans...,"* all eyes widened with glee, *"...are the salt of the earth!"*

The family broke into shrill whistles and foot stomping. The waiters traded worried looks as they ladled shrimps at the sideboard into thick glass goblets: *Another night with the shameless cousins.* The foot stomping, in the ancient Shelburne, caused the dusty chandeliers to quiver. Larry let things build, indeed he goaded them, mostly the young, with upturned palms; turned his ear to them, a plea for volume. The oak plank floor vibrated. Then he laid his hands on the podium and assumed a patient look. When quiet returned, he launched a review of the coming week: "A bus will be at the hotel tomorrow morning at nine o'clock, that's nine o'clock sharp, dear sister Jennifer, to pick up the sixteen who have signed up for golf, all pray that the rain stops. Dinner, tomorrow, is here at the hotel at eight. Sunday morning, we will take cabs to the Sport Stadium for Irish football beginning at eleven, all pray that the rain stops. Sunday evening, we have two entire rows, front and center, Paulie my darling, just as you requested, at the Gaiety Theatre where an Irish comedian will tell lots of filthy jokes. Or so I am told. All the college students in the crowd are expected to write down the best ones. For your Uncle Larry to take back to Chicago. Monday, should this rain stop, we..." He continued with such necessary announcements through the group's departure six days hence by motor coach to the airport. Finished, he paused, then whispered into the mike: "I want all of you, everybody now, to stand. *Not you, Dad."*

The family, with much pushing of chairs, rose. Barnaby, who had failed to hear, or perhaps to understand, struggled against the arms of his chair, but Atkins, with a large hand on Barnaby's shoulder, restrained him. Barnaby, mystified, smiled; his eyes darted about.

Larry intoned: "I wish to propose a toast." He lifted his glass: "We Sullivans, the mighty Sullivan clan, thirty-one strong, have come to Dublin

151

this evening to honor the only dry cleaner in the entire Midwest, the only dry cleaner certainly in the entire world, who never lost one single belt." He paused and looked to Barnaby whose breathing was shallow, his eyes cloudy. "And Dad still has a box full of belts to prove it! Don't you Dad?"

Applause from the young; guffaws from the middle generation. Barnaby, not comprehending the punch-line, pinched his nostrils, glowed to hear the cheers. MomsaBomb took his hand, patted it. Barnaby toasted the toastmaster. And the crowd. The crowd toasted him.

"But seriously now. You young ones never knew your uncle Kevin. We knew little of him too. Only from many, many years ago. It's a bleeping shame. But it's done and nothing we can do about it. How's about for Kevin? A minute of silence?" All bowed their heads, eyes closed. For the full minute.

Larry tapped the mike: "Okay, okay. I have a note here—a little quiet please?" Larry squinted at the note: "I have a note—a serious note-- from Aunt Jenny." He read: 'Dear Family, All of you will remember how upset the management at Disney World got just three short years ago. I do not want to put blame onto any one in this room.' Okay, you all understand that this is not Uncle Larry speaking? Not I!" Larry then continued to read. "'So, please, have fun but that family member who dares throw the first piece of food will answer to me.'" The cousins booed and hissed. Larry held the note over his head to show separation from its message. Jenny pointed to Dougie at the head table, mouthed: "You, buster, you." A scone soared on a high trajectory from a table of cousins missing Dougie's ear by a scant inch.

Larry tapped the mike again.

"And now, MomsaBomb, GrandmomsaBomb. I ask you to please stand." Atkins assisted Bridget. The party gave her steady, polite applause. The matriarch did not quite know what to do with her hands: first she clasped them, then hid them behind her back; smiled shyly.

"Sing it, Grandma," cried out a grandson in the party who, by long custom, knew what was to come next.

"GrandmomsaBomb, do it!" This cry arose exclusively from the youngest Sullivans. Bridget put two fingers over her mouth in a gesture of modesty. Larry crossed to her with the mike, held it while standing at arm's length. The tables fell quiet. Demurely, the doyenne of Whipple Street sang in a small voice, for the most part on key.

Picture a little love-nest, Down where the roses cling, Picture the same sweet love nest, Think what a year can bring.

Patrick scanned the room; all had succumbed—to nostalgia, the afternoon drinks, love—MomsaBomb winked, nodded, crooned on, then teasingly shook her derriere before aspirating a—final—breathy 'makin' whoopee.'

The family rose once more. Bridget waved and blew kisses until the last clap. Barnaby watched her; a man smitten, old scores, their bickering forgotten. *His Bridget.* No one else's. *Till death do us...* He sipped his Martini deeply, shook his head slowly. At their wedding, she had sung the same song. At her Grandfather's request.

Larry raised the mike over his head: "There is another announcement. I have been asked to allow an announcement. Seamus?"

Seamus O'Connor, Matt and Jenny's oldest, sprinted to the podium. Larry clasped a hand upon his much taller nephew's shoulder. Seamus looked down at his uncle, pulled the mic to his mouth: "Thank you, Uncle Larry. I know, we all know, how painful it must be for you to give up the microphone."

To applause and whistles Larry smiled then stepped aside. Seamus raised a hand. Waited judiciously, then spoke slowly: "Tonight there will be a cousin's reunion. At Mulroney's Publican House on O'Connell Street. Beginning at ten-thirty. *Cousins only.* " He held a finger high. "No family member *over* twenty-three will be welcome!" The cousins bellowed approbation; Seamus turned to his uncle, spoke over the din: "That includes you, Uncle Larry." Larry smirked through a wide grin.

Seamus gave up the mike and jumped from the stage. Crossing to his table Larry called after him: "You'll miss me, Seamus, you are making a big mistake."

Seamus called back: "Not after Las Vegas!"

Larry retorted: "One of the best nights of your young life!"

He waited for the tumult to settle; then, with the mike in both hands, whispered: "You lucky Sullivans, I give you... *Maureen Scanlon!*"

Rosemary's second-born, barely nineteen, toed her detested spiked heels under her chair, and glided—skipping once--to the stage and her uncle. Dressed in a navy blue silk chemise with a full-bloom crimson rose at the waist, she bussed her uncle's cheek on tiptoes and, declining the microphone, put her hands behind her back, cleared her throat and sang *a capella*:

> When Grandmother's eyes are smiling
> Sure it's like a morn in spring...

Listening to Maureen sing, Bridget's chin dimpled and her shoulders shook gently; she swiped at a tear, blew her nose politely, shook her head as if to say, 'How did I ever deserve this?' At song's end, she raised her glass to Maureen. Maureen moved to the head table and kissed

153

her grandmother. All cheered; all eyes, even Patrick's, brimmed. Helpless, he gave himself over to the maudlin sight. Who would not?

Larry began anew: "Now, I'm going to ask Dad, on this august occasion—this June occasion?--to say just a few words. As befits the man who started all this. How about it, Dad? On your feet, ok?"

All eyes turned to Barnaby. Dougie nudged him to stand, which he did unsteadily: he who never crossed the Illinois state line until he was forty-seven and off to South Bend to watch the Fighting Irish; a man of seventy now suffering intercontinental jet lag and more than a few adult beverages. The applause was not the plangent stomping, nor the fraternal hooting heard earlier, but the clan's respectful acknowledgment that the patriarch was rising. A few granddaughters stood. Then the grandsons. Followed by the siblings. Patrick was last to join. He was startled and embarrassed--though none saw him—with the onset of autonomous tears. Larry left the stage, carried the mic to Barnaby. Barnaby fiddled with the switch, and, in so doing, turned it off. Larry switched it back on. All heard him chide his father: "You turned it off." Barnaby, confused, turned it off again. Larry draped an arm over Barnaby's shoulder, held the mic at the level of his father's neck: "I'll hold it. You just talk."

The cheers ebbed, Barnaby swayed. Buffeted by invisible currents, he tried to clear his throat which created a hoarse cackle in the sound system. His lips quivered, opened, closed and opened again, but no words came forth. Sparing himself the shame of public tears, he emitted a croaky: "Great, really great."

All applauded quietly while Larry and Atkins assisted his return to his chair. Bridget kissed his hand. Barnaby retracted the hand, reached for his glass, drank. To the quieting clan, perhaps, his inability to make a speech was the purest emotion of all.

Larry, again at the podium and grinning proudly, proclaimed: "Some people here tonight, some of you out there, have been *kicking ass* this past year!" He scanned tables. "Liam Sullivan, stand up!"

Liam, no wall-flower, sprang to his feet, smiled expectantly.

"Two weeks ago—you were all there, most of you—when Liam got his sheepskin: *Bachelor of Arts, Loyola University! Dean's List!"* All manner of hoots and foot stomping broke forth; Liam, arms over his head, spread his index and middle fingers high in Nixonian victory. He took his seat to fading hurrahs and blown kisses.

"Maureen Scanlon!"

Maureen stood slowly, daintily and with dignity. "Maureen leaves in September, music scholarship--The *Juilliard School of Music.* I want to hear it for Maureen!" Applause built and held for the cousin who had accomplished so much—without a father. She was kissed and hugged by each of the cousins at her table; many others sallied to her. As the bussing went on Larry waited. "Maureen, there's good wine in your future—your

Uncle Patrick lives just about a mile from Juilliard. He asked me to let you know that you have an invitation for Sunday dinner—with him and Rebecca--every week of the school year."

Maureen blushed, looked to Patrick, who, finding himself without an option, waved. Blew a kiss.

Larry, with the mike held high, pursed his lips. There were titters. All guessing as to who would be next. Larry surveyed every table. Then began in somber, even ecclesiastical, tones: "Dad, what do you think of us? What all your messing around has caused? Dad?"

Barnaby, hearing his name, lifted his glass, toasted the toastmaster. He somehow got to his feet without assistance. Croaked, rasped. Tottered. Patrick remembered his boyhood chore when this voice was heard: to create, along with Dougie, with intertwined fingers, a conveyance to carry their father to bed. Barnaby had never weighed more than a hundred and fifty, but borne by the two sons, he was liquid stone.

This night Barnaby wobbled side to side. Atkins rose to catch him but tardily; the old man slid like a sheet of water beneath the white linen. The room was quiet until a muffled rasping emerged from beneath the table, a throaty giggle: Barnaby chuckled through a nasal thickness. Rosemary caught Patrick's eye and rolled hers.

MomsaBomb waved off Dougie: "Leave him. He's being bad. He can stay there. We'll have a nice party." Atkins, looking thoroughly disgusted, glowered at the table cloth, not seeing what lay beneath the linen folds; tonight's early departure by his father was hardly without precedent. Unusual only in that his slide had preceded the appetizer. Bridget lifted the linen and shook her finger: "Bad boy!" She dropped the cloth, looked back to the family, flushed and breathing heavily, addressed all in her small voice that was, in the excitement, breathless. "You know, all of you...how *bad* he can be." She clasped her hands nervously. Sat back. Swiped at her wet brow with a serviette. "Let's all just enjoy our party. Without him." Her moist cheeks and beaded brow gleamed and Patrick saw her dancing madly, her swaying breasts inviting a stranger in grey sharkskin at an overheated, smoky party; her face aflame then too from perfumed oils and sweat, so very long ago.

Larry, mike in hand said: "I think...that's all there is to say. Enjoy your dinner."

There came an appalling sound from the head table, the gasping struggle of life itself demanding to continue, MomsaBomb's last efforts at breathing. She tossed her head like one needing to but unable to sneeze. Her oval mouth and unseeing eyes screamed soundless terror. The children were quickly out of their chairs and crossing the room. Jenny, who had finished the Chicago marathon under three hours, arrived first. A whitish foam oozed from Bridget's otherwise sere lips.

Jenny said: "Another stroke. Somebody do something."

Dougie was already exploding through the double doors.

Larry tried for a pulse: "Am I doing this right?"

Patrick watched: *She is dying. Maybe dead already.* As once on a plane to Japan, an octogenarian Japanese woman. The crew never got her out of her seat. The corpse, in the sold-out flight, remained strapped beneath a blanket the entire flight to Narita. "I think she may be gone already."

Jenny proclaimed this a sacrilege: "No! We can save her."

"Jen, it's time, let her go."

XXII

THE UNNECESSARY MISSION OF
DR. FINBAR FINNEY

While the hotel staff sought a doctor, Atkins and Paulette's Sean and Douglas, Jr., both Lake County All Star linemen, hoisted Barnaby from under the table and conveyed him pasha-like to the Bridal Suite. So transported, the patriarch's eyes flared with injury. "Put me down, damn it, who are you anyway?"

"Grandpa, it's Sean."

"You are not!" His besotted voice barked then faded as they bore him down the corridor: "Put me down! I have an American passport!"

***

"I'll wager that in her day she was a beauty. You say she loved a good party?" Dr. Finbar Finney, as things turned out, was more of a consoling presence than a medical intervention for Bridget had passed quickly. "Sure it's a sad, sad day for you Mulligans. No. It's *Sullivan,* isn't it? Are you by any chance related to the Detroit Sullivans? Maurice Sullivan? Probably not. Maurice had a turrible heart attack right here at the Shelburne. Ten years ago. Today he's out and about like a colt. Has himself ten—perhaps it's twenty—of your pizza restaurants, he does. We visited Maurice and his wife, me Mary and I did. Delicious really—all those different toppings. His trade is mostly the coloreds and they can't buy enough. Your Detroit, tis like a wee Africa, wouldn't you say?"

Bridget was laid out on a divan along the wall. Her expression was neither sad nor glad, neither at peace nor war. Her fingers, intertwined with Jenny's rosary, became more translucent with each passing minute; the wooden beads in turn encircled Grandma Powers' star sapphire, a cloudy stone set in diamonds, a fabled jewel within the family. When Patrick was four, Grandma Powers held it up to him: "See the spider inside, Paddy? Can you see it? Just waiting to be let out to crawl all over your nose." Little Paddy had cupped his nose. To save it from that spider.

Rosemary said: "Jen, I already know: the sapphire is yours. She told me."

"You're not angry?"

"Not so angry that I'd kill you."

"I can't bear to take it off her finger."

"The undertaker will do it."

"She hasn't taken it off in years," Jenny said, "not since the arthritis."

"Your sister is right," whispered good Doctor Finney. "Leave it, dear, to the mortician."

"He...won't cut her finger off?" Jenny began a high pitched whine. "Just for the ring?"

"Such a thought!"

"I don't want it! I don't want it!"

Matt implored her: "Jen, however he does it--" He patted her shoulder.

"He'll amputate my mother's finger!!"

All demanded that she cease.

After a fashion she did.

Dr. Finney at the edge of the family circle, sighed and, with repeated elevations of his furred white eyebrows, counseled the survivors: "She's found a better place. Jesus has called your mither and, don't you know? She's in a better place. For sure now. The worst thing, you'll come to see, is her being absent from her own grand party. That's the real pity." Dr. Finney smiled sweetly, his rutted face a porcine ellipse, with a flat nose, perhaps he had been a boxer in his youth. "Bless her. Bless her. Now where are those mortuary lads?" The good doctor left to hasten the mortician one more time.

"Let's circle these wagons," said Larry, and the men pushed chairs around the sofa. In the quiet that followed, several contributed an utterance, a thought or two, none with any energy, like coins falling into a muddle of wet dirt.

Dougie and Constance returned from a visit to the grandchildren.

Jenny asked: "How are they?"

"They're in our suite," said Constance: "Pretty sad. Maureen is really broken up. Shannon too. The boys are quiet."

Constance said: "They all loved their GrandmomsaBomb."

"And Dad?"

"Out cold. Big smile on his face."

Dougie said, to no one in particular: "Me, I'm not afraid to say it, I'm glad she's dead." He drained his glass of Port; a black string of sediment clung to his lower lip.

"Douglas, shush." Constance dabbed at his lip.

But Atkins was, this night, not to be quieted: "Shush yourself."

No one argued.

Larry asked Patrick: "What are you going to do now?"

"Hmm?"

"I mean, unemployed...and all?"

"I was thinking I might buy a small hotel or a B&B. Someplace tropical."

158

"No, no." Rosemary, in the family as well as at the bank, often became the self-appointed interpreter of what people really meant. "You mean you have that fantasy. Many people have that one."

"No, big sister. I mean maybe *I will buy a small hotel*."

Jenny added: "*With* Rebecca."

"Don't, Jen, *please?*"

Jenny, always up to mocking, and recovered for the moment from her grief, said warmly, innocently: "I won't say a single, further word about Rebecca. Not about your wife Rebecca. Not about Rebecca whom I so dearly do love. And who you still love so dearly, Paddy. Not another word will I say. Despite your temporary insanity. I won't say another thing for at least one minute. Not about Rebecca. Uh uh."

Patrick said: "Matt, is there any way she can be controlled?"

Matt shook his head: "Not to my knowledge."

Larry glowed, a hot idea: "You buy the hotel. We'll all come and visit. I've got a customer, a pilot for American? He does charters on his days off. He will fly us all down on the cheap."

"There you go again, Larry," Paulette said. "Playing tour operator."

"Just one more thing that I am excellent at. Makes you love me even more, doesn't it? Paulie?"

She addressed—pleadingly--her in-laws: "All day long, he's buying tickets for hockey, baseball, the Bulls. At the showroom people come in and give him cash all day. You should live with this man."

"That would involve incest," said Rosemary. "Which at my age might be better than nothing."

Jenny reached to Rosemary's hand: "Hold out, Rosie Posie, Mr. Perfect's going to knock. I feel it in my bones."

"Maybe at your B&B I'll meet somebody," said Rosemary. "He can jump on *my* bones anytime. They have nude beaches. In the Caribbean."

This drew many eyes but no comment.

Jenny said: "Don't bring kids."

Constance said, "Jen's right."

"I have a good salary," Rosemary pounded a fist on a palm. "But no sex!!"

Matt, wide-eyed, said: "What?"

"My friend Helen told me to say that. And I do. Ten or twenty times a day. Men are supposed to pick up...on my vibe?" There was a pause: "It worked for Helen. She and her boyfriend do it almost every day. And they've been together for months."

Larry spit out: "It can't be done. Not every day."

"It's what Helen said."

159

"That's what Helen *bragged*," corrected Matt. "It won't work, Rosemary, everyday."

Jenny said: "I can vouch for Matt's."

Rosemary held a finger high: "I'll tell you this: Helen smiles all day long."

Caught up in remembering, or just imagining, their own days of frequent sex, the group fell silent.

Until Dougie changed the subject. "The Shelburne, this is a *great* hotel. Did you see all the meat at breakfast?"

Matt said: "I ate the blood sausage. Jen said it was for barbarians."

Jenny rolled her eyes: "First, it was disgusting to look at. Second, my cholesterol already is two-sixty-five."

Paulette returned to the Caribbean and Patrick's small hotel: "Maybe Patrick won't want the entire clan to invade?"

Larry spoke with patience to his wife: "Hotel operators, Paulie my love, want and need their rooms to be full. It's not like we wouldn't be paying Patrick. We would expect, and be entitled to, of course," he leaned toward Patrick, "a family rate?"

Patrick said: "I will be delighted to see you all at my new hotel. You guys are all that I've ever had. Really. You and Martin Luther."

Jenny whispered *sotto voce*: "Don't forget Rebecca."

"You said you'd cut that out."

"I did not."

Rosemary edged forward on her cushion: "Paddy, things tend to work out. First things suck and then they don't." She took Patrick's hand, an event last enacted walking when children to St. Monica's grammar school: "Paddy, you are with your family. We who love you to pieces."

Jenny blew a kiss: "Welcome back. It's been a long, long time."

Atkins said: "Yeah."

Jenny kissed him, wetting with her tears his chin and cheeks. "I'm so glad to have you back."

"I'm...catching a plane. Tuesday at noon."

"What?!"

"Maybe to Bermuda."

"Bermuda?" This query was collective, emitted in astonished unison.

"I know a hotel guy in Bermuda. He can tell me what properties are for sale."

"You're leaving already?"

"Leaving is what I do best."

"What a pea brain," said Matt.

"You can say that again," said Larry.

So Matt did.

***

In his room, naked in the wing chair, Patrick drained a miniature of Jameson's from the mini-bar. Then another. Followed with a Johnny Walker. Red for a red-letter day. After three Cognacs, he took to the bed, screamed into the pillow that he hated everyone and everything in the world. Had for all time. Would for all time. That, most of all, he hated himself. Naked as the day MomsaBomb pushed him forth, Patrick lost consciousness within the hotel linen: sailed a one-man sloop across the seven seas, flew strapped to a rocket from pole to pole, and, with seven league boots, strode boldly about the globe.

XXIII

Bora Bora

My hotel is a pink antithesis of Whipple Street.
I bought it after I reunited with Victoria. Oh the tears we shed that we had ever parted! With star crossed serendipity, we embraced after stumbling into each other in a hotel lobby. Within minutes we took a three hundred dollar room in the middle of the afternoon.

I gave my attorney power-of-attorney to spare myself of ever seeing Rebecca again. How wondrously simple to pay her off! On the third day in Bora Bora, Victoria and I bought Le Jardin: twelve guest rooms and a dining room. Everything changed for the better: I did not dwell on Rebecca, Melissa, or Martin Luther at all. I did not call Jenny, Atkins, Larry or Rosemary.

I am handyman, maitre d' and chef. The guests are wild for my cuisine. After the evening service I stroll among the tables in toque and whites chatting, shaking hands. The depth of the French wine list shames any hotel in all of Polynesia. In the kitchen, my secret is no secret: just plenty of butter! Ha ha. I accept the accolades of the guests while taking their credit cards.

Victoria and I live in a cottage that is set back from the hotel. Behind a pink gate there's a private lane bordered with oleander, bougainvillea and periwinkles that leads to a tranche of hidden beach we keep for our own pleasure.

Victoria takes up portrait painting again. She paints me in oil ten times, always late at night when the guests are asleep. I sip wine, pose. Until desire enters the room like a furtive cat and we move to a futon on the veranda beneath the stars.

We hire a chef, Jean-Claude, who enables me to escape the kitchen and, soon, my only worry is the receipts which do not tally. The accounts are a nightmare. Steeped in invoices and credit card vouchers I can only Sherlock one proof-positive deduction: the shortages started when Jean-Claude started. Bâtard. With ledger in hand, I climb furiously to the cottage to reveal this larceny to Victoria. Victoria and I will throw Jean-Claude to the sharks first and to the gendarmes only second. A taste for murder boils in me. Enraged I possess the necessary hate that will allow me to kill. I swing open the cottage door: Jean-Claude and Victoria are copulating against a wall. He cannot thrust violently enough for her, she screams to be hurt. A cry starts deep in me. I don't own a gun or I would shoot them. Or myself. Suddenly there's a small .22 caliber pistol in my hand. I shoot into their sweat-streaked bodies. Click. Click. No bullets.

Fucking like maniacs, they shriek and cackle, the hysteria of harpies. Next moment I too am naked, a whiny, shrinking cretin, covered with cancerous sores, with desiccated flaps of skin between my legs.

He had slept an entire night and day.

Opening his eyes the room was all shadow, no real light. He heard the sound of a key in the door. Housekeeping? "Go away!" He turned and hid his head in the pillow but heard the door open. Fabric sounds. "Go fucking away." He felt a presence staring a hole in the nape of his neck. Turned to see a female form in a trench coat in the gray light that lay upon the room.

Rebecca.

"I just got here."

He still wet, returned from Bora Bora; she stood over him with a moist curl stuck to her cheek like a question mark.

"My mother died. Kevin killed himself. Before Bridget...."

Rebecca exhaled. "Jenny called."

"She died during dinner. I didn't cry."

"She was a tyrant."

"How's Melissa?"

"She called yesterday. Screamed how pissed she was at me. Her floor counselor says her screaming is therapeutic and that I should be delighted."

Patrick could only see the outline of Rebecca in the dim light. He hugged himself to ward off chill brought on by the dream. "I socked Martin Luther."

"No."

"I don't know what's with me. Rebec, cut your losses. It will always be like this."

"Maybe. Maybe not."

His mouth was dry wool. "Carmine fired me."

"Good. I hate him."

"Actually I quit."

"Even better."

He smelled the wet of her trench coat. "Rebek...I..."

Her fingers pushed wet strands from her face slowly. He inhaled deeply: "Why are you here?"

"You shouldn't have to ask that."

"I need to."

"Your mother just died. And your brother..."

"That's why you came?"

"And I guess...to find out what is with you."

"I am so ashamed. So, so ashamed."

She whispered: "Patrick, I can't do it for the both of us."

"Becca baby, crawl in?"

"No."

"Warm me."

"I said 'no'. You're a rat."

"Maybe just a mouse?" He heard her exhale. *"Crawl in?"*

"You think that if we make love you'll feel better?"

"Maybe."

"And then?"

"I'll do better. Somehow."

"I don't think so." She stood before him without moving. Her coat an opaque shroud. "On the plane I kept thinking that I want out."

"Of our marriage?"

"I'm afraid I've picked another Mannie."

"That hurts."

"Sorry but...you've pretty much earned it." She turned.

"Where are you going?"

"I've got a room. Down the hall."

"I'm *hurting,* Rebek."

"Me too."

XXIV

THE GRAVE DIGGER'S PUB

That afternoon Patrick, recognized as the family's most experienced traveler, was delegated to negotiate coffins, air transport, and interment of both Kevin and MomsaBomb in Chicago. He visited the airport, the U.S. Consul's office, and two mortuaries. Back at the Shelburne he made his report over whiskeys neat in the oak paneled bar.

"It's expensive to die. No. To be buried."

Matt asked: "How expensive?"

"Caskets, first class ride in refrigerated baggage, two nights of showing in Chicago—all their best friends? We need to buy the plots they never bought. To get them underground in Chicago? Ball park? Come on, guess."

Dougie: "Ten million?"

"Thirty thou."

"Punts or dollars?"

"I didn't ask."

"Do they get mileage from United?" Dougie asked not too innocently. Constance rapped his shoulder with closed fist. He winced. "Ooh...that's my bad one. You should know that by now."

Patrick began his report once more. "We have to pay duty upon entry. In Chicago. The City gets a cut."

"Duty? They're an import or something?"

"Something like that."

Long silence. Then Matt offered: "We split it five ways. When we sell their house we get it back."

Jenny slapped her knees: "And where does Dad live? Not with you and me."

Rosemary said: "I just got the last kid out. I'm not taking another one."

Dougie held up a finger. Then took a long sip of whiskey, shook his head with the blast of single malt. "I know, listen: So you see there was this rodeo that went to London, England. Really. To show the English what the Wild Old West was like? And this 6 foot 10 inch 340 lb. Texas cowboy is riding this bronco they brought over to England. The bronco bucks him and the cowboy breaks his neck. Dies right there in the sawdust of the performance ring with a thousand limeys watching."

Matt's eyes narrowed: "And the point is?"

Dougie held his hands up like a traffic cop. Or the priest at Benediction. "Patience. You're always telling me patience? So the boss of the rodeo goes to every funeral parlor in London. But no one has a casket big enough for this guy." Dougie's head swiveled, caught everyone's questioning gaze. "Really they looked and called and called. Nobody in all England had that gigantic a casket. Then they figured it out." He raised his eyebrows and glass. "Gave the corpse an enema. Shipped him back to Texas in a shoebox."

Jenny shook her head slowly: "That is gross beyond gross."

Rosemary said, "Not to mention sick."

Matt with eyes squinted in disbelief asked: "This story--you have a point in mind?"

Dougie paused then offered: "Cremation?"

They located a crematorium in Glasnevin. Barnaby was against it. "Too pagan. But if it's what you kids think is best, then okay." The grandchildren, for the most part, thought cremation certainly ecological, that it had served the Hindus well for eons but rather than ride with grandmother and uncle to the crematorium, they opted for a memorial--they called it a celebration--picnic in the Wicklow Mountains from whence earlier Sullivans had reportedly emigrated during the time of the potato blight. B.J. whispered to Patrick: "Another fucking by the Brits. They were ecstatic to see us go."

Larry arranged for a limo to take the siblings and in-laws to Glasnevin.

Next morning they gathered in the lobby. Patrick saw Barnaby in the bar. "Wait. I'll ask him once more."

Barnaby was drinking his whiskey alone, staring into the amber which he sloshed gently in the glass. Patrick, at his side, interrupted him: "Dad, you're sure you won't come?"

Barnaby looked at Patrick with a forced smile: "No. You kids go."

"I'm afraid...that you're going to have...regrets? Because of the cremation and all?"

"Jesus, Paddy, really, you kids are in charge."

"Okay. I guess." He turned to leave. Then walked slowly back to the bar. "Dad, there's so much I've never said to you."

"Me too, Paddy."

"Really?"

"Sure. I wasn't the greatest father. I know that. Say it. It's okay." He looked up through bloodshot eyes. "You, all of you, deserved more."

"I...I have to tell you, Dad. It would have helped. Me and everybody. If--Jesus, Dad--if you had come home...at night?"

Barnaby sipped his drink. Winced. Looked to the mirror beyond the rows of spirits bottles. "I did leave her alone in a gin mill. Once. And she didn't come home."

At Glasnevin, not twenty meters as the crow flies from the field stone chimney of the crematorium, they sat around a heavy pine table in the Grave Digger's Pub. All sipping stout. The pub contained, besides the Sullivans and their mates, a huddle of black-suited hearse drivers at the bar.

"I figured out," said Jenny, "that MomsaBomb was pregnant thirty-six months of the first forty-seven months after their marriage."

"If the pill existed back then," Rosemary said, "there's no way she goes so nutso."

Jenny said: "She was not 'nutso'. Phyllis says 'nutso' is a judgment. She was only responding to stress."

Atkins said: "Wait. Nutso is nutso."

Larry couldn't figure out why it mattered.

Patrick offered—Georgetown's Jesuits would have been proud—a conundrum: "If Beethoven had been taking Valium, would he ever have written his Ninth Symphony?" They looked at him utterly puzzled.

Larry offered his own analysis: "I don't see how it's such a big deal to write nine symphonies. What kind of big number is nine? Ernie Banks had five *hundred* home runs, Hank Aaron and Babe Ruth *seven* hundred. Now that's a life's work."

"You ought to stick to Chevrolets," said Matt.

"You're the first to know, Babycakes: I'm talking to Toyota. *Sayonara.*" Larry lifted his glass, drank deeply. He, the house comedian, who as a toddler would cram cold mashed potatoes into his eye sockets. He who would jump off garbage cans, a North Korean Commie dying in flight. He licked his upper lip clean with one quick swipe and, invaded by a sudden mystery, hunched forward: "Does *sayonara* mean goodbye? Or hello?"

No one knew.

Lorries rumbled slowly past rattling the pub's window panes. Patrick asked: "Remember the piggy bank? How crazy she got because one of us robbed her pink piggy bank?"

Jenny said: "I've tried to forget."

"I remember: my butt is still cracked down the middle," said Atkins. He looked for a laugh but got none. Constance shook her head.

"I don't remember a piggy bank," said Larry.

Rosemary said: "You were there but you and Kevin were still babies. She had this piggy bank. For a rainy day. After the war, we really had a lot of nothing. The six of us slept in one bedroom. Do you remember that?"

"No."

"The police came because Jenny and Rosemary were hysterical, screaming bloody murder," said Atkins.

Rosemary wagged a correcting finger: "No. The police *called on the phone.* They didn't come."

Jenny eyes twinkled: "Norman Rockwell wanted to paint us. But he wanted a big fee and it never happened."

Larry asked: "Norman Rockwell wanted to paint the Sullivans?"

For this innocence, Larry was obligated to buy the next round. While at the bar, he bought a round for the hearse drivers. Back at the table, he confided with a wink: "I'll write it off. Customer development. Guys like them move to Chicago to live all the time."

Rosemary's mug resounded on the table: "My psychiatrist was convinced that Bridget was on the verge of a nervous breakdown. Not once. Several times."

Jenny sat up with indignation: "Wait just one second: *which* psychiatrist?"

"*My* psychiatrist. I never told you. I saw him in the Sixties, only three or four times. After Tommy died."

"You tacky, tacky bitch." Jennifer glowered. "Weren't you the one who gave me 'what for' when I went to Phyllis?"

Rosemary showed offense: "Phyllis was not a Catholic. I called Bishop Quinlan and got a Catholic one."

Patrick interjected: "Rebecca thinks that 'Catholic psychiatrist' is an oxymoron."

Rebecca said: "I said that?"

"Yes you did."

"Well, I shouldn't have."

Larry, who liked to show he could stay in any conversation with the college graduates, contributed: "I sold a Corvette to a psychiatrist who was a moron. He paid full sticker."

Patrick pushed again the question of the pink piggy bank: "Well one of us—not Larry or Kev--robbed her goddamned piggy bank. I'd like to know--for the record--who did it?" The faces around the table were as revealing as Jupiter's moons. "Tell you what: we close our eyes and the guy who did it raises his hand and then we open our eyes. Okay?"

All agreed and when they opened their eyes everyone--except Larry--had a hand up. Constance shook her head; Paulette cackled. Rebecca too shook her head, an anthropologist on a field trip.

"I seem to remember," Patrick said, "that if I shook the damned pig slowly, upside down, the coins would slowly spit out."

Atkins said: "Dimes came easy. Quarters came slow."

Paulette, a daily runner, forever reaching to touch her toes, even there in the Dead Man's pub (she, in sweats and running shoes, had contemplated running to Glasnevin, swore she could get there faster than the limo in the many bottlenecks of Dublin's traffic), spoke red-faced with her head almost to her ankles: "Constance, Rebecca: do we know these people?"

"Douglas and I," Constance said, "we'll be married twenty-six years this November. I thought that I had heard everything there was to hear about the Sullivans."

"Looking in...", Rebecca said shaking her head, "I mean I'm the latest in this family--but it can't be just blind luck that you all turned out so fabulous."

Jenny kissed her cheek: "Our luck is to have you, new sister."

"Hear, hear," said Matt, holding up his glass.

After they toasted Rebecca, Atkins smiled, said to Patrick: "Paddy, you missed it: Barnaby when we told him you were marrying a Jew: 'No! You're lying! Jesus, Mary and Joseph!'"

"He crossed himself," said Constance.

Dougie turned to Rebecca, offered proof that he was free of his father's parochial failings: "Our bookkeeper is a Jew."

"And we have a foreman," Constance added, "who is Black Muslim."

"He wants us to say 'Nation of Islam'", corrected Atkins. "I don't argue. He's bigger than me."

Rosemary touched Rebecca's hand: "Dougie's trying to welcome you. You're the first Sullivan...of your persuasion."

Rebecca tried to explain gently: "We're not really a persuasion. More like a tribe."

Jenny took Rebecca's other hand: "We're a tribe too." Jenny laughed and laughed at her joke. Could not stop. She put a finger in her stout, sucked the foam. Found herself hysterical. In a near paroxysm, collapsed on Matt's shoulder.

With a steady glower on the risible Jenny, Matt asked: "Rebecca, do Jews take converts?"

"If you find the right rabbi."

"Sammy Davis made himself to be Jewish," said Larry. "Now that man could sing. We saw him in Vegas. Right, Paulie?"

"At the Sands. We saw the floor show twice. He's a tap dancer too."

"He's got a glass eye. I talked to him in the lobby. It was hard, you know, because I wanted to stare and, of course, I didn't want to stare. The glass eye doesn't move but the real eye does. He was nice. Not at all conceited."

At noon, a thin line of white smoke began to curl from the crematorium's chimney. Matt saw it first; rose and pointed: "All give thanks. A new Pope."

Rosemary ruffled her hair: "There's going to be fallout."

171

Jenny grimaced, began to brim tears of sorrow. Again.

Larry, almost done with his grief, slid Murphy's Stout coasters to each of them. "Cover your mugs!"

Patrick raised his glass as if to catch an ash or two: "Here's to incest and to cannibalism rolled into one."

Rebecca kicked him.

"Really," said Patrick. "It happened during the potato famine. Families ate their Mums."

"Patrick says things like that to shock," said Rebecca.

"Paddy, no. That never happened," said Rosemary.

"Protein is protein, Rosie Posie."

Tearful Jenny, in the brogue she had tried to develop all week, said in a little girl voice: "'And what did you do during vacation in Ireland, Jennifer Sullivan?' 'I drank me Mum, I did.'"

A light wind dispersed the thin curl from the crematorium; there one moment, nothing the next. Matt held forth his glass, swirled to take in his mother-in-law's dust: "Here's to you, Bridget, Body of Christ."

Jenny kicked *him*.

"Mine tastes a little nutty, maybe a little like rye toast?" said Patrick gazing into the vanilla cream atop his stout: "Hi, Mom." Only slowly did they take in his words. Had it really been thirty years since Paddy had made a funny?

Jenny raised her glass: "I want you to know that I love you all madly." She giggled her little girl giggle: "Here's to madness," she said.

They raised their glasses, drank, and then settled back; the wisecracks having ended for the moment, they watched looping curls of white ash drifting across the week's first peek of blue sky. Above Glasnevin, Momsabomb and Kevin were united in smoke and ashes--a rebirth of sorts, together once more.

XXV

At Mulroney's

Late that night, the family—again without Barnaby--gathered in front of the old Custom House on the walled bank of the Liffey. Dougie held MomsaBomb's ashes in a porcelain urn. Patrick held Kevin's. The neap tide, black and full, dappled with the lights of Dublin and sloshed against the wall of the quay. Patrick, delegated because he was the oldest son (because the oldest sibling Rosemary had refused) knelt and shook Bridget Sullivan, née Powers, into the brine of eddying waters. Dougie did the same with Kevin.

With taxis roaring past and Maureen Scanlon's ghetto blaster flooding Verdi's Requiem over the waters and into the North Dublin night, the Sullivans stood and watched. No speeches. Just fingers squeezing other fingers. The urns, ash and lumps of bone receded, in undulant waves drawn by a low full moon out and into the Irish Sea. Patrick recalled a line from a poem but not from whence it came: *Streaming clouds of glory.*

***

In the quiet, Patrick thought about immortality, his soul's future. Thought seriously. For the first time since third or fourth grade that he had become as black as wet mud in the hell-bound state of mortal sin. Dead in Rebecca's way of thinking. And--in the old way of thinking--an enemy of the Holy Ghost, that Spirit Who is the outpouring of the love between the Father and the Son. The Holy Spirit Who loves all Beings with a perfect love. An immanent presence who wants and needs love in return. Thinking these thoughts, Patrick felt once again the comforts of Mother Church.

They entered Mulroney's, a prokaryote of quiet keeners, for a last supper of Dublin coddle and stout. The pervasive mood of mourning did not persist for already lodged within Mulroney's was a clamorous ruck in mid-jubilation over a football match earlier in the afternoon. By the time the fifteenth or twenty-fifth Sullivan entered the pub, like so many circus clowns emerging from a miniature van, the tipplers began cheering the long lost émigrés, both recognized and unknown.

That night the Sullivans engaged in an unspoken pact to drink up the full inventory of Mr. Mulroney's stout; they failed though Larry sent round after round of to tables and bar: "Sullivan Chevrolet, folks! Skokie, Illinois." The tipplers toasted the Sullivans; the Sullivans toasted in return. Many of the local Irish sat with the mourners, and, learning of their bereavement, were regaled with stories of the matriarch. And also the brother now and forever lost to them.

174

The dispersal of the ashes, the Verdi, all the happenings of the past week, and certainly too the stout, all conspired to bring a creeping sadness upon Patrick. Ancient sorrows gathered and—he quite helpless---began to pour forth great sorrow. About his entire life. He was a watering can, leaking, peppered with shot. He shook; started to reach for Rebecca, stopped, then reached again, took her hand, squeezed with all his might. She squeezed back. He collapsed into her,screaned into her breasts. The family did not fail to take notice. Jenny left Matt, came over and kissed him. Rosemary too.

All the while, a five-piece band played sentimental favorites: *Hennessey, Hennessey Toots the Flute. MacNamara's Band. I Left My Heart in San Francisco.*

Jenny and her Seamus improvised a jig atop their table. Atkins slow danced with Constance. Rosemary sat alone in thoughtful tears. Sometime toward midnight, Maureen Scanlon, complying with the clan's demands, stepped forward to the bandstand, conferred with a wiry piper, then sang to the maudlin delight of all. For both the family and the post-football regulars. All poured out their love to Maureen as they listened. Even the red-haired serving girl who leaned against a pine post covered her quivering lips.

> But come you back when summer's in the meadow
> Or when the valley's hushed and white with snow
> 'Tis I'll be there in sunshine or in shadow....

Maureen was applauded, then foot-stomped until she sang it again. Which she did. Three times. So sweet and pure was Maureen's singing, that night when ashes were cast upon the Liffey's waters, that the family and the locals both achieved a kind of sweet union. A union that swept sadness in the direction of tomorrows and yesterdays with the soft broom of Maureen's mezzo rendering. Rosemary and Patrick's were hardly the only tears shed. Not in that publican's house. Not that night.

Then it happened. Something only Patrick was aware of: the bar lights on the beveled mirrors, colored and blaring, seized him softly and he levitated. Hovered over the bench several feet. For just a second or two. *Lumen gloriate.* He never shared this moment. Not even with Rebecca.

XXVI
Return to Chicago

Back in Manhattan only a week, Patrick got a call from Jenny.

"He's in the hospital. He fell down. Cracked his head."

"Did they check his blood alcohol?"

"He was blotto. Pat, he's slipping away. It's best that you come. Right away."

Rebecca and Patrick flew into O'Hare and taxied to the hospital on the near North Side. Riding on the expressway Patrick was quiet; Rebecca offered him a penny.

"I was just thinking that my life is one of those made-for-tv movies. That—when I get to his bedside my father will suddenly--sober, unshaven and expiring—pour forth a *mea maxima culpa.* There'll be a big slobbering scene, my dear. I'll break down in lugubrious remorse."

"Will you? Break down?"

"I don't know. Maybe. He'll die and you and I will live happily ever after?"

She squeezed his hand.

***

They arrived ten minutes after Barnaby had been pronounced. Jenny sat with Matt, crying so copiously she could only wave a few fingers lightly to greet them. Rosemary was red-eyed but composed. Atkins sat with Constance down the corridor looking a bit worse for wear.

Atkins stood: "You even missed his dying. Paddy, you are a shitcake."

"I waited in the parking lot till I got the all clear."

"What a lifelong waste you are."

They stood nose to nose. It would be forever unclear who threw the first punch. Entangled, they hit the floor; Atkins' three sons piled on, then Matt, and finally B.J. B.J. jumped on the scrum not because he was at all angry but rather because he did not wish to miss a familial moment sure to be spoken of just about forever. A lasagna of Sullivans. Bloodied lips were here and there in the mound of men grown and growing, spitting curses, men trying to restore peace, men trying to sock each other with fists unable to get much of a swing.

Jenny ran from settee to mêlée, stood over them, and began a banshee scream of one nigh onto insanity. This morphed to a wail not of death but life, real life. An outcry somehow new to them all. In her

177

desperation and sorrow, a lifetime of limiting just how much pain was allowed to be felt. Up and down the hospital corridors curing stopped, food trolleys halted. An expiring coronary gained a brief reprieve on a life that moments before had begun to float out and over the rooftops of Chicago's Old Town. Jenny's wail gave the brawlers pause. The scrum halted. Without meeting anyone's gaze, extremities were extracted from divers embraces. They stood. No one willing to meet another's gaze.

Patrick, dabbing at a bleeding lip, asked: "How'd it happen?"

"We think he fell, hit the corner of the old dining room table."

The hospital chaplain emerged from ICU using a towel to wipe the holy oils from his fingers. They gathered round. "Your Dad's up there with the angels. You know that, don't you? We've lost a good man. Let us pray?" They knelt there in the corridor; nurses circumnavigated the gaggle, crossing themselves at the same time. Patrick struggled to remember the exact words of the Lord's Prayer. He recalled a fragment: *Hallowed be thy Name.* Then remembered what Barnaby used to say were his proudest moments: Seven a.m. Sunday mornings. After six long days on the floor of the cleaning shop. After holding court at The Play Pen with Bridget on Saturday night till the wee hours of Sunday. And then maybe on to a Blind Pig. After only a few hours sleep, there was the weekly wiggle with the gigglers outside their door hearing the bed springs ping and groan; when the headboard stopped its rhythmic knocking against the wall, Jenny was perennially the first to meekly peek in, the first to be welcomed. Then the others streamed in, till the bed was full, eight Sullivans, the kids atop the blankets and sheets--but not under--because it's a sin to see or touch your parents' naked skin. Barnaby was first to get up crooning the immortal hits of Bing Crosby as he served up breakfast, his weekly chef duties a gift to the Queen of Whipple Street where she remained, lying under the over-sized bronze crucifix, a wedding gift from her parents. Barnaby, in the kitchen, cried out, with cold beer in hand: "Hair of the puppy dog, you sleepyheads and sweethearts! No Communion today but all my kids are good kids, aren't you? Well, Douglas?"

Dressed for Mass, MomsaBomb too, the most beautiful mother in St. Monica's parish, the eight Sullivans embarked in the green van that moved the family, the shock absorbers perennially shot, slowly but faithfully for nineteen years, its side panel stenciled in white script:

Sullivan's Perfection Dry Cleaners

Let Barnaby Take You to the Cleaners

After the two minute ride to St. Monica's, Barnaby passed out quarters to each child as they exited the van's rear door. So that each would have a coin to put into the wicker basket when it was extended into their pew. Because the ushers kept count of who gave and who did not.

Such Sunday mornings were the proper glory of Barnaby and Bridget: the family together, the boys in Oxfords not Keds, all kneeling before their Creator. (If Rosemary did not make them late by discovering a run in her nylons, occasioning a stop at the drug store for another pair, her changing in the van, her dress at mid-thigh, Barnaby telling Patrick and Dougie, "No looking, you goons!") The eight Sullivans laved by Father Carolan's unworldly voice, the Latin liturgy chanted not sung, in competition with Bridget's Pall Mall hacking: *Gloria in Excelsis Deo...*
***

There was a Requiem at St. Monica's for Barnaby celebrated by three classmates of Father Aloysius (outlived by Barnaby now several years) followed by interment at Sacred Heart Cemetery. At graveside, amongst the foul wafting of day lilies, family and friends beneath a temporary awning heard the pastor's stentorian eulogy while a lone piper (Larry the Impresario had found him) squeezed and blew in a steady drizzle.

Martin Luther was there having flown in from St. Maarten with his girlfriend Veronique who was teaching him, among other things, French. At the airport, father and son in a private moment experienced a clumsy embrace and promised to stay in touch.

Jenny came to Patrick in the upstairs bedroom of Whipple Street where he and Rebecca stayed the few days following Barnaby's passing. She approached a bit like a supplicant, cradling a shoebox. Inside were many handwritten notes. "Paddy, I found these. He must have been writing down things." In the box there were scribblings in a jagged script no longer taught by the nuns.

"Things like?"

"Like letters. Maybe he meant to mail them—someday—maybe not. Two are yours. Here. You'd better read them alone. You got two. I only got one." Jenny stopped at the door: "I didn't mean to. No, yes I did. Of course I did. Read them I mean. It's important that you know...really that I don't know which was written first." She closed the door gently.

Patrick read:

> Patrick,
> I know that I have not been the greatest father to you that I could have been. But I did do my level best. Always. But you were such a bastard. You moved away and stayed away. And wouldn't even call. I hope your own son treats you the same goddamned way.
> Your Father

Patrick read the second letter.

179

Dear Patrick,

I don't think I ever said what, son, was in my heart about you. And I want to do that right now. Because...well, I have always been very proud of you. That you were a great salesman. And despite those bastards at Discipio, the whole world knows what great work you did to build their name. Don't ever have any regrets. You made them rich, the bastards. And though I hardly know your Rebecca, she is clearly a very good woman. You be good to her.

I have some great memories in my heart of our times together—like when we went to the Golden Gloves. And that beautiful day we went sailing together—just a Dad and his son—on Grassy Lake. Remember that broken sailboat they gave us? Anyway I have always in my deepest heart of hearts loved you. Remember that.

    Barnaby

XXVII

Going to the Dentist

Rebecca's shrink recommended analysis for Patrick. Patrick had forever refused the very idea of a joint session. In fact, refused any session whatsoever. Rebecca reconciled with Patrick only after securing his collapse to counseling. The shrink also recommended to Rebecca that she allow a lot of distance to Melissa.

"How far?"

"Far. The kid will figure things out. Or she won't. Get out of the way, that's all you can do." Melissa decided that she trusted horses more than people and found a job on a horse farm in Santa Barbara mucking out stalls for room and board.

Rebecca and Patrick departed the Apple for New Mexico. Bought an adobe in Tesuque, a bosky village with a year-round stream. Their property was lined with white blossomed desert willows and bent cottonwoods just north of Santa Fe. Patrick bought a wine store and sold Grand Cru Bordeaux and Napa Cabernet to Texans. (Bob Wolf, a truck dealer in Houston, was a major customer whose bragging of Patrick's palate brought many customers. Bob in particular wrote big checks and when showing his appreciation for a good wine always used the same words: "Patrick my boy, this here wine is damned good shit!")

Rebecca in Santa Fe became midwife to the mothers of the San Ildefonso pueblo and--while waiting for babies to slip down the chute--a Hospice volunteer to sit with the dying. Patrick dubbed her "Miss Womb to the Tomb". When people asked her about her unorthodox blend of professions she would say: "It's just like when you go fishing--catch and release?"

Patrick kept to his oath that had gained him reconciliation with Rebecca: therapy sessions. He groused, swore and bellowed his objections--but always showed up. Always showed up at the office of Dr. Dorothy Abramowitz whose office walls held many several diplomas: a B.S., an M.D., and a Ph.D. in psychology; certification as a shaman; and a Doctor of Divinity. She spoke and read Hebrew and was studying to become a rabbi. Of late she was conquering Aramaic to decode the Dead Sea Scrolls. She could also channel--for a not modest fee—while spouting an Irish brogue.

Patrick called her 'Dorothy The Dentist' and for him this metaphorical profession fit perfectly; because at each session Dorothy drilled into him, performed historical extractions, without the benefit of anesthesia. Thrice weekly.

Dorothy maintained on her desk a collection of Aztec figurines all with over-sized genitals and black-toothed snarls. Their hostile bearing, from their desk-top encampment between Patrick and the Dentist, his view over, through and around their mendacious visages, gave Patrick a worse mood, a bothersome bent toward violence even more so than upon his arrival.

At their twentieth session, Patrick shared with the Dentist that during the drive to Santa Fe and her office he had felt "murderous".

"'Murderous'? Do you feel like murdering me?"

"In point of fact, yes, Dorothy, I do. It's a strong feeling. No, Dorothy: it's a glorious feeling."

"Go on."

Patrick shrugged: "I feel that after murdering you, I will be exalted."

"Wow. More please!"

"You're safe. I know it's a fantasy. I'm full of them. All day, every day."

"Tell me all. I love fantasies."

Patrick gripped the arms of the club chair. Ready to flee to Bora Bora. "All right, Dorothy: first I kill you. Then I pulverize your fucking tribe of pre-Columbian friends."

Dorothy the Dentist clapped her hands. Applause? "This is marvelous, Patrick."

"'Marvelous'?"

His eyes narrowed, rifle slits in a fortress wall; hers puddled: "Don't you see? We're beginning to get somewhere."

"I don't think so."

Dorothy, all one hundred and five pounds of her, vibrated in her swivel chair: "Oh yes we are!"

***

Patrick learned to sniffle in Dorothy's presence. Not long after he was moved to bawl. Life—in fits and turns—got more livable. He flew solo to Saint Maarten and, in a spirit of renewal as if in the Confessional box, intoned *'mea culpa, mea culpa, mea maxima culpa'* perhaps one hundred times while making it up with Martin Luther. Next he and Rebecca flew to Santa Barbara where they were introduced to all Melissa's favorite horses.

*

Made in the USA
Middletown, DE
11 February 2021